ONCE MORE, WITH FEELING

A COLLECTION OF SECOND CHANCES

S.L. STERLING

Once More, with Feeling

Copyright © 2025 by S.L. Sterling

All rights reserved. Without limiting the rights under copyright reserved about, no part of this publication may be reproduced, stored in, or introduced into a retrieval system, or transmitted in any form or by any means (mechanical, electronic, photocopying, recording, or otherwise) without the prior written permission of both the copyright owner and the above publisher of the book. This is a work of fiction. Any references to historical events, real people, or real places are used fictitiously. Other names, characters, places, and events are products of the author's imagination, and any resemblance to actual events or places or persons, living or dead, is entirely coincidental. Disclaimer: This book contains mature content not suitable for those under the age of 18. It involves strong language and sexual situations. All parties portrayed in sexual situations are consenting adults over the age of 18.

Editor: Brandi Aquino, Editing Done Write

Cover Design: Thunderstruck Cover Design

DOCTOR DESIRE

I'd spent the last five years learning from some of the best doctors and surgeons so I could further my career. I'd also spent that time homesick and missing the only place I'd ever call home. When Eastport General Hospital offered me a position I took it. I was so happy to be returning home, but returning home met revisiting the ghosts of my past.

Brielle, my little sister's best friend was that ghost. We'd had a secret fling the summer before I left, a friends with benefits relationship, no strings attached. Despite that my feelings for her grew. Now I find out that she is now a mother. The woman I had crushed on for years was someone else's woman and I had no one to blame but myself, after all, I'd left her here.

Only the joke was on me, Brielle didn't have another man's child, she had my child. A child I'd known nothing about. How could she not have told me? I didn't know if I should have been angry or excited….because bottom line was, I was a Dad.

S.L. Sterling's Doctor Desire is a surprise baby, steamy second chance heartfelt romance.

BRIELLE

Late Summer 2017

My back arched off the mattress, every inch of my body on fire as Sawyer ran his fingers around each nipple before trailing down my stomach. His lips met my abdomen, and he traced my belly button with his tongue, sending chills through my body. He lowered himself down and gently spread my legs, placing a kiss on each inner thigh, gently biting each side before he moved to the inside of my knees. I could feel his rough hands gripping me, and I murmured something incoherent and bit the back of my hand as I lifted my ass off the mattress, practically begging him to place his mouth on me. He'd been at this for hours. Every part of my body was on fire, and I almost hit the ceiling when he finally sank his tongue into my soaked center. The instant his tongue ran over my clit, I let out a loud moan, arching my back even more than before. His hands left my ass, and I could feel his rough hands on both of my breasts. He pinched my nipples hard between his thumb and forefingers as he sucked my clit into his mouth, sending more shock waves through me.

"That's it, baby. Lose yourself," he whispered breathlessly as he ran his tongue over me once again.

My mind spun. The entire summer with him had been like this. I'd spent many nights in his bed and in his apartment, as he fulfilled every need in my body, needs I didn't even know I had at the age of twenty.

"Do you want more?"

"Yes," I cried as I held back my release.

He grabbed my legs and placed them on his shoulders, and then sunk himself into me. He held on to my legs as he pumped into me with deep thrusts, pulling out just before I climaxed. He quickly flipped me onto my stomach and pulled me back onto my hands and knees and buried himself deeply into me, fucking me roughly as he held on to my hips and pumped hard into me.

"Don't you come yet," he said, his jaw clenched, each word forced out with a breath.

I closed my eyes and enjoyed every deep thrust he

delivered, fighting my body's want for release when I felt him reach around and rub my clit, only heightening the need for release. He slowed each thrust to match the rhythm of his fingers. I buried my face into the pillow and bit my hand, doing my best to mute my moans.

He trailed kisses over my back, and without warning, I felt myself tipping over the edge, my body trembling, my moans loud. Sawyer McKay was going to be the death of me.

"That's it, baby," he moaned as he gripped my hips tight, and I felt his cock throb inside of me as he let go as well.

I collapsed onto the mattress, my body unable to hold itself up any longer. I felt him get up off the bed, the light from the bathroom spilling into the darkened room. In a matter of minutes, I felt the mattress dip back down as he crawled back into the bed beside me. He gently scooped me into his arms and lay back against the messed pillows.

He should have been against the law for me. I'd crushed on Sawyer for years, and I never dreamt in a million years that this would be happening. That we'd be laying in one another's arms, sweaty and out of breath. I closed my eyes and curled into his side, praying he wouldn't let me go because, deep down inside, I knew he had ruined me for any other man. Yet, I knew that good-bye was coming.

"I'm going to miss this," I mumbled, breathing hard, wiping my eyes, and looking at him as he came into focus.

"Summer isn't over just yet, baby," he whispered, placing a kiss on the side of my neck. "We have lots of time."

I nodded, giggling as his scruff tickled me. He kissed my neck and moved to my ear before meeting my lips, kissing me gently.

"Brie, I have a question for you."

"What's that?"

"You haven't by chance missed your pill, have you?" I looked over my shoulder at him, his face taking on a serious look.

"No, why?" I asked frantically, searching my mind to see if I could remember looking at the packet this morning to see if I could recall if all the pills had been taken.

"I don't want you to panic, but the condom broke."

"That's the third one this week." I swallowed hard.

"Perhaps the box was defective." He shrugged and chuckled as he pulled me closer.

"Sawyer...It's not funny. I can't get pregnant."

"Relax, Brie, that's why I asked. As long as you haven't missed any pills, I am certain we will be fine."

"How do you know that?" I questioned, feeling the panic rise in me. If I got pregnant, our secret would be out. My best friend would hate me, and my mother would be furious.

"I'm a doctor. I know these things. Trust me." He winked and smiled.

It was always that sexy smile that pulled me down from panicking—that and those dimples. I relaxed back into his arms and blew out a breath. I looked up at the ceiling, still not sure how to digest the fact the condom had broken again. "You're a soon-to-be intern. You're not a doctor yet."

"Actually, I am. I've graduated medical school," he whispered, his breath on my neck, his scruff tickling me once again.

I closed my eyes as his lips connected with my skin. "I could always help you take your mind off everything. Perhaps call it a prescription of sorts, and you know you need to follow the doctor's orders." He chuckled as he pushed himself up on his elbows and met my lips. I could already feel his growing erection poking into me.

I looked up into his eyes and slowly lifted my head to meet his lips. His tongue forced my lips apart and washed through my mouth, as his hands travelled down between my legs, his fingers slowly rubbing me with small circles. It took him only mere seconds to make me forget all about the broken condom, and soon I was once again writhing on the mattress as he brought me to the brink.

BRIELLE

I COULD HEAR the murmur of guests out in the living room as they left, while I quietly set the book I'd been reading to Emma down on the table. She was sound asleep against me, and I did my best to pick her up without waking her. I lay her down in her bed, pulling the covers up around her, then made my way to the door, looking back at her sleeping face one more time before shutting the light off. I pulled the door closed behind me. Where had the time gone? It seemed like only yesterday that I looked down into her scrunched-up little face the day she was born and instantly fell in love with her.

I looked around the apartment at the mess in the living room and let out a breath. It had been an amazing day. Emma's fourth birthday party had been a success. My sister and her husband had brought their three kids over, and my brother and his wife had brought over their two. We'd had dinner, and when I presented Emma with her cake, we all sang Happy Birthday. Mom and Diane, my best friend, had both snapped a picture of the cake I had made at the same time Emma sank her little hands into the soft icing and shoved a fistful of cake into her mouth.

I laughed at the thought as I looked around at the mess of paper plates all over the living room table. I was about to grab them when I heard Mom's laugh coming from the kitchen, followed by Diane's. Ignoring the mess, I wandered into the kitchen to see them both sitting at my little kitchen table, a glass of wine in front of them.

"She go down okay?" Mom asked, patting the chair beside her as she grabbed the bottle of wine and filled my glass.

"Yeah, she was fighting, but eventually, she calmed down. Everyone left?"

"Yep, we ushered them out, so take a load off, would you?" Diane said, shoving the full glass over to the only empty chair.

"I can't. I need to get everything cleaned up. I have to be at the bakery tomorrow morning at five. If not, then orders will not get filled." I sank my hands into the hot water in the sink and began washing some glasses.

"Brielle, honey, come now, take a rest. You've been going all day." Mom came up behind me, forcing the cloth out of my hand and taking over at the sink. "Sit down."

"Mom, I'm fine."

"Brielle, don't argue with mc. Go sit down. It's bad enough you've had to raise that child on your own. Now, it's time to learn to accept some help when it's given to you."

"Fine," I said, holding my hands up in defeat. "Knock yourself out."

Diane let out a laugh. "She never accepts help."

"Don't you start on me too!" I cried.

"It's true. I'm always offering to help."

"Trying to fix me up is not what I call helping," I said, sipping on my wine.

"Your daughter is impossible. I've been trying to fix her up with some doctors from work. Every single time I mention it, she turns me down. I honestly don't think she wants the help. I think she likes to suffer."

I looked over at Diane. "Way to sell me out. Besides, I've told you I don't have time for a relationship right now. I have Emma, and The Cooling Rack, and..."

"And needs, Brielle. You have needs." Diane laughed. "You are twenty-five years old! You have needs."

My mother looked over at me with what appeared to be concerned. She didn't fool me though; it was always the same look, one of disappointment. She'd never let me forget I had made a mistake when I decided to raise Emma on my own. However, I hadn't exactly been honest with her. Instead of the truth, I'd told her that the father had been a one-night stand.

"Diane, I'm fine. Honestly. I have enough on my plate. I don't need some guy coming in here and making my life more of a mess."

Diane gave me a knowing look and shrugged. "Can't say I haven't tried."

"I'd never say that. Besides, I still have that date with Drew in a couple of weeks—the pediatrician. I didn't cancel like I wanted to."

"Good! I think you will really like him. I'm glad you agreed to that."

"What choice did you leave me? He stood right in front of me as you went through my phone, looking for an available date."

Mom looked at Diane, an amused smile on her face as Diane giggled. "All right, fine, perhaps I was a little pushy. Anyways, I have to get going. Early morning for me tomorrow as well." Diane finished her glass of wine before making her way to the door.

"Okay, well, thanks for coming. It meant a lot that you were here."

"I wouldn't miss it for the world. I love that little nut," Diane said, leaning in for a hug before grabbing her purse off the back of the chair. Then she stopped and hugged my mother before she made her way to the door.

"I, too, should get going," Mom said, drying her hands on the towel, all the dishes now washed. "However, before I go, I could help you clean up the garbage."

I turned and looked over my shoulder into the living room and shook my head. "I'll be fine. Honestly."

"All right, suit yourself, sweetie. You have a good night then."

"I will. I'll get this cleaned up and then get to bed."

"Make sure you do. You look exhausted," Mom said, kissing me on the cheek, then slipped into her coat and shoes.

As soon as I locked the door, I grabbed the garbage pail and quickly made a beeline for the living room. Within five minutes, I had all the plates, forks, and plastic cups in the trash, and I quickly straightened up the living room before grabbing my glass of wine and placing it on the end table. I then changed into my shorts and T-shirt.

Before sitting down, I went over to the hall closet and reached up for the blanket I had put away earlier. I gave it a tug, but it was stuck on something, so I tugged a little harder. My eyes went wide as I saw a shoebox come crashing down along with the blanket. I quickly stepped back and caught the box just before it hit the floor.

Once I had caught my breath, I looked down at the

old pink shoe box. I smiled to myself as I looked down at the familiar stickers covering it. I had totally forgotten I had shoved that up there as I ran my fingers over the stickers.

I carried the box over to the couch and curled up under the fuzzy blanket, placing it on my lap. I took a sip of wine and carefully lifted the lid. There were some pictures on top of my sister, brother, and me on summer vacation the year before my brother got married. I pulled out an old concert ticket stub and smiled. I remembered the concert. It was the last one I'd been to before Emma was born.

I reached into the box and pulled out a little black book. I flipped it, my fingers running over the gold *Diary* written on the front. I flipped open the cover and a soft smile fell on my lips. Hearts were drawn in sparkly pink ink all over the inside the front cover.

I turned the page and leaned back against the couch cushions and began reading the first entry.

Two hours later, I sat gripping the diary. I reached for my glass, picking it up. I went to take a sip and noticed it was empty. I got up off the couch and walked to the kitchen, pouring myself another glass. "So much for an early night," I mumbled to myself, looking at the clock. It was already one.

I made my way back to the couch and sank down into the cushions, picking up the diary. The date October 2, 2017 was scrawled on the blank page. I flipped to the next page to notice it, too, was blank. Not that I had forgotten because I would remember that date forever.

I stood in my bedroom, looking out the front window. The bright-orange and yellow leaves danced in the sunlight as I looked at the clock. It was almost seven. I took one last look at myself in the mirror and smoothed my skirt. I was meeting Sawyer for dinner, but first I headed into the washroom and looked down at the pregnancy test I'd taken only a few minutes earlier. Two dark-pink lines looked back at me as I ran my fingers through my hair, panic filling me. I took a moment to gather my thoughts and figure out how I was going to tell him. We were only supposed to be having fun, nothing serious.

I grabbed the pregnancy test off the vanity, wrapped it up in tissues, and buried at the bottom of the garbage can, then I pulled the bag from the can and tied it closed. That was the last thing I needed my mother to find, I thought to myself as my thoughts ran rampant.

I ran down the stairs, yelling good-bye to my mother, and made my way out to the car, first dumping the bag into the garbage can that sat at the curb. I backed down the driveway, wondering how stupid I could have been. What had I been thinking, hooking up with my best friend's brother, mutually agreeing to be friends with benefits for his last summer at home. Just because we were both single didn't give us permission to screw around. We had been careful, but the last three times we had been together, the condom had broken, and I had somehow missed two birth control pills. I mentioned nothing to Sawyer about missing those pills and really tried not to give it much thought, until my period had been almost three weeks late.

Sawyer and I had a quiet dinner at one of the fancier restaurants on the other side of town. Tonight was our good-bye dinner. Sawyer had spent the summer applying for internships, and he had finally been accepted; however, the hospital was out of state. Sawyer leaned back against the chair and looked at me.

"It looks like something is weighing on that pretty little head of yours."

I shook my head. "No, just going to miss you is all. When are you're planning on leaving?"

"Monday. I wanted to tell you sooner, but I wanted to make sure that everything was solid first before telling you. You know that I had an apartment and everything."

"So, basically, we only have tonight?" I questioned.

"Unfortunately," he said, studying my eyes. "I know

it's been hard on you to keep this from Diane, but I want to let you know that this summer was...amazing."

Keeping the fact I'd been sleeping with my best friend's brother quiet from the only person I ever talked to about my private life had been stressful. It was going to be even more stressful now, especially since she thought I had been single all this time. I couldn't hide the fact I was pregnant for very long, and I feared I would crack when she confronted me about it. She would want to know who the father was, and I knew that if she found out it was her brother she may never speak to me again.

I smiled. "It certainly was. I really can't believe that tonight is it. Our last night together." Our eyes locked as the words fell from my lips, and I shifted in my seat. I knew the look in his eye all too well. He was hungry...for me, as I was him.

"It doesn't have to be the end, Brielle. I mean, I will come home occasionally. Plus, you could always come visit me as well, especially if you need a break from school."

I thought for a moment. "I'm sure I could, but only if you would want that."

"Brielle, of course I want. I wouldn't suggest it if I didn't. I don't want to be away from you, but I haven't gotten a response from any other internships that I applied for. If only Eastport General had taken me, then we wouldn't have to be apart, but perhaps this being apart will allow us to explore the possibility of something more. Give us a chance to miss one another."

I swallowed hard. We hadn't talked about anything permanent, and with the information I had just found out, I wasn't sure I was ready to be talking about it either. It was in this moment I wished I could call Diane and ask her for her advice. However, after we had finished desert, that thought flew from my mind as I followed him back to his condo and spent the next three hours wrapped in his sheets.

Monday morning, his family drove him to the airport. I'd wanted to go with them but didn't think it was appropriate to interrupt the personal family time. Instead, I drove to the airport and parked on a side road and watched his plane take off from the front seat of my car, never getting another chance to say good-bye.

Once he landed, he called me to give me his address and number, and then we talked on the phone for a couple of hours. Over the first few weeks he'd been gone, I gave us a lot of the thought. I missed him something terrible, and that was when communication between us had shifted. He no longer spent nights on the phone with me; he was either working, sleeping or was just too tired. I knew he had been working hard, and I knew that the move had been a huge adjustment, but for some reason, those excuses weren't enough for me, but I, too, was going through a huge adjustment. My hormones were going crazy as his baby was growing inside of me—a baby he knew nothing of.

Mid-October, I'd started my first semester of Law School. I was out with my friends one Friday night, and as the conversation shifted to school, a realization came over me that there was no way I could complete even this semester with a baby on the way, never mind once she or he were born. The course load was already heavy, I was behind, and I was already exhausted. There would be no way I could keep up with all the case studies. I could barely keep my eyes open during my later afternoon classes. I cried all weekend over it, and the following Monday, I dropped out of school. My plan was to go to Seattle and tell Sawyer about the baby. It had been a long, emotional day, giving up my dream, but it got worse once I returned home and told my mother that I'd dropped out of school.

I'd never seen my mother look at me with such a mix of anger and disappointment before. She sat silently at first, staring off into space. Then the screaming began, and once she'd said all she had to say, I went to my bedroom where I lay in bed with tears streaming down my face, longing to feel Sawyer's arms around me. Once the tears stopped flowing, I got up and opened my laptop and booked my flight to Seattle.

I flew out three days later, finally feeling confident enough to tell him about the baby. I spent the entire flight going over what I was going to say in mind. I also imagined his response to the news and was actually excited about it by the time the plane had landed. I grabbed a cab and gave the driver Sawyers' address, and soon we were off making our way through the city.

I glanced down at my watch. It was almost four. I knew Sawyer was off early tonight, and I should arrive just as he got home. I watched out the window as the cab sped down the road, finally pulling to a stop outside of a three-story walk-up.

"Here you are, miss. That will be ten dollars."

I grabbed my purse, fishing through for my wallet, and had just grabbed a bill when I saw Sawyer round the corner up ahead. My heart stopped; he wasn't alone. There, hanging onto his arm, was some brunette in scrubs. I continued watching them, my heart in my throat, as they talked and laughed. I could feel the tears burning.

"Miss, ten dollars."

My eyes blurred with tears as I continued watching them together. I swallowed hard and looked down at the money in my hand, and quickly shoved it back in my purse. "You know, silly me, I just realized that I forgot one of my bags at the airport." I swallowed hard, not taking my eyes off the two of them. "Could you take me back?" I questioned, meeting the driver's eyes.

"Sure thing, miss. Is everything okay?" he questioned.

I nodded, afraid if I said anything, I would break down in tears. I sat back in the seat, and as he pulled away from the curb, I looked back over my shoulder and watched as Sawyer and the brunette climbed the stairs to the door. He opened the door and placed his hand on the small of her back, allowing her to enter the building, just like he'd done with me so many times.

I'd been stupid to believe I was special. I closed my eyes and rested my hand on my lower abdomen and swallowed hard. I really had no right to be upset. We were friends with benefits and nothing more, and I had been stupid to think we were more than that. I rested my head against the seat and watched the buildings pass by, until we had pulled back up to the airport.

Three weeks after I'd returned, I'd finally broken down and told my mother the real reason for me dropping out of school. I was pregnant. She yelled at me for hours, at how irresponsible I'd been and that I'd ruined my life. Then she demanded to know who the father was.

"Let me guess, it's Sawyer, isn't it?"

"What?"

"It's Sawyer, Diane's brother. You two spent a crazy amount of time together this summer."

"Mom, no, it's not Sawyer." Since no one really knew he and I had been sleeping together, I decided the only way to deal with this was to lie to her, and so I told one enormous lie.

"It's a guy I meant one night out with the girls, just a one-night stand. I don't even have his number." That only made her more furious.

I was not proud of the lies I'd told, but I felt at the time they were necessary. That night I'd made a call to Diane. I needed my best friend now more than I ever thought possible, and so I told her the same thing.

I LEANED my head back against the couch cushions and took in a deep breath, and that was when I noticed I'd been crying. I wiped my cheeks. I hadn't spoken to Sawyer McKay since I'd gotten out of the cab. Still, to this day, no one knew he was the father. I remembered him calling me for weeks after I'd flown to Seattle. He left me messages, begging for me to return his calls, but I couldn't. Soon, the calls became fewer and fewer, and just like that, whatever our relationship had been had died.

Time passed, and eventually I had gotten over him, and Emma had been born. I now had this perfect little baby that soon became my world, and I was scared shitless. Eventually, I'd gone back to school and gotten my pastry chef degree, while Mom watched Emma. Then I'd opened The Cooling Rack and gotten myself into this apartment. I looked around at the furnished apartment and blew out a breath. Even though every year had been a struggle, I had done pretty well for us.

Suddenly, I heard Emma begin to fuss, and I threw the blanket off my lap and quietly entered her room. I gently pulled the blanket up over her and looked down at her. I was kidding myself if I said I never thought of Sawyer again because, looking down at Emma, she was the spitting image of him. I had a daily reminder of Sawyer every single time I looked down into her face. I missed him, and I'd have given anything to have another chance with him.

I blew out a breath, reached over and clicked off the lamp and turned on her little night-light, then walked to the door and pulled it half shut. I walked over and shut the lamp off beside the couch and wandered into my bedroom, setting the alarm for five and crawled into bed.

SWAYER

Five Weeks Earlier

"Hey, Sawyer."

"Brenda, good to see you."

"Think perhaps we could have a night cap tonight?" she asked, stepping up beside me and sliding her hand into mine as she continued walking with me toward my office.

"Ah, not tonight. Apartment hunting," I answered, stopping outside of the change room door and resting my arm on the doorframe over her head as she looked up into my face.

"Maybe another time, then," she whispered.

"Only if you promise to wear that sexy little number you had on the other night," I said in a low voice as I kissed her lips.

It was totally against hospital policy to fraternize with other staff members, but I'd become used to breaking that rule. In the five years I'd been here, I'd been with most of the nurses in the emergency department.

"I promise," she said between kisses. "Call you later."

"Sounds good," I murmured and leaned against the wall, watching her walk away from me. I waited until she disappeared down the hall and then made my way into my office. It had been a hell of a day. My body ached, and I was tired. It had started the second I had walked in this morning, like usual. I'd barely sat down when I was called immediately to the emergency room for a multi-vehicle accident, and just as we got that cleared, two life-threatening gunshot wounds had come in.

Once I was out of surgery, I'd made my way back to my office. I walked in, sat down, and took some time to continue my search to find some crappy, overpriced apartment. I'd found out two weeks ago that I was being kicked out of my current apartment thanks to my room-mate's girlfriend. The pair of them had decided on a whim that she wanted to move in with Mark and had told me over coffee and pancakes one morning. I'd quickly checked for any new listings and became frustrated at the fact I still couldn't find anything suitable. Then I turned to the pile of paperwork on my desk. I sifted through medical documents mixed with my mail when one envelope caught my eye. Instead of opening it, I packed up my bag, took the letter, and made my way to the doctors' lounge.

I'd just gotten out of a hot shower, wrapped a towel around my waist, and walked over to my locker. Reaching into my bag, I pulled the letter out of my bag and sat down on the bench. I looked over the envelope, my eyes darting to the Eastport General Hospital Logo in the top right-hand corner. Excitement filled me as I ripped the corner of the envelope.

I'd applied to Eastport General regarding an opening in their emergency department over three months ago. After not hearing from them, I'd figured they filled the position. I took a deep breath, ripped the envelope open, and pulled out the letter. Sitting back against the wall, I unfolded the letter looked down at the first words, 'Congratulations." That was the only word I needed to read. I had gotten the job.

I leaned back against the cool wall and blew out a breath. I'd been living in Seattle for almost five years, and I'd hated every single solitary moment of it. My parents were getting older and needed more help, and being this far away didn't allow me to help them as much as I'd like, but now I held my ticket back home in my hands.

I re-read the letter, looking down at the last paragraph. I had until today to respond. I quickly pulled my cell phone from my bag and dialed. As soon as I heard another voice on the end, I typed in the extension for a Dr. Ryan Richards.

"Hello, Dr. Richards."

"Yes, it's Dr. Sawyer McKay. I'm calling about the letter you sent me regarding the position open at Eastport General."

"Ah, yes. I was beginning to think I wouldn't be hearing from you and that I'd have to return to my applicant pile."

"Sorry about that. It's been a crazy few days. If you haven't already filled the position, I am looking forward to starting at Eastport General."

"Glad to hear it. Your resume speaks for itself. How long will it take you to get here?"

I tapped the corner of the letter quickly, going over in my mind all I'd need to do. "A month too long?"

"See you then. In the meantime, you have my number should you have questions. Let me know once you arrive in Eastport. I would love to give you a tour of the hospital."

"Sounds good."

I hung up the phone as excitement filled me. I was going home.

"I CAN'T BELIEVE you are finally home," Diane said, coming into the kitchen of our parents' home. I looked up from the paper I was reading and smiled.

"Hey, sis. How's things?" I said, getting up and hugging her.

"As well as I can be with an asshole of an ex-husband making my life a living hell, but let's not talk about him right now. So, my big brother is going to be working with me at Eastport. Everyone is so excited to have you there," she said, sitting down at the table across from me.

"So, I've heard. What about you? Are you excited to have me there?"

My sister and I hadn't always been on the best terms. She'd married an asshole, I'd tried to warn her, but she was determined to prove me wrong. My inter-fering had only made our relationship worse. She was now separated, but he still worked hard to make her life a living hell. I was just glad she was finally away from him, and now that I was back in Eastport, I was determined to try and have some sort of a relationship with her.

"Oh I guess. It will be an adjustment taking orders from my brother in the workplace." She laughed.

"No, it won't. You won't be working directly with me. I made sure I told them that we were related," I said, sitting back in the chair taking a drink of my water.

"Have you seen some of the old guys since you've been back in town?" Diane asked. "I know Lions asked about you the other day, and so did Paul."

"God, I haven't thought about those guys in a long time. Probably since the party they had back before I left for school. I sort of drifted apart from everyone when I left."

"Lord, don't remind me of that. That was the party I met Leo at. I thought he was so hot." She buried her face in her hands in embarrassment. "Little did I know what he would turn out to be," she said, screwing up her face in disgust.

"Yeah, well, had I of known you were running off with him when you did, I would have put a stop to it."

"You wouldn't have won. I mean, Brie did try and stop me, and I didn't listen to her either."

A funny feeling ran through me. Brie—a name I'd not heard or thought of for a long time. I thought back to the night of that party. That was the night that began a summer I'd not forgotten. "Yeah, well, Brie isn't me, now is she," I said, looking at my sister.

"No, but..." Diane looked away, and I knew she wanted to change the subject.

I cleared my throat. "Brie, how is she? You still talk to her?"

"She's my best friend. Of course I still talk to her."

I nodded, softly smiling at the memory of her. "Is she still in Eastport?"

Diane nodded. "Yes."

"What's she up to now?"

"What's with all the questions?"

"Look, you don't want to talk about Leo. Can I not be curious about people?"

Diane let out a breath. "If you must know, she runs a very successful business here in town, and she has a little one."

I nodded, disappointment filling me. The first girl, maybe the only girl, I'd fallen in love with was now someone else's woman, and I had no one to blame but myself. I could have had her. I had every opportunity to have her, and I'd blown it by leaving her here.

"That's good. Guess I'll have to give those guys a call, maybe get the old crew together for a poker night or something," I said, changing the subject immediately.

"Just don't invite Leo, okay." Diane laughed.

"Don't think you need to worry about that," I bit out.

We both grew silent as we sat at the table, my mind going back to Brielle.

"Good to have you home," Diane said, getting up and coming around the table to give me a hug.

"Good to be home," I said, hugging her back.

"You guys ready to eat?" Mom asked, coming into the kitchen and making her way to where the roast was resting on the counter.

"Absolutely," we both said in unison and made our way to the dining room table.

I KISSED HER LIPS, gently forcing them open with my tongue. Her body was pressed against mine, and her hands rested on my ass, pulling me closer.

Our lips parted, and I opened my eyes and brought my hand to her face, brushing her hair back. I looked into her blue eyes, hoping to see something in them other than of want and need, but there was nothing.

I met her lips again, this time taking my time with that kiss. Perhaps she would pick up on how I was beginning to feel about her. As our lips danced over one another, I pulled her close to me, and then gently rolled her onto her back. I reached for the condom that lay on my nightstand, pulling away from her long enough to slip it on.

I took my time with her. This wasn't just about sex anymore for me. I wanted her, every single inch of her, in every way possible. I slid myself into her, and the moan she released went straight through me. I loved it when she made that sound.

I pumped slow and deep, grabbing her ass with one hand, as I held her with the other and kissed her lips. We stayed that way, her legs wrapped around my waist, until we both came.

I walked her to the front door, the sun shining through the windows. I leaned against the wall and watched her as she slid her shoes on and then grabbed her jacket before turning to me. She looked so sexy in the sunlight with her disheveled hair and that 'I just got laid' look in her eyes.

"Thank you for dinner, and a fabulous night," she said, taking a step closer to me. I could already smell a mix of her coconut body lotion mixed with her natural scent.

"My pleasure."

She leaned in and kissed me.

"What are you doing later tonight?" I asked.

"Diane wants to hit the club tonight."

Alarm filled me at the thought of her going to a club. I needed to tell her how I felt, no matter if she didn't return the feelings. I looked down to the floor and then back up to her eyes. "Oh, I was going to see if you wanted to maybe watch a movie or something."

I watched as a soft smile came to her lips. "What am I going to tell your sister?" She giggled.

"Tell her you have the flu." I shrugged.

"But I already told her I'd go."

"You know you shouldn't lie to your best friend." I chuckled, leaning in and kissing her lips.

She leaned in and kissed me and then pulled away, her eyes still closed.

"Brie, I..."

I woke with a start and looked around the dark room. I ran my hand across my face. I was covered in a sheen of sweat. I blew out a deep breath and kicked the covers off me, getting up to get a drink of water. I looked at myself in the mirror and shook my head. I'd been back in Eastport one week, and I was already thinking of her and all I'd allowed to slip from my fingers.

BRIELLE

DREW PLACED his hand on my back and guided me into the restaurant. Once we were seated, I pulled my phone from my purse and checked my messages. I had nothing from the sitter, only one from Diane telling me to relax and enjoy myself. I rolled my eyes, shoved my phone back in my purse, and picked up the menu.

"Everything okay?" Drew asked, looking over the edge of the menu at me.

I nodded. "Yes, of course. Why?"

"Well, for starters, you've checked your phone more in the last half hour than you have spoken to me."

"I'm sorry. Emma is with a new sitter. It's just making me a little uncomfortable." I'd almost canceled when I was unable to book my mom. Diane was working, and my normal sitter couldn't watch Emma either. Instead,

Brenda, one of my employees, had heard I was in a bind and offered to sit with her for the night.

At first, I had said no, but with Diane sitting across from me in the kitchen of The Cooling Rack giving me the look of death when Brenda offered, I decided against it. Now I sat across from a very attractive young doctor perusing a menu, while my knee was continuously hitting the table from nerves.

"Brielle?" he questioned, not looking up from the menu.

"Hmmm..." I mumbled, pretending that I didn't notice that the table was shaking.

"You're nervous. Your knee has hit that table more times than I can count."

"I'm sorry. I'm not used to leaving Emma late at night."

"I'm sure she is in very capable hands."

"She is. I'm sorry. I will try and get a hold of myself. Sorry."

"It's okay. No need to be sorry. I understand. Just try to relax and have a good time. Now, what are you eying on the menu?"

"The chicken looks good. What about you?" I said as I felt my phone vibrate in my purse.

"I think I'm going to have the steak."

"That sounds good too," I answered as, once again, my phone vibrated.

We were halfway through dinner and were in deep conversation when I felt my phone vibrate against my leg for the third time. I did my best to quell the anxiety I could feel building inside of me and continued listening to what he was saying. It worked until I felt the phone begin to continuously vibrate. I knew he could tell something was wrong because he sat there looking at me with concern in his eyes.

"Brielle, just answer your phone," he bit out, raising his glass and taking a sip of wine.

It was that moment I felt the phone vibrate again. "I'm sorry. I'm worried that something is wrong with Emma. Just give me two seconds."

Drew nodded, placing his napkin on the table, and glanced around the restaurant. He was annoyed, and really, I couldn't blame him. This was extremely unfair to him, but I didn't care. I ignored the looks he was giving me and dove into my purse. I unlocked the phone and read the text that sat on my screen, my heart in my throat.

"Oh my God, Emma is on her way to the emergency room. She fell off the jungle gym at the park," I said, panicked as I dialed Brenda's number.

"Just relax and breathe, find out what is going on," Drew said, trying to keep me calm. "I can always call ahead and notify the doctor to update you," he offered.

I could barely contain myself and gathered my purse.

"Sorry, I'm going to have to go," I mumbled, trying hard not to panic as I waited for her to answer her phone.

"I don't think we need to go," he said, annoyed.

"You're wrong. We do," I said.

I looked at Drew just as he rolled his eyes and let out an annoyed huff and signaled the waiter for the check. This was the exact reason why I didn't date. Aside from having no time to build a relationship, I didn't need some guy trying to tell me to calm down. Emma was and would always be my number-one priority, and as a pediatrician, he should have understood that. Instead, I felt as if I were sitting here with a guy who'd never met a parent before. I never left her with strangers, and this was why.

Drew drove straight to Eastport General and followed me in against my wishes. He led the way to the emergency room and over to the nurse's station, and immediately, they directed me to the room where Brenda sat with Emma.

"I'll go try and find out who's looking after her," Drew said, heading off in another direction.

The moment Emma saw me, she held her little arms out and tears began pouring down her cheeks. "Emma, sweetheart, what happened?" I said, sitting down beside Brenda, taking Emma from her and pulling her into my lap, trying to console her.

"She fell off the jungle gym and started crying. Her arm started to swell, and no matter what I did, I couldn't get her to stop crying. I panicked. I didn't know what else to do."

"It's okay, hon, you did exactly what you were supposed to do. Here..." I said, digging in my purse for my wallet, "You don't need to stay. I can take it from here." I handed her the money I owed her for the night.

"No, Brielle, I won't take it. I ruined your date, and on top of that, I broke your child," she said, refusing to take the money from me.

"Brenda, it's okay. It was sort of boring, and Emma will be fine." I winked at her, encouraging her to take the money. A slight smile landed on her lips as Emma began to fuss.

"Seriously, Emma is going to be fine. These kids are made of rubber," I said, pulling her closer to me as Brenda finally took the money I'd offered.

"Thanks, Brielle."

The curtain opened, and Drew smiled down at Emma and me. "So it looks like you'll be in good hands. You'll be looked after by the new transfer. He should be in shortly. I've worked with him a couple of times. He is excellent. Very, very good with kids."

"Thanks, Drew," I said, looking up at him, suddenly feeling bad for how the night had ended.

"Should I call you to reschedule?"

I didn't have the heart to tell the man no, so I just nodded and smiled at him. I knew I'd never hear from him again, I could tell, so I didn't really worry about. "I look forward to it."

Drew gave me half a smile and then looked to Brenda. "Did you need help finding your way out of the hospital?"

Brenda nodded, quickly hugged me, and then followed Drew. I pulled Emma against me, as she rested her head on my shoulder. I smoothed her hair and closed my eyes, waiting for the doctor. I'd finally gotten her calmed down when the curtain parted and Diane rushed into the room, panicked and muttering to herself under her breath.

"Brielle, oh my goodness, I saw Emma's name and rushed in as soon as I could. I must have been with a patient when she came in or I'd of been here right away. I didn't expect to see you here though. They said she was brought in by Brenda."

I let out a laugh. "Brenda called me. She didn't know what else to do."

"What about your date?" she whispered as she took Emma from me and placed her on the exam table, looking her over just like she did every time she got hurt.

"Let's not talk about it okay. He was more annoyed at the fact that the date was interrupted. I can't date someone who can't understand and accept that she is my main priority," I said as Diane continued examining her.

"I understand. All right, I have to get back to work. I

don't know who you are seeing, but the doctor should be in shortly. Here, if she is cold you can use this blanket," Diane said, pulling a blanket from under the exam table.

I grabbed Emma off the table and sat back down in the chair, wrapping the blanket around her. She shoved her thumb in her mouth and buried her face in my neck. Diane smiled at me, tousled Emma's dark hair, kissed her on the cheek, and then left the room.

SAWYER

I'D BEEN BACK in Eastport three weeks, and this had been the first ten-day stretch I'd done. I was exhausted and looking forward to my days off. Every night for a week I'd dreamt of Brielle, but they had finally stopped. I walked in behind the nurses' station and handed the current patient file over to one of the nurses.

"Please order these tests and put a rush on them."

"Sure thing."

I'd just sat down and taken my first sip of hot coffee when I heard my name.

"Dr. McKay, your next patient is over in room three." Mandy, the nurse I had been partnered with tonight, handed over a file to me.

"Mandy, please, it's Sawyer. Now, what's it look like?"

"Possible strain or break. Little girl fell off a jungle gym at a park."

"Age?"

"Four."

"Did you order x-rays? You can't be too careful with a child that age."

"I wasn't sure it would be necessary, but I can if you'd like."

"It's okay. Just wait until I take a look. Can you please set up an IV on the patient in room five and start the paperwork to admit Mrs. Rodriguez in room seven. I'm also waiting on a list of tests for room one. Please let me know as soon as those come in."

"Of course. I was just going to take you to room three."

"No need, Mandy, it's fine."

"Well, it's just she is Diane's best friend. She asked me to update her."

"Diane, as in my sister?"

Mandy nodded. "Yes, she just stopped by before you got here."

"My sister is best friends with a four-year-old?"

"No, she is best friends with the mother."

"It's fine. You go, take care of that, and come back when you're finished. I will update my sister," I said, turning and making my way toward room three.

I stopped outside of the room and washed my hands,

then opened the file, quickly reading it over, paying no attention to names and ages. I parted the curtain and stepped into the room, and immediately sat down at the computer without making eye contact.

"I'm Dr. McKay. I will be looking after Emma tonight. So, looks like we have a right-arm injury, or more specific, wrist. Fell off a jungle gym, is that correct?" I said as I logged into the computer and pulled up the patient's electronic chart.

When I didn't get an immediate answer, I put my pen down and turned to look at the patient. The little girl with hair as dark as mine sat huddled against her mother's chest. I raised my eyes to her face, and when they met hers, I froze. Brielle sat across from me. It was almost as if I had been transported back through time, and every feeling I'd ever had for her hit me straight in the gut. She was more beautiful than I remembered.

"Sawyer?" she questioned, her eyes wide, her flushed cheeks turning pale. "What are you doing here?"

"Brielle?" I looked at her, and then glanced down to the little girl on her lap. In a matter of seconds, I was transported to the last few times we had been together. Then I looked back at the computer screen, my eyes skimming over all the information in front of me, looking specifically for the birthdate. I finally found it: June 19, 2018. I quickly did a little math and then the realization hit. It had been a little over four years since I had last laid eyes on her.

I checked Emma's birthdate again and swallowed hard. Was I staring at my child? The condom had broken twice…or had it been three times? I couldn't remember. Could it be possible? Did I have a child I knew nothing about? Had she kept this a secret from me? Suddenly, anger came over me that I could barely control. I slammed the folder shut, got up, and walked out of the room without a word.

I walked down the hall with purpose to the nurses' desk and looked at the girl behind the counter. "Where is Dr. Richards?" I demanded.

"He's in the middle of an emergency that just came in. He says he will be a while and asks that you take over the couple of patients he has so that he can leave once he is finished. Is something wrong?"

"What about Reggie?"

"He, too, is wrapped up with a patient."

As quickly as the idea had flown into my head to have one of them look after Emma, it had been cut out from under me. I was the only doctor available tonight, and I had no choice but to deal with the situation.

"No, everything is fine. I just had a question, but I can figure it out. Thanks."

I needed to get myself and my emotions under control, I thought. I turned and began making my way back down to room three. I blew out a breath. I had no proof that that gorgeous little girl in that room was indeed mine. For all I knew, Brielle had met someone shortly after I'd left and was now happily married, just like Diane had said.

I stood outside of the room and let out a breath before walking back in. I needed to push all that nonsense to the back of my mind so that I could do my job. After all, she had been the one not to call me back.

I blew out a breath and went to the sink and washed my hands again and was just about to head back in when Diane came around the corner.

"Is everything okay, Sawyer?" my sister asked quietly.

I stepped into the supply room without saying anything, pretending to look for a couple of forms, pretending I didn't hear a word my sister had said.

"Sawyer, didn't you hear me?"

"I heard you, Diane. I'm fine."

"You seem bothered with something."

"I guess you could say I am bothered with the way fate has come back to haunt me. Perhaps coming back to Eastport was a mistake." I pulled the forms I had been looking for.

"What the hell is that supposed to mean?" she questioned, a confused look on her face.

"Brielle, is she by any chance married?"

"Brielle? Gosh no. I've tried to fix her up, but I've been unsuccessful. It's too bad. She is such a nice girl."

I nodded, still searching for a form. "Do you happen to know who her child's father is?"

Diane was quiet for a moment. "Sawyer, what is wrong with you? Those are some pretty personal questions." Diane frowned, looking at me as if I'd lost my mind.

"I realize that. It's just her file has no father's name on there. I think the father should know about the incident, don't you?" I said, looking at her for any sign she may give me that the child was mine.

"Why would that be?" she said, crossing her arms in front of her.

I looked to my sister and then to the floor. How was I going to get myself out of this? I shifted my weight from my left to right foot.

"Sawyer, you and I have both known Brielle since school. If you think she did something to that little button, you are crazy."

"That isn't why I am asking," I bit out.

"Well, that should be the only reason you are asking, and since there is no sign of that, you haven't any right to ask. Look. I have no right to say anything, but I was with Brielle when Emma was born. I can assure you that the father is not now, nor was he ever in the picture. He was a drunken mistake, a one-night stand, completely gone the next day. She hasn't had it easy, and for you to think such a thing would crush her. Besides, Brielle has emergency contacts listed, her mother, and myself," Diane said, shaking her head and turning away from me. "Oh, and any other information you feel you need ,I think you should speak directly with Brielle. Now, I need to go and check on some tests that Dr. Richards ordered."

I leaned against the doorframe and watched my sister walk down the hall. Diane was right; I had no right to ask her any of those questions. I blew out a breath, gathered myself, and walked into room three. Emma was lying on the exam table, covered with a blanket, while Brielle sat beside her holding her little hand and singing a nursery rhyme. She immediately stopped and looked at me.

"Sorry, I had to take care of something. I'd like to examine her wrist if I may," I said, meeting Brielle's eyes.

"Of course." She moved over so I could get in beside Emma.

I looked down at Emma, her bright-blue eyes staring back at me. I gently took her little hand in mine and moved her wrist, but the slightest movement resulted in Emma screaming out in pain.

"I will put in a call to radiology to get some x-rays," I said, frowning as Emma let out another loud scream.

"You don't think it's broken, do you?" Brielle asked, worry lining her voice.

"Better to be safe than sorry. Judging from the way she just screamed, I'm thinking it might be," I murmured and quickly began filling out a form while Brielle comforted Emma.

It seemed to take forever as I filled out papers I'd filled out millions of times over the past five years. I could feel myself getting hot as I scribbled my signature on the bottom of the form. The tension in the room could have been cut with a knife. I really just wanted to get out of here, and then I heard her clear her throat.

"When did you get back in town?" Brielle asked, finally looking my way.

"A month ago or so. I didn't figure you'd still be living here. I imagined you were off somewhere in some big court room fighting cases left and right." I scribbled out a couple of notes and then closed the file, finally meeting her eyes, only to see sadness in them I'd not seen before.

"Yeah, well, let's just say things didn't turn out the way I thought they would." She set Emma back down on the table, covering her with the blanket.

I looked to Brielle and nodded. "Radiology should be down in a few minutes. You can go up with her if you'd like, or grab a coffee in the cafeteria. Totally up to you. They will bring her back here, and then I'll be back after the x-ray results are here."

"Thanks, Sawyer."

"You are welcome," I replied and picked up the file. I was about to leave the room, but instead I just stood in the doorway for a moment, before turning back around to look down at them. Brielle sat holding Emma, rocking her gently back and forth, humming away to her.

AN HOUR LATER, Brielle walked beside me carrying a sleeping Emma in her arms: "So, as I said, nothing was broken. It's just a bad sprain."

Brielle nodded. "What about pain?"

"You can give her some children's pain medication every six hours or so. Otherwise, I think she will be okay," I said, looking into her eyes; they were lined with worry. "She may get a fever, so, if you're worried about anything, you can always call me," I said, holding out my card for her to take.

"Thanks, Sawyer. You've been great," she said, taking my card and looking down at it.

"My pleasure." I took hold of her hand and looked into her eyes as a moment of silence passed between us. "Listen, there are some things we should probably talk about."

She pulled her hand away and looked to the floor. "What did you have in mind?"

I had done my best to put the thought out of my mind that Emma was possibly mine, but somehow, deep down, I knew I needed to know for sure. "Tell me when you are available, and we can meet somewhere?"

"Hmmm okay, well, how about Wednesday afternoon? Could you meet me at Eastport Park around two?"

I nodded, "Sure. I will see you then."

"Okay, I'm going to get her home and into bed. Good night."

"Good night, Brielle."

I watched as she turned away from me and carried a sleeping Emma down the hall and away from me. Once she was out of my sight, I heard my name being paged. I stood there for a moment, thinking of what the probabilities were that Emma was indeed mine, and then shook the thought from my head once again. There was no way she would have kept something like that from me.

Diane was probably right; a one-night stand shortly after I'd left was more than likely the truth. She probably was open to meeting me because she wanted closure, I thought to myself, closure I had never been able to provide, even for myself. I had two days to figure out how I was going to give that to her. My mind was riddled with thoughts when I heard my name again over the paging system.

"Doctor McKay, please report to Emergency."

BRIELLE

I'D WORKED on autopilot over the next few days. Emma had been cranky and clingy and only wanted to be with me. I'd been super busy at The Cooling Rack with large orders, but none of that compared to the stress I'd felt after seeing Sawyer. Not only had the journal brought back memories, but now that I'd seen him, I'd dreamt about him every single night since.

I arrived at the park early and set us up along the edge of the beach. I threw down the beach blanket and umbrella and then sat Emma down and dumped out her beach toys in front of her before setting up my chair.

"Emma, did you want a drink?" I asked, watching as she dug her little shovel into the sand.

She looked up at me and nodded her head and raised her little sand-covered hand to me. I quickly pulled out her cup and handed it to her and watched as she took a drink and then handed me the cup back. I then pulled my book from my bag, turned to where I had left off, and sat back, trying to take my mind off everything.

Emma was finally playing and I had just gotten into the chapter, when I caught movement out of the corner of my eye. I glanced in the direction of the parking lot and saw Sawyer walking across the park in our direction carrying a chair. I couldn't help but take him in. He looked different than he had the other night. Of course, in my panic, I hadn't really taken a close look. He was built a little heavier than when we had been together, like he had been working out. He wore dark-blue jeans and a light long-sleeved shirt that hugged him in all the right places. However, no matter how good he looked, I'd be lying if I said I had been looking forward to this meeting. How I went from being absolutely sure I would never see him again to meeting up with him alone I didn't know. I swallowed hard and put my face back in my book. The last thing I wanted was for him to see me watching him.

It only took him mere minutes to cross the park, and now he stood beside me. He set up his chair and placed it close to mine, then sat down. He said nothing at first. Instead he just sat there studying Emma, probably to see if he could see himself in her actions. Sawyer wasn't a stupid man, and I was surprised that he didn't ask me the other night in the emergency room. He was going to be in for a big surprise because as she sat there struggling with her little shovel, every expression that lined her face was his.

"How is she today?" he questioned, still watching her.

"She had a bit of a fever through the night, but it eventually broke this morning. I've followed your suggestion with the medication, and she says her arm doesn't hurt anymore."

"I'm glad to hear that."

He was silent again, still studying her, a small smile on his lips as he watched her dump over her bucket and begin filling it again. He could tell, I knew he could, and I swallowed hard, trying to come up with a way to tell him.

"Why didn't you tell me about her?"

So this was how we were going to do this. Neither of us able to swim, we were going to jump right on into the deep end of the pool without a life jacket. I let out a deep breath and placed my book down on top of my bag. "I guess you could say I didn't want to interfere with your dream or your goals."

"Are you serious?" He glared at me with disbelief. "Like really serious?"

I nodded. "Yes, Sawyer. I couldn't do that to you. You had worked so hard."

Sawyer chuckled to himself and ran his hand across

the back of his neck. "So in your mind it's okay that you kept something like this from me? It's okay that our daughter would grow up never knowing her father?"

I didn't say anything. I could see the anger in his face.

"We aren't talking about a puppy, Brielle. We are talking about a child."

"I am fully aware of what we are talking about."

"Are you? I'm not sure you do. Do you have any idea how I feel about this? Let me tell you, I feel like shit because I wasn't there for you when you needed me. I also haven't been there for her. I've missed out on raising my daughter, missing birthdays and holidays, because you chose not to tell me."

"There is no reason for you to feel like shit, Sawyer. I made the choice—for both of us. Being a doctor was your dream, and you have the right to live it."

"Well, you had no right to make that choice for me. None. We could have made it work, and besides, you had dreams too, Brielle. What makes it right for you to give up yours?"

I thought for a moment. "I didn't give them up. I just slightly altered them. I didn't really have a choice, but you did."

"Oh come on, like I said, you made the choice for you, but you had no right to make it for me." Tension lined his shoulders as he looked off into the distance.

"Sawyer, we spent one summer together screwing

around. It wasn't like we were in a serious, committed relationship. There wasn't a soul who knew about us. Hell, to this day, Diane still doesn't know. You were leaving, and to be honest, I was very unsure of what we even were to one another, if anything at all."

"So my hints weren't strong enough?"

"What hints?"

"Movies, dinners alone, making excuses not to go out with friends or to leave a party early. That I still wanted to see you?"

I couldn't help but chuckle. "You wanted someone to keep your bed warm, and sure you wanted to see me when you came home on break."

"Brielle, don't you dare try and downplay this. I never ever treated you like you were an object, *ever*. You also know that I didn't mean it like that either."

"How did you mean it then?"

Sawyer ran his hand over his face, and I could see the tension in his jaw. "Jesus, Brielle, if you must know, I was in love with you. I didn't know how else to broach the subject. I had planned on returning from that internship, figuring by then we would be serious, and then we could get married and start a family. Instead, I never heard from you again."

"Is that right?"

"Yes."

"Well, Sawyer, perhaps you should have been a little more clear on what you meant," I bit back.

"Tell me one thing: why is that I never heard from you again?"

I looked down at the book that sat in my lap.

"Tell me the truth, was there someone else?"

"No, Sawyer, there was no one else." I was hurt that he would even think that way of me.

"Then what was it?"

"Sawyer, after I dropped out of school, I flew out to Seattle. It was about a month after you had left. I wanted to surprise you, and that was when I planned on telling you about the baby. I had it all played out in my mind, that you would be happy and ask me to move in with you. Instead, when I arrived, I saw you with a nurse. You were walking back to your apartment, she hung off your arm, you were both laughing and talking. I didn't have the strength to even get out of the car after seeing her all over you. Instead I had the driver take me back to the airport. My heart was crushed. It wasn't as if I didn't expect that you would date, but seeing you with her, well, I couldn't face it. So you can tell me whatever you want. You can say you loved me, but I have a hard time believing that."

"So you think because you saw me with some girl that my feelings for you weren't true."

"Sure looked like it."

"Well, Brielle, you are wrong. She was the sister of the doctor I was rooming with. She asked if she could walk with me so she could see her brother, and on the way, she twisted her ankle. That was why she was holding onto my arm and she was walking with me because the neighborhood that we lived in wasn't exactly the safest place on the earth."

I felt my stomach drop at his admission.

"And, just so you know, I tried to call you, Brielle, a lot. You never took my calls, nor did you once ever call back. I came home many times in the five years I was gone, and every single time I thought about coming to see you but knew damn well I'd be wasting my time because you wouldn't see me."

He was right, I wouldn't have seen him, because then he would have known about the baby.

"You weren't fair to me, Brielle. But regardless of what happened between us, together or not, I still had every right to know about her," he said, glancing to Emma. "Every right."

I didn't know what to say. I had planned on him never finding out because I had planned on never seeing him again.

I looked down to where my hands were clasped in my lap. "I know," I whispered.

"I feel like I need to do something, to help you out in some way."

"The last thing I need or want is charity, Sawyer. I've done fine supporting both of us all this time. We are fine."

Sawyer looked at me, a frown coming to his face. "Brielle, she is my daughter. I have a right to be involved somehow."

I looked down to Emma and then leaned forward toward Sawyer. "You were involved for about fifteen minutes."

"That isn't what I meant, Brielle, and you know it. Stop acting as if I am the enemy here. I am trying to tell you I want to be a part of this," Sawyer bit out, looking me directly in the eyes.

I turned and looked out at the water, doing my best to calm myself down. There was nothing to fix. He had no right to start demanding to be a part of her life, but on the other hand, I had no right to deny him either. I also had no right to treat him the way I was.

"I can only imagine what your mother must think of me," Sawyer mumbled.

I turned and looked at him. I could see the hurt splashed across his face. "My mom doesn't know."

"How does your mother not know? Let me guess, you were like those women on that show *I Didn't Know I was Pregnant*."

"I mean she doesn't know that Emma is yours. As I said, Diane doesn't even know. I kept our secret, just like you wanted. All my mother knows was that we hung out sometimes with our friends. She did ask me if you were the father because she thought something was going on between us, but I flat out denied it. I told my mother that Emma was the result of a drunken one-night stand and that the father wanted nothing to do with me or the baby afterward."

"Lord, Brielle, I'm sure your mother could do math."

I shook my head. "Once Emma was born, she questioned it again, but I made up a date and told her the one-night stand happened right before you left."

"Are you ever going to tell her?"

"I wasn't planning on it, no. Besides, you were never supposed to come back to Eastport."

"Well, I'm here now," Sawyer said, "and I know about her, and I want to help. I want to be a part of her life. I deserve to be a part of her life."

I closed my eyes for a moment and dug deep inside to pull myself out of this pit I felt I was in. I knew I had been wrong by not telling him, and I realized now how much of a mess I'd really dug myself into. It hadn't just been Sawyer I had lied to, but my mother and my best friend as well.

"Are you planning on staying in Eastport?" I asked, looking to Sawyer.

When he didn't answer me right away, I knew the answer. He had probably taken the position at Eastport

General as a stepping stone to get into another position in another hospital somewhere in the world. If that was the case, I wouldn't let him near Emma.

"What is that supposed to mean?"

"Look, I don't want you to be in and out of her life. I know firsthand what it's like to have a father walk out, so I refuse to do that to her."

"So you're going to paint me with the same brush I see."

"No, I never said that, but if you are going to be her dad then you need to understand it's a full-time job. You are either here or you're not. Once a routine is established, she won't understand why you don't show up when it's your turn to have her, and she certainly won't understand why all of a sudden you aren't around anymore either."

"If you are asking me if I'm back in Eastport for good, Brielle, the answer is yes. I missed home too much to leave again."

I looked into his dark-brown eyes, trying to read them. It had been so long since I had seen him, and I was feeling so out of touch with myself after all that had happened over the past few days that I couldn't quite tell if he was just saying that or if he meant it.

"I don't know, Sawyer," I murmured.

"Mommy, look!" Emma shouted.

When I didn't immediately look, she stood up and

came over to me, pulling my shirt. I tore my eyes from Sawyer and pulled her against me, kissing her forehead. "Yes, I see it, baby. It's a bird."

She pulled her little hands into her chest and laughed as the bird ran down the beach.

"Why don't you get back down and play in the sand," I whispered, kissing her forehead.

She looked at Sawyer with curiosity. "Mommy, who that?" She pointed to Sawyer.

Sawyer smiled at her. "That's just an old friend of Mommy's," I said, pulling her hair from her face. "Now how about you go back and play."

She slid off my lap and went back to digging in the sand and playing with her toys. I smiled at her, until I realized that by forcing her back down, I was back to the reality and that the conversation Sawyer and I were having was still staring me in the face. I turned to face him only to see the pain in his eyes.

"Brielle, please, let me try. Let me try and prove to you how serious I am about this."

"How would you like to do that?"

"How about a date? Just you and me where we can talk."

I couldn't help but laugh to myself, at how naive Sawyer truly was when it came to what it was like to have a child. "Well, Sawyer, as wonderful as that sounds,

I just can't leave a four-year-old unattended, and I don't have a sitter."

"All right, well, then why don't we take Emma to the fall fair? You and me."

I had planned on taking her myself the following weekend. I shrugged. "I guess we could do that."

"Okay, so I will pick you both up early next Saturday morning."

I quickly ran through my schedule and shook my head. "It will have to be after eleven." I had orders to prepare at work. Plus, I had to open the bakery.

"Okay, how about two o'clock?"

"Fine, Sawyer, two o'clock," I said, meeting his eyes.

"Now will you do me a favor and introduce me to my daughter," he pleaded.

SAWYER HAD CALLED every day since we had met a week ago to check on Emma. It was Wednesday morning and I was expecting him to call and cancel our day trip on Saturday. Yet he shocked me when he'd come by on Wednesday night and brought dinner with him after Emma was already tucked into bed.

That time together had given us a chance to clear the

air between us. We spent the evening getting reac-quainted, not arguing. After he had left, I sat in the dark-ness of my living room wishing that somehow things had turned out differently. I was tired of struggling. I was tired of upholding a lie to the people who mattered. Perhaps this was the chance.

A little after two on Saturday, I saw his car pull up out front of my apartment building. I carried Emma out to his car and was just about to tell him I would drive, so I didn't need to grab the car seat, but when I poked my head in the window, I was surprised to find there was a car seat already in the back.

"I picked it up from the store yesterday," he said, climbing out of the driver's seat and coming around to grab my bag and stroller.

"Wow, Sawyer, you didn't have to do that."

"I did. I told you I wanted to be a part of this and I meant it." His eyes meant mine.

I watched him for a minute as he loaded everything into the trunk and then came over to my side. "Here, give her to me."

"I can put her in the car seat," I said, but I could tell he wasn't going to back down, so I handed Emma over and watched as he strapped her in and then placed her blanket over her legs.

"All set," he said, stepping around me and pulling my door open, waiting until I climbed into the front seat. I watched as Sawyer ran around the front of the car and climbed into the driver's seat.

Once we arrived at the fair, Sawyer insisted on heading over to the rides that were geared for small kids. He purchased tickets and went with her on every ride, holding her on his lap while I watched from a distance. I could tell she liked him; she never made a fuss and was always smiling any time he would show her any attention. Then she wrapped her little arms around his neck and hung onto him as we made our way to the next ride. She would throw her head back and laugh while he held her tight.

Once he'd taken her on every ride, he stopped and grabbed tickets for the games. There was a little magnet fishing game that she was insistent on playing all because she wanted a big Minnie Mouse stuffed toy. When she didn't win, she burst into tears.

Sawyer looked at me and then down to Emma whose chubby little cheeks were streaked with tears. "Do you really want that Minnie?" Sawyer asked, kneeling down to her eye level.

She nodded.

"Then just you wait." He took off in the direction of the ticket guy before I could stop him.

I remembered he had done this with me one night. Of course I never broke down into tears, but I remembered he had spent over a hundred dollars trying to win my something at this exact fair, when finally the guy behind the counter took pity on him and just gave him what he had wanted because of all the money he had spent.

I picked Emma up and wiped her tears, then grabbed her juice and handed her her bottle. Within minutes, Sawyer was back with another handful of tickets. He looked around and saw a ring toss game that had the exact same Minnie hanging from the rafters. "Let's go over there." He nodded.

"All right." I strapped Emma into her stroller and covered her with a blanket, and then followed Sawyer over to where he stood, with a handful of rings, already beginning to play.

"Hopefully, you've gotten better at this game," I called, smiling at him.

"I'm surprised you remembered. Now let's hope I am." He laughed.

A half hour later, he finally landed the third and final ring on the bottle needed to win the Minnie Mouse. He turned and smiled at me, then pointed to the stuffed animal. The game attendant reached up and grabbed it and handed it to Sawyer.

I smiled and shook my head. "I can't believe you did that for her."

"She will be so surprised when she wakes up."

"So tell me, how much did that end up costing you?" I questioned.

"Believe me, you don't want to know." Sawyer laughed and glanced down at his watch. "Did you want to go and watch the fireworks before we head back?"

I smiled and nodded. "That sounds wonderful."

Sawyer reached over and placed his hand over mine, and a surge of electricity pulsed through me. I slowly let go of Emma's stroller and let him take it. He lifted his left arm, waiting for me to slide mine through his, just like he always did when we had gone anywhere. I was hesitant at first, and then slipped my arm through his. We walked that way to the end of the beach where we found an empty bench away from the crowd.

SAWYER PULLED into the parking lot of my apartment building and pulled into one of the visitors spots and cut the engine.

"Thank you so much for today. I had an amazing time."

"No, Brie, thank you," he said, his voice quiet and deep as he stared at me.

A funny feeling went through me as he used the short form of my name. He was the only one I'd ever allowed to call me that. I met his eyes and then glanced in the back seat at a sleeping Emma. "If you give me a couple of minutes, I will just take in all the stuff and then come down to get her."

"I can bring her up if you like," he whispered.

"It's late, Sawyer, and you have to work in the morning."

He shrugged. "It's okay. I've spent many days being tired at work because of worse choices. I'll be fine. I don't mind."

I smiled and nodded. No doubt he was telling me the truth. I was tired anyway and could use the help. We climbed out of the car together, he pulled the stroller, bag, and stuffed animal out of the trunk, then walked around to the passenger's side of the car and reached in. He gently picked her up, careful not to wake her, and rested her against his chest.

My stomach flopped at the sight of him holding our baby, her little fist up to her mouth as she sucked on her thumb. He carried her up to my apartment, and I was shocked that she still hadn't woken. I opened the door and walked in, flipping the light on in the corner of the living room.

"Where is her room?" Sawyer whispered, looking around my small but cozy apartment.

"Right over there," I whispered, pointing to the far door.

He slipped his shoes off and carried her over to her

bedroom door. He was just about to step inside when she started to whine.

"Did you want me to take her?" I questioned, beginning to make my way over to them, but Sawyer shook his head and gently bounced her. She immediately stopped fussing.

"I'm fine. Why don't you make us a cup of coffee or something while I put her down."

I watched as she ground her small fists into her eyes, but Sawyer didn't stop. I stood and listened for a moment. He didn't need to get her in her pajamas because I had done that before we had left the park. Instead, I heard him start to read the same book I had read to her the night before. His deep voice took on this soft tone, and as I stood there listening, I knew that I really had made a mistake keeping her from him. Tears came to my eyes as I listened for a few more minutes before finally tearing myself away.

I carried two steaming mugs into the living room and placed them on the coffee table. I could still see the soft glow of the light on in Emma's room but could no longer hear Sawyer reading to her. I took a sip of my coffee and was about to get up and go make sure everything was okay when he stepped out of her room, pulling the door closed partway behind him.

He smiled as he made his way over to me and sat

down. He picked up his cup and took a sip, then sat back against the couch, not saying a word.

"Everything okay?" I questioned.

"Of course," he said, smiling at me. "She's amazing."

I smiled. "So why did you come back to Eastport?" I questioned as we both took a sip of coffee.

"Honestly, as good as I've made my life in Seattle sound, it was lonely. Plus, Mom and Dad are getting up there. Dad just had knee replacement surgery and had a few complications, and Mom needed help looking after him. I can't do it from there, and Diane has her own problems with that dick she married, which I am sure you know all about, so when the opportunity came up to apply, I did."

"Is your father okay now?" I questioned. I hadn't seen him in a while. His mother sometimes stopped into The Cooling Rack on occasion, but I was always in the back when she came in.

"He's doing better, thanks."

"That's good," I said, picking up my mug. "What about your significant other?" As the words slipped out of my mouth, I wished I could swallow them back down. I didn't want him to think I was interested in anything with him. I more wanted to know what she thought of all this.

"There isn't anyone at the moment. I dated some of the nurses at the hospital in Seattle, but my work schedule was heavy and didn't really permit me to have a private life."

I nodded in understanding.

"What about you? How have things been for you?"

I picked up my mug of coffee and leaned back, pulling the pillow that had sat behind me in front of me as if it were going to form some sort of protective shield around me.

"Things are good now. I won't lie that it's been rough. I had no idea what I was doing when I dropped out of school shortly after I found out I was pregnant. There was no way I would have been able to keep up with the demand of law school, I'd already known that. It took me months to figure out what I was going to do. I knew my mother was angry and there was no way she was going to let me move through life without education.

"After Emma was born, I enrolled into the community college here. I took night courses in business management. When I finally graduated, I worked for a couple bakeries in town but had a hard time keeping the jobs. Mom couldn't always be with Emma, Diane was having issues with her ex, and of course the owners didn't want a baby in my office. I couldn't just leave her with anyone. It needed to be someone that I could trust. So, after six months of shitty pay and a lot of work, I decided that if I was going to be able to support us, the only way I could do it and be successful was by being my own boss.

"So, I went back to night school, completed a pastry chef program and an entrepreneur program. Once I was graduated, I took the remaining money I had saved for law school and got a small business loan and put it all towards opening The Cooling Rack."

"Diane said you owned a successful business, but I had no idea that it was The Cooling Rack," he said.

"Yep, that's my baby. I pour all my blood, sweat and tears into that place."

"How did I not know that? I stop by there almost every morning for breakfast, and sometimes for dinner when I tire of cafeteria food. I've never seen you there."

"So do most doctors. I'm surprised you didn't know because Diane tells everyone." I giggled. "I'm normally in the back doing bookwork, baking, and running the kitchen. I leave most of the front of the store to the staff."

Sawyer looked down to where his hands rested in his lap. "Is it going okay? I mean, are you making enough to support yourselves?"

"It's been challenging, and had its moments. I almost lost it twice, but after a few tweaks, yes, I am doing better each year. It's a lot of work, but it makes it easy now that Mom is retired and she can stay with Emma most of the time—her or Diane—and when they can't be with her, she just comes with me."

He glanced around the apartment, growing quiet, and then he turned his eyes to me. He sat there a funny look on his face. I watched as his jaw tensed, and then he cleared his throat. "Are you seeing anyone?" he questioned.

I shook my head. "No, Sawyer, I'm not. Diane keeps trying to fix me up with people, even though I beg her not to bother. Most of the men my age are looking for fun, and that is something that I can't do with the responsibility of a baby and a cafe," I said, quickly bringing my hand to my mouth to cover as I let out a yawn.

"I see, well, you have another sitter if you need," he said, glancing down at his watch. "I really should get going. It's almost eleven, and you probably have to work in the morning."

I nodded. "Yes, I have to be at the café for five." I smiled and watched as Sawyer stood.

I followed him to the door and watched as he slipped his shoes on. Then he turned to me.

"We need to figure out a plan, some way that I can spend time with Emma."

"Sure, why don't you text me your schedule and we will figure something out?"

He turned and looked my way. When our eyes met, an odd silence fell between us. Sawyer looked at me and slowly brought his hand up and brushed away a loose strand of hair that had fallen into my eyes, his hand resting on my cheek. I could feel my heart pounding in my chest at the feel of his warm skin on mine. "I never wanted to be apart from you," he whispered, and without any warning, he leaned in and met my lips.

All the feelings I had worked so hard to bury came rushing back, and as his lips danced over mine, it was like I was transported back five years. His hands rested on my hips, and he brushed his thumb over the soft, bare skin of my abdomen. I could feel a part of me awaken that had been asleep for so long. I wrapped my arms around his shoulders and felt him press his body against me, pushing me into the wall, as his tongue washed through my mouth. Both my body and conscience was screaming simultaneously, one warning me to stay away from him, the other craving him. I closed my eyes, shutting out the first, and allowed myself to get lost in the kiss I'd missed so much.

Suddenly, Emma let out a scream, and I pulled away from his lips, placing my hands on his chest. "I've got to get her," I said breathlessly.

His eyes were heady and filled with want and he pushed forward for more, biting my bottom lip. I welcomed him once again, forgetting all about my screaming baby. His kiss got more forceful, more heated, and I met his rhythm with the same heat and want. I could have stayed this way forever, but Emma once again let out a full-blown scream.

"Guess that's my cue," he whispered against my lips, his dark eyes meeting mine.

I nodded. He kissed me one more time, and then I watched as he walked out of my apartment door, pulling it closed behind him. Every part of me wanted him to come back. I stepped forward and glanced out the peephole to see if he was still waiting on the other side of the door, but he was gone. I leaned against the cool door, trying to gather my thoughts when Emma let out another loud shrill.

I picked her up and sat down in the rocking chair, adjusting her to a laying position, and comforted her while gently rocking her. I rested my head against the chair and thought back to moments ago, still feeling his hands on my body.

As the cloud lifted, I realized that I couldn't allow him back into my life, not this way. I needed to protect as much of myself as I did Emma, and allowing him in to be a father figure for his daughter was troubling enough. The last thing I needed was to have my heart broken because I allowed myself to fall for him all over again. I needed to be strong for my daughter, just in case he decided that the idea he had of playing family was no longer all the fun and games he thought it was.

SAWYER

---

3 Months Later

"Good morning. How's my two favorite girls?" I said as I walked into the kitchen and poured myself a cup of coffee.

Brie sat with Emma at the breakfast table, feeding her oatmeal. I leaned down and placed a kiss on Emma's head, and then turned to Brie and met her lips with a morning kiss.

"Morning. Sleep well?" I whispered to her as I kissed her again.

"Very well, once you stopped torturing me." She giggled.

"Funny, that's not how I remember it." I chuckled, reaching my hand down between her legs and grabbing her inner thigh.

Brie swatted at my hand and laughed, meeting my eyes. "You are so bad," she chastised.

It was only quarter to six. I had to be at the hospital for eight, and I planned on dropping Brie at The Cooling Rack a half hour before that.

"There is oatmeal for you as well," Brie said as she smiled at Emma's messy face.

"Thanks," I said, sitting down beside her. It had taken a long while, but I had finally proven myself to Brie, and at first we worked out an arrangement so I could spend time with my daughter. It had taken much convincing, some back and forth conversation, and a lot of begging to get her to agree. The more time I spent with Emma meant the more Brie and I saw one another, and soon we were right back where we had been before I had left for medical school, only this time it wasn't just a casual relationship. We had begun to see one another on a more serious level, still privately, the only difference being that this time we'd decided to take things slow.

I scooped up a spoonful of oatmeal while watching Emma and Brie. The more time I spent with them, the more I felt like kicking myself for never growing the balls to go and knock on Brie's door when I'd come home. As I watched Emma giggling away, I realized just how much her laugh reminded me of Brie. I had missed out on the first four years of her life; however, I needed to focus on moving forward. That was in the past.

"What time are you finished tonight?"

"Ah same time, between seven and eight."

"Did you want to come by afterward? Maybe watch a movie?"

"I'd love that. I'll bring dinner."

"No need." Brie smiled. "I'll have something ready. I'm going to hop in the shower. You both be okay?"

"We will be fine." I smiled as she leaned down to kiss me before making her way into the bathroom. The second I heard the door click shut and the water turn on, I looked at my daughter and made a silly face, which caused her to break out in a fit of hysteria.

I DRIED the last of the dinner dishes and placed them up in the cupboard, while Brie picked Emma up off the floor.

"I'm just going to put her down."

"Could I do it?" I questioned, placing the towel I had dried the dishes with on the counter. It had become my favorite way to spend my nights. Reading her a story and watching her little eyes close as she relaxed against me was the best feeling in the world.

Brie smiled. "If you'd like."

She carried Emma over and passed her to me. As always she reached her little arms out and wrapped them around my neck. "Daddy," she squealed.

I looked at Brie, my heart in my throat. This was the first time Emma had called me Daddy. "My God, did you hear that?" I asked, swallowing hard.

"I did." Brie smiled at me, her eyes full of happiness. "Take your daughter and put her to bed," she whispered, kissing Emma good night on the cheek.

I hugged her tighter to me and carried her in her bedroom. I sat down in the rocking chair, sitting her on my lap, and then grabbed two of the books I had gotten her off her little bookshelf.

"Which one would you like to hear tonight?" I said, holding them out in front of her?

She quickly pointed to the bright-pink book, and so I flipped it open and began reading it to her while gently rocking. At first, she was glued to the book, pointing at the pictures, looking up at me, and then she quieted down, and before I had reached the end, she was sound asleep against me.

I carefully scooped her up and placed her in bed, then I covered her up and placed the Minnie Mouse doll I had won for her beside her.

I looked down at her and watched her sleep for a moment. I didn't want to be apart from her any more than I had to, nor did I want to be away from Brie. I wanted to make them a permanent part of my life. I bent down and placed a kiss on Emma's forehead and then switched the light off. Now I just needed to figure out a way to let Brie know I was serious about them.

I made my way back out to the living room and found Brie on the couch almost asleep. I sat down beside her and brushed the hair from her eyes. She stirred and looked up at me with sleep-filled eyes.

"Hey," I whispered.

"Sorry, I must have fallen asleep," she said, trying to push herself up. "Did you get her down all right?"

"Of course I did. Daddy isn't going to fail her." I smiled as I met her eyes.

She studied me for a moment, and then a soft smile came to her lips. "You look so happy."

"I am happy. She is everything, and I can't believe in the short time I have known her that I already feel that way."

"I know that feeling. It's like your entire world changes."

I nodded and looked at her for a moment, then without warning, the words fell from my lips. "There is only one thing that would make me happier."

"What's that?"

"You."

I wasn't sure how she was going to respond to my answer, but she surprised me by meeting my lips with hers. As she kissed me, she rose onto her knees and pushed me back against the couch so she could straddle me. I kissed her deeply, allowing my hands to run up her back as I pulled her against me. I could feel my cock starting to harden as she lowered herself onto my lap. She surprised me by pulling her shirt off over her head and reached behind her to undo her bra. My eyes roamed her body as she allowed the fabric of her bra to fall away from her body. Her nipples were already hard, and my mouth watered at the thought of sucking one of those perfect buds into my mouth.

I reached behind my head and pulled my shirt off and leaned back on the couch, my eyes meeting hers before they ran over her body once again. I brought my hands up and cupped her breasts, then leaned forward and took one in my mouth. I gently bit the hardened peak. She let out a tiny gasp and wrapped her hand in my hair.

My cock ached behind the zipper of my jeans. I'd felt like I'd had permanent blue balls for the past couple of months. We'd had yet to go further than a little fooling around. I had made a promise to myself that nothing more would happen between us until I was sure she was ready. As I kissed her, I held her hips tight against me, grinding up into her.

I looked into her eyes and traced my fingers down her stomach to the button on her jeans. I flicked it open with one hand. She rose up onto her knees, and I roughly pulled her jeans down her legs. She placed her hands on my shoulders and looked down into my eyes. I allowed my fingers to gently dance over the fabric of her panties, her body shuddering as I did so. I placed a kiss on either thigh and gripped her ass in my hands.

My cock throbbed as I held her there, teasing her with my tongue through the fabric of her panties. Her fingers dug into my shoulders. I was about to pull the fabric of her panties to the side when she lowered herself back down onto my lap. She looked at me, her eyes full of want, but without another word, she got up off my lap, allowing her jeans to fall to the floor. I frowned as she walked over to her bedroom door and looked back over at me.

"Where are you going?" I questioned, unsure of what was happening here.

But she didn't answer. She just smiled at me and cocked her head toward the bedroom. "Aren't you coming?"

I COULD STILL HEAR the sounds of her orgasm as I sat in the quietness of my office. It was a little past eight, and I was working hard to finish up the final bit of paperwork I had before I made my way home for the night, which was proving to be difficult, since I couldn't get her out of my mind. I let out a breath and set the patient file to the side when I heard a knock on my door.

"Come in," I called, not looking up as I heard the door open.

"Sawyer, I am surprised you are still here," Dr. Richards, said looking down to his watch. "I was just going to drop this on your desk, but since you are here, I may as well talk to you about it."

"Sure, come on in. Please have a seat."

Dr. Richards pulled the chair out on the other side of the desk and took a seat, looking a little perplexed at the paperwork in his hand.

"Sawyer, your work in this hospital over the past few months has not gone unnoticed."

"Thank you, sir."

"And I wish there were better opportunities here for someone as hard working as yourself. That being said, at the same time, it would be a shame to lose you. However, there is a position open in a hospital in Florida and they are looking for a supervising doctor to head up their ER."

I sat back in my chair, giving Dr. Richards my full, undivided attention. This position he referred to had been my dream. "When does the application period end?"

"In a couple of weeks, but as your supervisor, I took

the liberty of sending in a referral. You are a tremendous doctor, and I would hate to see you lose out on this position."

I looked at Dr. Richards. "I don't really know what to say."

Dr. Richards leaned forward and threw a thick envelope on my desk. Then he sat back and crossed his arms in front of him, smiling.

"What is this?" I asked, looking down to the manila envelope.

"Your offer. The hospital administrator sent this to me this morning. They want you. Take some time and look it all over. You've got lots of time."

I looked down at the envelope that lay on my desk, almost afraid to touch it. Then I looked back up at Dr. Richards just as his name came over the intercom.

"I'll have to think about it, of course," I said.

"Of course. Give it some thought, look over what they sent, and I will see you tomorrow, Sawyer. Congratulations on the offer. It's an amazing opportunity," he said, walking to the door of my office and opening it.

The second he was gone, I looked back down to the thick white envelope that sat on my desk. I picked it up and fiddled with the flap, letting out a deep breath. I knew this envelope held the contents of what I had worked so hard to achieve. I just couldn't bear to open it right now, so I took it and shoved it into my bag and packed up my things.

It was almost nine by the time I got home. I showered and got changed then sat down in the kitchen. I emptied the contents of my bag and sat there with the envelope staring back at me. I blew out a breath and opened it. I sifted through the papers. I was about halfway through the package when my cell phone rang. A smile came to my lips as I saw Brie's name flash across the screen.

"Hello."

"Hey, sorry, I know it's late and you're probably exhausted, but Emma's been crying all evening. She wants to say good night." I could hear the exhaustion in her voice and a crying Emma in the background.

"Put her on." I smiled as I heard Brie say something to Emma.

"Hi, Daddy." She sniffled.

My eyes went right to the package in front of me that held the offer, and I swallowed hard. I shouldn't have bothered even reading it. I should have just flat out denied the offer.

"Hey, angel. You getting ready for bed?"

"Yes, Daddy. When are you coming over?"

"I'll see you tomorrow okay. Now be a good girl for Mommy and crawl into bed."

"I want you to read me a story, Daddy." She sniffled.

This kid was literally breaking my heart. I closed my eyes. "I will read to you tomorrow night. It's Mommy's turn tonight."

"Okay, Daddy."

I could practically see her little face all scrunched up in a pout. I blew out a breath and pinched the bridge of my nose with my fingers as all the stress piled onto me.

"Hey, sorry about that. She's been screaming for you all night. How was your day?"

"Busy as usual. What about yours?"

"Crazy. Will we see you tomorrow?"

I pulled the newspaper overtop of the offer and got up to grab a mug from the cupboard. "You bet you will."

"Okay, we'll see you then. Night, Sawyer."

"Night."

I hung up the phone, made a cup of tea, and stood looking back to where I knew the offer sat. Finally, curiosity got the best of me, and I sat back down to flip through the offer.

BRIELLE

EMMA SAT PLAYING with her toys in my office while I began preparing some orders that were to be picked up for the late morning. The Cooling Rack was buzzing this morning, and I had more orders than normal to pack up. I set up some boxes on the counter and began packing them as I hummed along to the song that played on the radio.

"Someone is rather happy this morning," Brenda said, coming into the kitchen with a bin of dirty mugs and began loading them in the dishwasher.

I giggled. "I guess you could say that."

"All right, spill it. Did you have a date with that guy again? What was his name..." She put her finger up to her lips in thought. "Drew?"

I let out laugh. "No, that ship sailed long ago."

"What has gotten into you then?" Brenda questioned, turning to look at me.

I was about to answer when the back door opened and Sawyer walked in. He was dressed in dark jeans and a white T-shirt that hugged every muscle he had. "Morning," he said, walking over to me and placing a kiss on my lips. "How's it going?"

"Good. Little busier than I expected, but all the baking is finally finished."

Just then Emma let out a loud squeal of excitement. I glanced over and watched as she balanced herself as she got up off the floor, running in Sawyer's direction. He bent down and quickly scooped her up in his arms.

"She probably needs to be changed. She just woke up a little bit ago," I said, wiping my hands on my apron.

"I got her. Where is her diaper bag?"

"Just inside my office door." I nodded.

"All right, let's go, Emma bear," Sawyer said taking her into my office and closing the door behind him.

I looked over at Brenda, who stood there looking at me. "Oh my God, Brielle. I can see why you are so happy... He is hot."

I smiled and nodded.

"Is he..." She nodded to the closed door.

I was about to answer her but stopped speaking when the door to the kitchen opened and Diane walked in wearing her scrubs.

"Good morning!" she sang as she sat down in her usual spot with a cup of coffee in her hand. She reached across and grabbed a freshly baked cookie off the sheet I was emptying. Diane had been away on a course the past few weeks. In some ways, I'd been thankful because it had given me the chance to spend time with Sawyer without her asking me all kinds of questions.

Brenda took one look at the two of us and excused herself, heading back out to the front.

"What's up?" I questioned once the door had closed behind Brenda.

"I was going to call you, but with the course, I haven't had a chance. I should have told you a long time ago but didn't, and now I pray it isn't too late."

I frowned. "What is it? What's wrong?"

"The night you were in the hospital with Emma, Sawyer was the attending doctor?"

I nodded, focusing on packaging the cookies in front of me.

"Well, he was asking me all kinds of questions about you and Emma. He wanted to know who the father was so he could call him. He said he needed to be notified of the incident."

"It's not what you think," I said, reaching for the next tray of cookies.

"I don't know, Brielle. I thought he was acting weird at first, but I have seen this before with young single parents who come into the hospital with injuries on their children. The attending physicians end up reporting them for abuse. I just want you to be ready in case..."

"Sawyer isn't going to report me, Diane."

"Don't be so sure. I tried to talk him out of it that night. I have been talking with him while I was away. He's been acting funny. He always has to go, and anytime I mention your name, he gets even more weird. I don't trust that he isn't going to. I mean he won't tell me because he'd know I'd kick him right where it counts, not to mention I'd tell you."

A funny feeling hit me in the pit of my stomach. Diane was going to hate me forever, but she needed to know the truth. She sat there shoving another cookie into her mouth with a worried look on her face. "Diane, I have something I want to tell you."

A look of anger came over her face. "Did he already do it? I swear to God I will break every finger on his hands. He'll never operate again." She got up from the seat she was sitting in, pacing back and forth as she ripped another cookie off the sheet in front of me.

I was about to tell her when the door to my office opened and Sawyer walked out carrying a happier Emma in his arms. "She's all changed," he announced, and then looked over to where I stood with Diane.

Diane looked to Sawyer, then to me, then back to Sawyer a confused look on her face. "What is going on here?" Diane asked, her eyes moving back and forth between us.

I looked to Sawyer and held my hand up, letting him know I would handle this. "Diane, I know I told everyone that it was a one-night stand that produced Emma, but it wasn't."

"What! Brielle, what are you talking about?"

"I know who the father is," I said, looking at Diane and then back to Sawyer.

"Who?" she questioned, the color draining from her face as she looked between us, finally figuring it out. "No, don't you dare say it."

"Your brother is Emma's father. It happened the summer before he left for Seattle. We were both single, we were both alone. We were at John Lion's party—you know the one you met Leo at and left early. Well, one thing led to another. Neither of us were ready for a relationship, but we hit it off and one thing led to another, and without warning, we decided to spend the summer messing around. We didn't tell anyone. I found out I was pregnant right before he left for Seattle."

Diane sat there, shock lining her face with the information I'd given. "You're kidding me, right?" she asked, looking at me.

I shook my head. "No, I'm not kidding. Don't be angry with me, please," I begged. "I couldn't handle you being angry with me."

"I'm an aunt?" she asked, shock lining her voice.

"Well, you always have been her Aunt Diane," I answered, looking over at my best friend. I had insisted that Diane be her aunt for a reason.

"No, I mean, like her real aunt?"

I nodded, biting my bottom lip and laughing as I allowed the shock of the information to settle into her mind. I glanced over to Sawyer, who stood there smiling.

"Why didn't neither of you tell me?" Diane asked.

"It's complicated," I answered, pulling another tray of cookies so I could avoid her eyes. "I never told Sawyer about her."

"Wait, you never told him? That's why you were all over me that night with those questions?" she asked, turning to Sawyer.

"Yes. I told you I wasn't going to report her," Sawyer said, coming over to stand beside me. "I took one look at her birth date and put it together. I wanted to know if what I thought was true, but without coming out and asking."

I was silent, and once again I could feel all the guilt climb back into my shoulders.

"Brielle, why wouldn't you have told him?"

"We were young, he was just starting his career, we were only messing around. There are so many reasons. But I am not going to lie, when he came in the room that night at the hospital, I was shocked. I never expected to see him again. He figured it out pretty fast. Your brother never was a stupid guy," I said, leaning into him and placing my hand on his chest. "We met up a few days later and had a talk. We've started seeing one another."

"And?"

I softly smiled while I finished loading the remainder of the cookies into the box and sealing it. "We are working things out."

"That's why you've been acting weird," Diane said, looking to Sawyer.

It had been good for me to have Sawyer back in my life. I was happy to see he really wanted to spend time with his daughter, and in return he was building a relationship with me. At first, I was hesitant. I was so afraid to let him into our little twosome. I didn't want to be hurt again, but I would be able to deal with the heartbreak if he no longer wanted to be a part of us. Emma was a different story. She would never understand if he no longer came around, and until her reaction last night, I didn't realize how quickly she attached herself to him.

"I'm gonna take Emma out to the park and let you two talk. We will be back in an hour," Sawyer said, placing a kiss on my temple.

"Okay, have fun."

I watched as Sawyer made his way out the back door with Emma in his arms. Then I turned back to Diane.

"How is Emma reacting to him?" she questioned.

"Well, last night she wouldn't stop crying until she said good night to him."

Diane let out a laugh. "Sounds like Emma." She grew quiet and then took on a serious look. "What about you?"

"What about me?"

"How are you reacting to him?"

I didn't want to admit what I was feeling to anyone, mainly because there was no way my feelings for him should already or perhaps still be so strong. I'd crushed on Sawyer growing up and I'd never let Diane know. Even after we'd started whatever it was that went on between us, I had done my best to protect my heart. I had been in love with him, and even though I had never wanted to admit that to myself then, I couldn't hide that from myself any longer. Every one of those feelings I'd had before were starting to resurface.

"As I said, we are working on things," I answered before biting into one of the fresh cookies.

I thought about all the time we had been spending together. He was the same guy he'd always been, only now his attention was focused on Emma, which was how it should be because she was the most important person in all of this. I was constantly second-guessing my thoughts on whether or not we would both be able to fit in his life.

"Working on things? Are you two sleeping together?"

I turned around to place the racks into the dishwasher

and grabbed the next rack of croissants only so I could hide my face from her. We hadn't slept together yet. We had messed around but that was the extent of it.

"Brielle? Please, I'm not trying to pry. I just want you to be careful. I know you need to protect Emma, but protect yourself too okay. My brother can be...selfish."

I closed my eyes tight and fought back the tears for the first time since Sawyer had returned into my life. Diane's words hit me hard. Diane and Sawyer didn't have the best relationship—they never had—and deep down, I knew her warning came from a place of protection. I think that was one of the major reasons why I'd never told her about us to begin with, because she would have swayed me away from him. It hurt me not to tell her because there wasn't much in our lives that we didn't or hadn't shared with one another. He was the first man in my life, since…well, since himself, and the hurt from before was still there, and I knew that at any time the scab could be ripped off to expose the old wound.

"Brielle, please," she said, coming up behind me and wrapping her arms around me.

"Don't worry, I'll be careful."

[illegible]
[illegible]
[illegible]
[illegible]
[illegible]
[illegible]
[illegible]
[illegible]
[illegible]
[illegible]
[illegible]
[illegible]
[illegible]
[illegible]
[illegible]
[illegible]
[illegible]

I LOOKED at my reflection in the mirror, then picked up the bottle of cologne. Tonight Brie and I were going alone on our first official date as a couple. I'd arranged to have my parents watch Emma for the night.

Everything had been crazy over the past week. Diane had found out about us. We then told Brie's mother. Brie had stood up to her, telling her she'd made up the story and that I knew nothing of Emma. She didn't take the news all that well and the look she gave me was one of death. My parents, on the other, hand were ecstatic. Emma was their first grandchild and they snatched the opportunity to have their newfound granddaughter for the night.

I quickly straightened up the living room, just in case

Brie decided to return with me for the night. I'd hope she would. I wanted us to be able to move our history behind us and move on to bigger and better things. I could still feel that connection we'd had when we were younger, and I knew that if given the chance, we had the possibility of being great.

I quickly straightened up the pile of papers and mail on the kitchen table, setting them in one neat pile off to the side. Then I made my way to pick up Brie from The Cooling Rack.

I pulled the car up to the front door and she stepped out and quickly locked the door behind her. The burgundy dress she wore hugged every curve of her body, and I felt my dick twitch as my eyes traced every curve of her body.

"Hey. Sorry about that," she said as she climbed into my car.

"About what?"

"Having to close up. Brenda called in."

"Brie, it's fine. I dropped Emma at my parents' earlier this afternoon and stayed with her until she was comfortable."

"Thank you. I hope she will be okay," Brie said, a look of worry on her face.

"I think she will be just fine. When I left, they were sitting down to have a little ice cream."

Brie nodded. "Should we call and check on her?"

I reached over and took her hand in mine. "Mom and Dad have my number. They said they would call if they needed anything. Tonight I just want us to focus on us."

She softly smiled and nodded, slipping her hand into mine.

"I HAVEN'T BEEN HERE in ages." Brie looked around at the dining room of her favorite Italian restaurant in all of Eastport—The Lantern House.

"I wonder if they still have your favorite dish?" I said, opening the menu that was in front of me.

She quickly opened hers and perused the menu, looking for her favorite lobster ravioli. She ran over the menu again, slower this time, only to look up at me with a defeated face. "They must have gotten rid of it." She pouted.

"I think you and my sister lived here when you were in your late teens. They probably stopped carrying it after you stopped ordering." I winked.

"Yeah, you are probably right." She giggled.

Brie went back to the menu just as I glanced up and saw the server standing behind Brie just like we had planned, and I gave a soft nod. He reached around her and placed a bowl down in front of her and smiled. "Your lobster ravioli, miss."

Brie jumped and then looked at me, her eyes bright, and smiled. "How did you do this?"

"I pulled a few strings. The chef is a personal friend of mine."

"Go right ahead, miss," he said, handing her a fork.

I watched as she picked up her fork and dug into the dish, placing piece of ravioli in her mouth and closing her eyes.

"Oh my, Sawyer, it's delicious. Exactly how I remember it," she said, wiping her mouth with her napkin.

I couldn't help but smile as she polished off the bowl while we waited for our main course.

The dishes had just been cleared away, and I had just poured us each another glass of wine and smiled gently at Brie.

"What's on your mind?" she questioned.

"Just thinking about how stupid I was not to tell you how I felt all those years ago." I swallowed hard. I didn't normally talk about my feelings, but I knew this was something she needed to know.

"It's okay, Sawyer. You weren't the only one who was wrong."

"I know, Brie, but I want you to know I am serious.

Emma means the world to me and you, while I still feel the same way about you that I did before. These past few months have shown me that. I want to give us another go. A real relationship, not what we were before."

I SAT THERE, torn between wanting to say yes, and guarding my heart. The look in his eyes told me he was serious, and the undeniable ache I felt in my chest told me to go for it. Now, if any, was the time to trust him.

I was about to answer him when the bill was placed on the table, and Sawyer quickly inserted his credit card into the slip and turned back to me.

"Say something."

As much as I knew protecting us was important, if I didn't begin to trust him with something, there was a chance I never would.

I looked down at my hands and remembered how I felt every single time we'd been together over the past few months. I'd been happy, for the first time in a long time. I could see how much he loved Emma. He never said he was too busy to say good night when she'd cry, he spent most of his days and nights off with us. He'd gone with me when I went to tell my mother, and he stood there and took the heat from her and he defended me when she turned on me for lying to her. He was totally invested, I was sure. "I want that too," I whispered, my insides shaking.

We left the restaurant and were halfway across the parking lot to his car when I reached for his hand. He stopped and turned to look at me. "How long did you ask your parents to keep Emma?" I questioned.

Sawyer turned to me. "They offered to keep her overnight."

"Hmm. I was just thinking that if we are to give us another try, perhaps spending the night alone would be a good idea," I whispered shyly, looking at him.

He placed a hand on my cheek, coming in for a deep kiss. His lips danced over mine in that parking lot. Instantly, my center started to ache, and as soon as he gathered me in his arms, I knew I wanted more.

"Come, let's go," he whispered, pulling me into him as he guided me to his car.

I STOOD IN HIS KITCHEN, making a late-night snack for us. Soft music poured through the living room speakers, and I took a sip of wine as I listened to him speak with his mother. I added a few crackers to the plate, and then grabbed a bunch of grapes and added them as well, just as Sawyer stepped into the doorway of the kitchen.

"Any problems?" I asked, focusing on the task at hand.

"She went down no problem. Mom and Dad have no problem keeping her the night. They are thrilled."

I gently swayed to the music as I picked my glass up off the counter and took another sip.

I'd just set the glass down when I felt Sawyer step behind me. The warmth of his skin and scent of cologne enveloped me.

"You almost finished?" he asked, his breath tickling my ear as he brought his hands around and rested them on my abdomen.

I froze at his soft touch. My body was on fire as he pulled me into him. I could feel his hardened cock pressing into my ass as he gently swayed us to the music that played. "You look amazingly sexy in my T-shirt, you know that. That cute ass of yours swaying to the music is going to be my undoing," he whispered.

I closed my eyes and leaned my head against his chest as he brought his lips to the side of my neck. He kissed, at first, and then nibbled as he brought his hands up to cup my breasts. I reached behind me and fisted his shirt as he ran his fingers over my nipples and sucked on the lobe of my ear.

"I think I'm falling in love with you," he whispered into my ear.

I closed my eyes and allowed myself to succumb to him. I, too, felt what he was feeling, only a huge part of me was still afraid to say it. I felt his fingers graze my hips as he lifted his shirt up and over my head. He grabbed and pulled me against his hot skin. I turned my head and met his lips. My skin pebbled as his hand travelled down and slipped inside my panties, running his fingers through my already soaked center.

I reached behind me and palmed his hard cock through his pants.

"Come with me," he whispered.

I turned to follow him and was surprised when he picked me up in his arms. He carried me through the living room and into his bedroom, placing me gently on the bed.

He stood before me, looking down at me, then grabbed my panties and slipped them down my legs. He licked his lips as he took me in, his hand going to the button on his pants. I watched as his fingers flicked it open. He allowed his pants to drop to the floor, and then he dropped his boxers, his cock springing free.

I swallowed hard as he took himself in his hand and began to stroke himself.

"Rub yourself," he whispered breathlessly.

I felt heat surge through my body at his request as I lay there watching his hand form a steady rhythm as he jerked his cock. I closed my eyes and reached down between my legs, sliding my fingers between my lips.

"Fuck, Brie...you're fucking gorgeous," he whispered.

I opened my eyes and looked down at his hand gripping his cock. Sawyer stood there, his impressive cock in his hand with his head cocked back, every muscle in his body tensed, and I could see a bead of precum forming at the tip. I sat up and scooted to the end of the bed, keeping my eyes on him. I didn't touch him. I leaned forward and licked the tip of his cock and then placed my lips around the head. He dropped his cock and brought his hands to the back of my head, lacing his fingers through my hair as I took him completely in my mouth, all the way to the back of my throat.

"Fuck, Brie, slow down," he hissed.

I held onto the base of his cock and let him slide in and out of my mouth a few times before he pushed me back. I dropped his cock as he knelt on the bed and laced his arms underneath my knees. He leaned down and kissed me hard, taking my hand and placing it between my legs.

I knew what he wanted, and I rubbed my clit slowly for him while he reached into the nightstand drawer and pulled out a condom. Our eyes locked as he slid the condom over his cock. I felt him at my opening, slowly pushing at first, and then finally he slid all the way in. I gripped his arms as he pumped into me, kissing me as he went.

I could already feel my climax building and could feel myself tightening around him when he pulled out. He rolled onto his back, breathing heavy.

"Is something wrong?" I questioned.

He bit his lower lip and shook his head. "Get on."

I'd forgotten how Sawyer was: his sexual appetite was insatiable. That, and he loved to change positions. I glanced to his cock and shook my head no. This position was always my undoing, and he knew it.

He rolled over and gently kissed me, placing his hands on my waist he gently coaxed me to straddle his lap. I felt him position himself at my opening, and then with both hands on my hips, he slowly guided me as I lowered onto him. I let out a loud moan as his cock filled me, and I held back my orgasm while I allowed myself to adjust to him.

He gripped my hips and looked up at me. "Rub your clit."

I could tell by the gruffness of his voice that it was more of a command than an request. I slowly began to rock my hips, and I brought my fingers between my legs, slowly rubbing my clit as Sawyer lay against the pillows and watched.

I dropped my head back. I could feel my orgasm building as Sawyer pumped up into me. I leaned forward, and he took my breast in his mouth, gently teasing my nipple with his tongue and teeth. One more time, he ran his teeth gently over the sensitive bud, and I clenched tightly as my orgasm took over my body. I gripped the pillows behind his head as he wrapped his arms around me, pumping up into me until I felt the throbbing of his release.

I STARED at the green lights of his alarm clock. It was only three thirty. I looked over my shoulder to see Sawyer sound asleep. I gently kicked the covers off and slipped his robe on, making my way to the door. I made my way to the washroom, and then made my way into the kitchen to get a drink.

The food still sat on a plate on the counter where we had left it. I grabbed a grape and shoved one into my mouth. As I stood there, my mind quickly ran back to his seduction in the kitchen. I smiled at the thought as my center began to throb again. I blew out a breath and filled a glass with water and sat down at the kitchen table.

I clenched as I sat down. My body hurt. I took a sip of water, thinking back to earlier. I couldn't help but feel the familiar ache between my legs start again as I thought back to last time we'd had sex tonight. It had been different than any other time; this time there was more feeling behind it. It was slower and more sensual. For the first time ever, the man had made love to me.

I blew out a breath. I needed to clear my mind before I went back and crawled into bed. I reached for the grocery fliers that sat in a pile on the table and quietly looked through each one. I was just about to put them all back when a letter addressed to Sawyer caught my eye.

I got up from the chair and looked around the corner toward the bedroom. The light was still off, and I could hear Sawyer gently snoring. I went back and sat down, picking up the letter. It was from a hospital in Florida.

I flipped the page and read the first line, a frown coming to my face the further I read. I flipped the page. It looked like a compensation package. I flipped back to the letter, looking at the date. It was dated a month ago. I flipped through the pages, finally coming to the last page. They needed an answer by next week.

My stomach flipped as I stared down at the papers in front of me. Then, out of the corner of my eye, I caught glimpse of a half-written letter in Sawyer's handwriting.

It was addressed to the same hospital. I read what he had written and dropped the letter to the floor. He was taking the job. He'd not mentioned a single word to me about it.

My heart sank and my stomach turned as a flood of panic and hurt filled me, finally turning to anger. Tears filled my eyes as I stared at the letter, finally throwing it down on the table. He'd worked his way in to our little bubble, and now he was leaving. He'd lied about everything.

SAWYER

I woke just as the sun began to peek through the blinds. I stretched, reaching for Brie, only to find her side of the bed cold and empty. I frowned and lifted my head, looking around the bedroom and listening hard. The apartment was silent. I kicked the covers off, slipped into my shorts, and made my way into the living room.

Brie sat on the couch staring off into space, ignoring the fact I had even walked into the room. "There you are," I said, smiling, making my way over to her. I leaned down to kiss her lips, but she turned her face away from me. I frowned. After last night, this wasn't exactly how I imagined this morning going.

"Here I am," she whispered, still not looking at me. The silence was deafening as I looked down at her emotionless expression.

"Did you sleep okay?"

She shrugged. "As well as I could," she muttered. Her chest rose as she took in a deep breath.

"Would you like some breakfast? I can make you whatever you'd like, bacon, eggs, pancakes, waffles, eggs benedict. You just name it and I'll whip it up," I said, clapping my hands together, a worried feeling coming over me that something was very wrong.

Brie shook her head. "I'm not hungry. Besides, I need to get Emma. Brenda is sick again, which means I have to be at work."

I looked around the room. "Oh, well, why didn't you say so. No need to be stressed. I'll take you to work, and then I'll pick Emma up, take her to the park, and then bring her to The Cooling Rack this afternoon after you're finished."

Brie still didn't look at me. "No, we have time to go get her now," she muttered, getting up from the couch and stepping away from me.

I didn't know what to say. I stood up and looked around the living room and then glanced at my watch. "Emma will have more fun with me than waiting for you at work. That way she won't be underfoot," I said, moving in behind her and running my hands over her chilled arms.

"I said it's fine. I'm used to her being underfoot." She ripped herself away from me, moving over to where her shoes lay on the floor. She slipped her feet in.

I wasn't sure how to respond. She stood there with her back to me. "Brie, is everything okay?"

"I said everything is fine. We have to go."

She stood there sifting through the contents of her purse, her body tense. I didn't have a clue what the problem was. I blew out a breath and then made my way into the bedroom and got dressed.

We drove in silence to my parents' and then to The Cooling Rack. Brie sat beside me staring out the window, while Emma sat in the back of the car chattering away to herself.

I pulled up to The Cooling Rack and parked the car, shutting off the engine, and looked over at Brie. She reached for the handle of the door and climbed out of the car, not once saying anything. She opened the back door and unbuckled Emma, taking her from the seat, then grabbed her overnight bag and shut the door, not saying so much as a word.

I climbed out of the car and walked around to the sidewalk where Brie struggled with both Emma and the bag. I went to grab the overnight bag from her, but she pulled it away. "I'm fine, Sawyer," she bit out. "I've done this alone for years. I've got it."

I held my hands out in front of me. "I was only trying to help."

"And I've told you I don't need your help."

Her eyes said it all: she was angry, and I didn't want to provoke her any more out in the street. Whatever was bothering her would surely come to the surface sooner or later.

"All right, well, call me when you're ready to head home. I'll come and pick you guys up." I could hear the defeat in my voice.

"No need."

"No need? Brie, you don't have your car. You live over fifteen mins away by car. It will take you an hour to walk home, not to mention you don't have Emma's stroller either."

"I said there is no need. I'll have one of the girls take us home."

Brie went to take a couple of steps forward when Emma let out a cry. "Daddy...I want Daddy." She held her little arms out, reaching out for me, tears streaming down her cheeks, but Brie ignored her pleas, still heading for the front door.

"I'll see you later tonight. I'll bring dinner and help put Emma to bed."

Brie stopped walking, turned and looked at me. "Don't feel like you need to come by, Sawyer. Actually, I'd prefer it if you didn't." I caught a glimpse of tears in her eyes as she turned back around, only this time she didn't look back. Instead, she moved forward and pulled the door open, while Emma screamed, still reaching out for me, tears streaming down her face.

"WHAT THE HELL DID YOU DO?" Diane screamed into the phone.

"What are you talking about?" I asked, getting up off my couch and making my way to the kitchen to grab another slice of pizza.

"Brie called me. She was in tears, mumbling something about how I'd been right. What did you do?" my sister questioned.

I could imagine her standing in front of me, looking at me with a look of death.

"Diane, I didn't do anything. I woke up this morning and she was acting weird." I grabbed a coke out of the fridge, cracking the tab on the can and drinking down the cold liquid.

"You had to have done something. She's a freaking mess. When she called me this morning, she begged me to come pick her up and take her home. I had to leave work. Martha took over my patients. Reggie was pissed, we were so busy."

"What did she say?"

"She wouldn't talk to me. She just said things were over between the two of you. She refused to tell me why, and then said she didn't want to talk about you anymore. So I want to know what it was that you did."

I leaned against the counter and looked down at my feet. I had no idea what had happened. When we'd gone to bed last night, everything was more than fine. I sat down at the kitchen table and put my head in my hands.

"I don't know. We had dinner last night, she spent the night, everything was fine. Emma stayed with Mom and Dad. This morning she was…well, you saw it."

"Sawyer, whatever you've done, you better fix it. That's all I'm going to say. You can't hurt them like this."

"Just wait a minute here. I haven't done anything and I would never hurt either of them. If I knew what the hell I'd done wrong, I would fix it."

"Figure it out! I've got to go."

She didn't even let me say good-bye; she was gone. I needed to get out of here. I needed to clear my head. I stood up, anger coursing through my body but accidentally knocked the pile of papers onto the floor. "Fuck!" I shouted as the papers fell to the floor scattering everywhere.

I bent down and gathered up the papers, placing them on the table. When I stood up and looked down, it hit me.

There, staring up at me, was the offer and letter I'd begun to write to the hospital in Florida. My stomach flopped. Brie had seen it and thought I was accepting the position.

FIVE DAYS Later

I moved about the halls of the emergency room almost as if in a trance. Sleep hadn't been my friend this past week. I had spent most waking hours trying to get Brie to answer her phone. I'd even gone by The Cooling Rack on my break in hopes she would be there.

"Brenda, I know she is here. Please, you need to get her for me," I'd pleaded.

Brenda just looked at me with pity in her eyes. "I'm sorry, Sawyer, she isn't here. What can I get for you?"

"A coffee," I huffed. "Fine when will she be in?"

"I don't know," Brenda said, setting the coffee I'd ordered in front of me.

"Come on, please. You have to know where she is."

"I'm sorry, I have a line and it's getting longer by the second," she said, barely looking in my direction.

"Can you just leave her a message for me?"

"Fine, here, write it down," she mumbled, ripping a piece of paper off her notepad and placing it on the counter in front of me. "I'll leave her the message okay." She called the person behind me to the counter, pretending to forget I was still standing there.

I scribbled down the note and then headed out the door. I'd done that exact same thing three times this week with the exact same result. I now sat behind the main desk, going over some reports, doing my best to concentrate.

"Earth to Sawyer?"

"Hmmm???" I looked up to see Diane standing beside me holding a few lab reports.

"These are for you. I told you three times they were here."

"Oh, sorry, I was concentrating," I said, taking the papers from her, going right back to the paperwork I was working on.

"You okay?"

"Yep, fine. I've got to go. I need to consult Dr. Richards on a case."

I got up from the desk, knowing full well Diane was watching my every move, and I made my way down the hall to Dr. Richards' office. I stood outside and took a deep breath before knocking on the door.

"Come in."

"Hey, Ryan, do you have a minute?" I asked, stepping inside.

"Hey, yes, come on in. Please take a seat. So have you made your decision?"

I took a seat and nodded. "I have."

"And?"

"And I am going to have to turn it down. I've already written to them."

Ryan looked at me, a little perplexed at my decision. After all, I had shared with him my intentions to advance my career when I had first arrived. "Oh, have you changed your mind about advancing?"

I shook my head. "No, I haven't. I would just prefer to advance my career here."

"Sawyer, you can tell me to mind my own business, but I am curious about the change in your decision," Ryan said, sitting back against his chair. "I figured I would only have you for a little while especially with your goals."

I blew out a breath. "There's been a change in my personal life, and right now I need to stay put."

Ryan flipped his pencil between his fingers and looked at me. "Is everything okay?"

"I'm a father," I bit out.

I swallowed hard, praying I would be able to get Brie to talk to me again so I could be a father to Emma.

Ryan looked at me, a smile coming to his face. "Congratulations, my friend. We are definitely going to have to celebrate at some point. So I guess that means you will be joining us at the Christmas party this year?"

"I will." I smiled.

"I'm somewhat relieved, to be honest. I didn't want to have to hire someone again," Ryan said as I stood up.

I'd just gotten to the door when my name was paged. "Guess I have to go," I said, opening the door.

"Have a good day, Sawyer."

SAWYER

One week Later

EMMA SAT at the kitchen table eating Cheerios while I loaded up my bag with snacks for her. It was almost six. I'd been late to work almost every day this past week. Emma hadn't been sleeping. All she did was cry for Sawyer, and my nerves were shot. I'd spent every night tossing and turning.

I popped a couple boxes of juice into my bag as Emma looked up at me. "Baby, why don't you eat?" I asked and jumped when the phone rang.

Emma looked up at me from where she sat. "Daddy?"

she questioned as she brought her hands up and rubbed her tired eyes and began to cry.

I turned to the phone, looking at the display, and closed my eyes. It was Sawyer, all right, calling from the hospital once again. I blew out a breath and went back to packing my bag.

"Daddy, Daddy..." Emma chanted.

It was like she knew it was him. As I stood there listening to her, a tear slipped down my cheek. It was best to just let him float on out of our lives, I thought to myself. It would be easier that way. If I were able to do that, I knew that Emma would eventually forget him—or so I hoped. I, on the other hand, would have a harder time getting over him.

"Eat your breakfast, sweetie," I said, wiping the tear from my cheek and placing my hand on her head and smoothing her hair. "We have to go soon."

Emma sat there and cried, then picked up the small plastic bowl of Cheerios and dumped it onto the kitchen floor. I looked down at the mess, tears filling my eyes, and grabbed the broom, sweeping them into a little pile as Emma screamed.

The Cooling Rack was already busy by the time we arrived. My patience was on the short side, and I was happy that when I put Emma down in my office with her toys she began playing with them instead of crying. Exhausted and feeling sick to my stomach, I began my day, prepping sheets of cookies and croissants to proof then decorating cakes and cupcakes. It was a little after eight when the door to the kitchen opened and Diane popped her head in.

"Morning," she called, a soft smile falling on her lips.

"Hey."

"You have a minute?"

"Not really," I said with a defeated sigh, looking around at all the orders I still had left to bake and box.

"You look exhausted. You're coming to sit down," Diane said, taking one hard look at me.

I didn't know who I was trying to fool. Anyone who took one look at me would see the exact same thing. When I didn't move, she came over, took my shoulders, and guided me into my office. I plopped down on a chair and looked up at her.

"What?" I asked.

"Have you eaten this morning?"

I shook my head. I hadn't eaten dinner last night either because by the time I'd finally gotten Emma to sleep, my head ached so badly I knew food would only make me sick.

"Brenda," Diane called, "could you bring us two coffees and a couple croissants please." Diane looked down at me. Brenda appeared at the door in seconds with everything Diane had asked for.

"Would you mind taking Emma for a second?" she questioned.

"Of course. Come on, munchkin," Brenda said, holding her hand out to Emma. "Let's go outside for a moment."

As soon as they were gone, Diane closed the door and sat down beside me. "Now what happened?"

I looked at her, refusing to break down, even though every fiber of my body was screaming just to cry and get it over with. "You were right."

"About..."

"About your brother being a selfish prick. I should have known better."

"I never said he was a selfish prick. I simply said he could be selfish. Now what happened?"

"I found a job offer in his kitchen from a hospital down in Florida. Did you know he applied? He promised me he was here for good, yet here he is applying for positions that take him away. I also found the beginnings of a letter saying he was accepting the job." I placed my face in my hands and drew in a deep breath. "I never should have let him in. I certainly shouldn't have let him into Emma's life. I curse the day I ever laid eyes on him."

"Whoa, now just a minute. Don't you do that. If you hadn't of met him, then you wouldn't have Emma."

I got up out of the chair I was sitting in and paced back and forth. "I know, I just..."

"Brielle, I know for a fact that Sawyer turned down that job offer."

"How do you know that?"

"Brielle, things spread like wildfire through that hospital. He didn't even apply for it. The hospital submitted a recommendation on his behalf because he shows so much promise to move up and there were no positions open here."

I blew out a breath and looked at my best friend. "I don't know, Diane."

"I do. Look, as much as Sawyer and I don't see eye to eye on things, I can say that he has changed since he found out about Emma. It's almost as if overnight he became a completely different person. Everything he's been doing lately has been for both you and Emma. I saw him at work yesterday. He's an absolute mess. I've actually never seen him this upset and worked up before."

I sat quiet for a moment, letting Diane's words sink into my mind. Sifting through everything she'd said about the job offer he'd received. Then I looked at her. "Did he tell you to come here?"

"Do you think for one second that I would come here if he asked me to? That I would lie to you for him if what I were saying isn't true?"

Never in my life had Diane ever done anything Sawyer had asked, especially if he were being deceitful. "No, I guess not."

"Exactly. I'm here because I care about you, and I care about my niece. If he makes you happy, then you should be with him. If he doesn't, then that is okay too, but don't throw away something because of something you saw. Especially when you don't have all the information you need to make a proper decision. You need to talk to him."

Just then the door to my office opened. I looked up to see a disheveled looking Sawyer. He looked at both of us before giving me an awkward smile, for the first time he didn't exude the confidence he'd always had. "Can I speak to you?"

Our eyes met and a funny feeling ran through my body as he stood there looking back at me.

"I'm going to run," Diane said, hugging me. She stood up and turned toward the door and stopped, leaning into Sawyer and whispering something before leaving my office.

Sawyer waited until Diane had left and then he took a seat beside me. He took hold of my hand and looked up at me. "We need to talk, Brie."

I looked down at my hand in his and closed my eyes, fighting back more tears.

"I know you saw the offer and the letter."

I nodded and swallowed hard. I was afraid that if I spoke, my voice would crack and give away how hurt I was. I reached over and took a sip of the coffee Diane had gotten for me, and then I looked to Sawyer. "Why didn't you tell me about it?"

"Because there was never anything to tell. I was never going to take that job. I never even applied for it. The letter you saw, I wrote it just to get it out of my system." He squeezed my hand and looked at me. "You know you could have just asked me about it," he whispered.

I looked at him with tear-filled eyes. "It wasn't my place."

"Yes, it is. I told you I wasn't going anywhere. I am fully committed to us, to this family."

"Yeah, but..."

"No, no buts. You and Emma mean everything to me. I swear to you, I'm not going anywhere. I'm in love with you, in love with us, in love with her."

"You are?"

"Yes, Brie, I am. I wasted a chance with you once. I'm not doing it again. I'm not going to throw away another chance with you."

I looked at him, unsure of what he was talking about. I figured what he had said to me when we first got together was just to get me to speak with him again. I didn't think his feelings were real. "Sawyer, please, I don't think you were ever in love with me."

"I was so in love with you I didn't date for almost two years. I'm head over heels in love with you." Sawyer leaned in and placed his hand on my cheek, wiping away the tear that had strayed from my eye with his thumb. He leaned forward and placed a kiss on my lips.

As we parted, the door to my office opened, and Brenda walked in with Emma. She was carrying a flower in her little hands. "Here, Mommy..." she said, holding out the flower to me, and then she spotted Sawyer.

The second she laid her eyes on him, she dropped the purple flower and brought her little hands up to her mouth in surprise. "Daddy!" she screamed, stomping her little legs in excitement.

Sawyer took one look at her and scooped her up into his powerful arms, bringing her in for a hug. "Baby girl..." he said, kissing her forehead as she wrapped her arms around his neck. "I missed you."

I stood up and looked around my messy office, then looked out to the mess of the kitchen. I wiped the tears from my eyes, then looked to Sawyer who stood there holding Emma in his arms. I'd missed him so much, and I hadn't been able to fully admit to myself how much he had truly met to me until he hadn't been around.

"I'm sorry, Sawyer."

"Don't be. We just need to get better at communication. Both of us do. It's going to take time, but we will get there."

He reached out and pulled me into him. I placed my head on his shoulder and took in a deep breath, the scent of his cologne filling my nostrils. The feeling of his arms around me put me at complete ease. Just then Brenda walked into the kitchen and signaled to me.

I smiled and popped my head out the door. "What's up?"

"Is Mrs. Benson's order ready yet? She's here to pick it up."

I looked around, feeling completely defeated. The pile of orders was a mile high, and I would never get everything done with Emma underfoot.

"Give me twenty minutes," I said, pushing the hair out of my face, running for the order form.

"Look, why don't I take Emma out of your hair and let you finish up here. When you get home, we can talk, sort things out?" Sawyer said, coming up behind me.

I bit my bottom lip and looked down to where Emma sat playing with her toys. "Are you sure you don't mind?"

"I'm positive." He leaned in and placed a kiss on my lips. "We'll see you at home."

"See you at home."

BRIELLE

Six Month's later

"Pick a hand," Sawyer said, holding both hands out in front of me in a closed fist.

I looked at him and smiled. "What are you up to?"

"Just pick a hand."

Emma looked up from where she sat on the floor with her toys and giggled. "Daddy's being silly isn't he," I said, reaching out and touching his right hand.

He flipped it over and opened his hand to reveal a silver key. I frowned as he held the key out in front of me. "Here you go."

"What is this?" I questioned, still looking at the dangling key he held in front of me.

"This is the key to our new place. The condo we went to look at a month ago is ours."

My jaw dropped and excitement ran through me. We had been discussing moving in together for the past three months. My place was too small for us, and his place was on the other side of town, too far from The Cooling Rack if I needed to walk. We had looked at some places but weren't able to agree on one, until we had seen this condo. Problem was there was a bidding war going on between two other buyers.

"How did you do this? I thought that our agent didn't want to us to get in the middle of it."

Sawyer gave me that cocky smile I loved so much. "When have you ever known me to listen." He winked.

I laughed. "What happened?"

"Well, I couldn't help it. I put in an offer. Of course, both couples raised theirs. I offered again, one dropped out. The other person raised his offer, and I decided to let him have it, but he couldn't get the financing, so it's ours!"

Excitement overtook me. "When do we move?"

"Place closes in sixty days. Get packing, baby!" he said, grabbing me and picking me up off the floor, kissing me hard.

FOUR MONTHS LATER, we held our first family dinner in our dining room. We had a lot to celebrate. Mom had finally forgiven me for lying to her all those years ago, and she had finally accepted Sawyer. Diane had finally finalized her divorce from Leo. She had moved into her new place and had started her new role at the hospital in the Pediatric Intensive Care Unit. Sawyer's parents now took turns with my mother babysitting Emma. Mom would take her the days she went to kindergarten, and his parents would take her the days she didn't. It worked well.

Sawyer and I worked hard on our relationship every day. We were well past the hurt stage, and we had learned to trust one another again. He stayed right where he was, in the emergency department of Eastport General. Emergency was his passion—he loved the fast pace, the challenge, and the fact that every day was different.

The Cooling Rack was finally really booming. Everyday there were more and more orders, and finally I had to hire a second baker, especially when I could no longer keep up with all the other work.

Sawyer would propose to me the following Christmas. It had taken us a long time to get where we finally were, but we were here, and I couldn't be happier.

I'd always had a strong feeling that one day he would be mine, even from the time I had been a teenager. There was no doubt about it, Sawyer would always be my one and only Doctor Desire.

DOCTOR RIGHT

After the worst breakup of my life, I'd needed a change. I needed to get my focus back on my life and my career. That was how I ended up in Eastport, Rhode Island. I was in the beginning stages of purchasing a large OB/GYN practice from a local doctor who was retiring. It was also where I met Bella.

She was working at the local bakery I frequented, The Cooling Rack. Being with Bella was unexpectedly liberating. There were no rules, no expectations beyond the current moment, no demands. She was loving, and so gentle with my broken heart.

That summer became all about recovery, not only for me, but for her as well. I'd told myself that was all it was. We weren't supposed to get serious, and at the end of summer we would go our separate ways.

Months passed, summer ended, and Bella left Eastport. Thoughts of her consumed me, and I realized that there was no getting over Bella. Then one morning, I walked into my next patient appointment and was shocked to find Bella standing in frnt of me.

It started by accident. Then it became more intentional. Know what wasn't intentional? The resulting pregnancy.

S.L. Sterling's Doctor Right is a surprise pregnancy romance in the Doctors of Eastport General Series.

BELLA

January

"JUST SIGN HERE AND HERE." The stuffy lawyer who sat across from me pointed to the spots on the paper with the lid of his pen.

My stomach rolled as I looked over to Miles, who sat there with an impatient look on his face, waiting for me to sign us away forever. The constant ticking of the clock that stood in the corner was grating on my nerves. *Tick... tick... tick...*

I looked down at the forms in front of me, my hands beginning to sweat as I thought about what life was going to be like without him in my life.

"Miles, I—"

"Bella, just sign. Don't make this worse than the last few years. This part is simple and painless," he bit out.

I could feel the tears burning behind my eyes. "Miles, there has to be another way. Please, reconsider," I cried. "We could always look at adopting—"

"Bella, the time for options is up. You didn't want that and, unfortunately, I don't want this anymore," he said, waving his hand back and forth between us. "The last five years have taken a toll. I can't live another day of my life being miserable. It's time we just move on. We are over."

I looked across the desk at the emotionless face of the lawyer. *Tick... tick... tick...* It seemed even the clock was getting impatient with me. I wiped my hands on my jeans, picked up the pen, wiped the stray tear from my cheek that had fallen, and signed my name through blurry eyes.

I placed the pen down and reached for a tissue. The lawyer grabbed the papers and placed them in front of Miles. He nodded, picked up the pen, and confidently signed the paperwork, a hint of a smile on his face. He probably already had someone on the side, someone he could easily plant his seed in and produce the children he'd always wanted. Perhaps she already was pregnant. I'd never really know the truth and wasn't sure I wanted to.

After I walked out of that lawyer's office, I didn't look back. I went home to my small apartment and cried my eyes out one last time. Then I picked up all my broken pieces and focused on putting one foot in front of the other.

Three months later, I was right back where I was now—on the couch, crying my eyes out. My boss had laid me off.

May

THE FIRST FOUR months of being newly divorced was about uneventful as the first week we'd been married. However, the first week of being unemployed was hell. I'd spent countless hours looking for employment, and by Saturday night, I was burned out. I'd curled up on the couch in my pajamas and was watching an episode of my favourite show when my phone rang. I let out a sigh, debating not answering it. After eight, I knew it wouldn't be a job offer, so I glanced at the call display. It was the first time a smile had come to my lips all week.

"Brielle? Is it really you?" I cried into the receiver, happy to hear from my best friend.

"Bella! How are you, gorgeous?"

"I'm good. Just plugging along," I answered, turning the volume down on the TV.

"How's work?" she questioned.

I'd talked to Brielle over the past few months about the divorce, but I'd yet to tell her about losing my job. It wasn't the way I wanted to start a conversation with her. I blew out a breath. "Well… it isn't. Cutbacks, you know," I said simply, trying hard not to allow the stress to creep up.

"Oh, Bella, I'm so sorry. How long?"

"I found out on Monday."

"God, I feel so bad now. I was going to call but figured you might need time to yourself to get over everything, and now I feel like I abandoned you."

"Don't be silly. You didn't abandon me."

"Yeah, but you needed me."

I grew quiet. I always needed Brielle. It had been hard since leaving Eastport. We'd been through so much together over the years. The fact that she wasn't right here had probably been the hardest part of going through this divorce. Not that Boston was that far. I'd headed back to Eastport right before we signed the divorce papers and spent a weekend. We'd had a great time, yet I felt bad adding extra work for her. She was busy running The Cooling Rack and looking after Emma. I didn't want to add my stresses to her day.

"Thanks. I always need you, but I needed some time, too. As for the new wrench in the gears, well, I'm just taking it day by day. Searching countless job websites for the same responses."

"Day by day is good. It's easier that way."

"So, to what do I owe this surprise?" I questioned, wanting to turn the attention off me.

Brielle was quiet for a moment. I could hear Emma in the background chattering away, then I heard Sawyer's deep voice answer her back. I was so happy for Brielle that she'd finally gotten back together with Sawyer.

"Brielle? Is everything okay?" I asked.

"Could be better. My assistant manager has left The Cooling Rack. She quit the day before yesterday."

"Oh, Brie, that is awful. I'm so sorry."

"Yes, especially with the baby on the way."

I could hear the panic in her voice. She'd found out she was pregnant again just last month. "Have you put out an ad to hire someone else?"

"I need someone I can trust. That's why I am calling you."

"Brie, I can't. I—"

"You told me yourself that you're looking for a way

to start over. This would be it. Even if it's just for the summer. I mean, it would help you and me. Besides, you are the only one I know I can trust with my business, and you have great managerial experience."

She wasn't wrong. I was looking for a way to start over. I also had managerial experience, thanks to my last job promotion. I really didn't have an excuse, since I was now unemployed. Packing up and moving would not be that difficult.

"Well, when would you need me there?"

"Whenever you can be here for. Seriously, you do not know how much this would help me out. Plus, if you come now, you can get into the swing of things. If you don't want to stay or your boss calls you back, well, it will also give me time to find someone."

I had a small clue. I also knew how much it would truly help me put everything behind me. Perhaps a change of scenery was exactly what I needed, and the one thing I knew for sure was that my ex-husband wouldn't be back in Eastport because he was here, in Boston, with his newfound love. I could run into them anywhere. "Alright, let me organize some things and I will be there in the next couple of weeks."

"Oh, and no need to worry about a place. There are two condos available in the building we are in. Sawyer and I will get things started for you."

Brielle and I said our good-byes, and I hung up the phone and looked around my small one-bedroom apartment. I'd barely unpacked in the few months I'd lived here, almost as if I knew that something else would come along.

ASHER

July

It had just stopped raining as I pulled up outside of The Cooling Rack. I cut the engine, unclipped my seatbelt, and stretched. It had been a long day. I'd had my meeting at Eastport General to see about office availability for what I'd hoped would become the home of my new private practice.

Afterward, I went to meet up with a doctor in the area who was looking at retiring. I already knew that a private practice was more my speed than hospital life. I'd spent my fair share in hospitals delivering babies, and I'd seen the shit that went on in ERs. I didn't want to get my hopes up, but I was excited about the idea of a new practice and a chance to start over.

I picked up the file folder containing all the details on the medical practice I was looking at buying. The doctor had been kind enough to put the file together and had given me at this meeting and headed inside the diner. I frequented the place in the last few weeks and loved it. At this time of the day, it was quieter, so it was a good place to sit down and go over these documents before contacting my lawyer, I thought to myself as I walked to the front door. However, when I stepped inside tonight, it surprised me to see that more than half the tables were still occupied.

After looking around, I spotted my usual table and made my way over. I'd just opened the folder and began looking over the notes I'd scribbled down when a menu was placed down in front of me. I looked up to be greeted by the same beautiful brunette that was normally here. The one I was certain I knew but still couldn't place.

She smiled. "Hello, welcome back to The Cooling Rack."

"Thanks," I replied, picking the menu up off the table. "What's the special today?" I questioned, looking over the menu to decide what it was I wanted for dinner tonight.

"Well, you look a little tired tonight, so I'm

thinking you need a cup of coffee, followed by the turkey club that's on special, and perhaps finish it with a couple of my favorite cookies—the double chocolate chip."

I smiled. Everything she'd suggested sounded wonderful. "That sounds great," I said, setting the menu off to the side, meeting her eyes. "I'm Asher." I held my hand out for her to take. "I figure it's time we formally introduce ourselves. After all, you can tell what I need to eat." Besides, I hoped that once I knew her name, I could place her.

"Bella. I'm the assistant manager here," she said, sliding her small hand into mine.

"Well, Bella, it's nice to meet you." I smiled, letting go of her soft hand.

"You too." She smiled and turned to walk away when suddenly it clicked.

"Bella, did you, by chance, go to Eastport High?" I questioned.

She nodded. "I did."

"You dated… Oh God, what was his name…. Miles Langdon, quarterback for the Eastport Lions."

"Yep, that would be me," she said, glancing over her shoulder as the jingle of the bell above the door rang out and two teenagers came in. "I'll be back with your order shortly." She grabbed the menu from the table and took off toward the kitchen.

I turned my attention back to the file in front of me and was soon deep into reading some of the information when a cup was quietly slid in front of me.

"Your coffee and cream." She held up a small basket full of creamers. "As always, there is sugar on the table."

"Thanks," I said, smiling. She'd learned how I liked my coffee the first time I'd had it and had never once forgotten, even when I hadn't seen her here for a few days. Most times, she'd even bring it over with the menu.

"So, did you play on the team with Miles?" she questioned.

"Yep, running back. We were always together."

"Oh my God, now I remember you. Asher Harrison, right?"

"That's me."

"You took me home the night after the huge win. The night Miles got super drunk." She giggled.

I remembered what a nightmare that night had been.

"I remember he was quite angry with you at the time for that." She smiled. "He'd gone on and on about wanting to hurt you. He thought you'd made a move."

The light blush across her cheeks caught my eyes, and I smiled. "Yep, he wasn't thrilled with me for that." I chuckled. "Him and I actually had a fight about in the locker room before the next game. The coach had to break it up." I chuckled.

"I know, I remember." She giggled. "I'll be back in a few minutes." She turned and made her way over to the table that had just left and began clearing it off. I tore my eyes away from her soft, curvy hips and went back to reading the file before me.

Shortly, a large plate was placed beside me, and I glanced over to see a large turkey club with a side of sweet potato fries in the center of the plate. "Thanks," I mumbled, placing the documents aside.

"Those look important." She glanced to the thick stack of papers while placing a set of silverware on the table.

"Somewhat…" I shrugged. "Just some business documents. Looks like the place kind of cleared out," I said, looking around the diner. Only one table on the opposite side of the room was now full.

"Normally does. Our next busy time is coming up though, close to seven, right as the doctors start their break at the hospital."

"I was going to ask what time you closed. I didn't want to be holding you up from something more important just because I need to eat. No reason I couldn't take this to-go."

"We close at nine. You have lots of time. I'm normally here until ten." She softly smiled. "You're welcome to stay as long as you need."

"Care to sit down and join me?" I questioned. "You must have a break coming up or something."

"I do, but I couldn't." She glanced around to, I assumed, see what she had left to do. "I just normally work through my break at night."

"That's not a good practice. Take a seat," I said, nodding to the empty bench across the way. "We're practically friends, having gone to the same high school." She slowly sat down, looking around as if someone might see her. "So, you work here long?"

"About a month and a half now."

"And you, are you from around here? Wait, of course you are. That was a silly thing to ask."

I shook my head. "Not anymore. I moved away for school. Then, you know, life happened. I'm just renting a small place here for now. There are some things I need to sort out in my personal life and my work life. Once I've got those things figured out, I'll decide where it is I'll end up."

"Well, you chose a good place to figure things out in. Eastport has always been great for clearing one's mind," she said, smiling. "You know, in case you forgot."

"Ah, so you're still a local?"

"No, Miles and I, we moved to Boston after college. He got a job, and we got married. I've just came back to help a dear friend of mine and to do some soul searching of my own."

I nodded, shoving a fry into my mouth. "Seems like we are both on the same sort of path. How is Miles? Is he here with you? It would be great to catch up. We lost touch after high school."

Bella glanced over at me and slowly shook her head. "I wouldn't know how he is. We divorced seven months ago."

"Oh, I'm sorry to hear that."

"Don't be, I'm not."

The bell rang out above the door again as someone came in, and she jumped, looking over her shoulder. "I've got to go. Enjoy your dinner."

Once she was gone, I turned my attention to my dinner. Occasionally, I'd look over at her and watch as she dealt with one customer after another. When my plate was clear, I shoved it to the side and turned my attention back to the pile of documents, reading over the contract this doctor had drawn up.

Reaching the last page of the contract, everything looked good, but I'd still needed to have my lawyer check it over before I signed. I was just about to send him an email requesting a meeting when Bella appeared at the side of my table.

"Would you like your desert now with another coffee?" I heard her soft voice ask.

I looked up and met those gorgeous dark eyes and nodded. "Only if you'll join me," I said, winking.

She softly smiled and shook her head. "I'd love to, but I'm the only one here tonight. It's going to get busy."

I couldn't get over how much I loved that soft-pink hue on her cheeks. She was attractive in high school, and had Miles not gotten to her first, I'd have gone after her, but now there was something even more attractive about her. I wanted to get to know better. "Well, that is a problem," I said.

"It is?" she questioned, looking around.

"Yes, well, I love desert, but I hate eating it alone." There was that blush again.

"Oh, that is a problem." She giggled. "How do you suggest we solve it?"

"Well, I was thinking, perhaps we could share a dessert later, after your shift is over," I replied, meeting her eyes. It wasn't like me to be this forward.

"Oh, I don't know." I watched her throat as she swallowed hard. She began fidgeting with the watch on her wrist as she stood there. "I'm really not looking for—"

"Just as friends. I'm not looking for anything either." I winked, trying to make her feel a little more comfortable at my suggestion and not think I was some creep.

She thought for a minute, then smiled. "All right, I guess… we could do that," she said, playing with the thin gold chain around her neck.

"Okay then. I'll be right here." I pulled my phone from my coat pocket, getting ready to email my lawyer.

"I'll sit here until you kick me out, then I will wait for you in the parking lot." I winked.

She nodded, smiled, and turned away from me. Occasionally, I'd notice she was looking over my way, a soft smile on her lips as she served the rest of the customers through the evening.

BELLA

I'D JUST LOCKED up the back door after letting all the staff out and went back out to the front to exit from the front door. I looked out the front window and could see Asher sitting in his car. Reaching into the display case, I pulled the last four double chocolate chip cookies and placed them into a bag, then I poured the last of the coffee into two paper cups, placing a lid on both. I shut the lights off, except for the ones behind the counter, and carried everything over to the door. I carefully punched the code into the alarm and then unlocked the front door, slipping outside.

Asher met me on the sidewalk, grabbing the bag and coffee from my hands so I could take my keys and lock the door. Together we walked to his car, where he opened the passenger side door for me and handed me the coffee and cookies. Then he ran around the front of the car and climbed in.

"I noticed you don't have a car here?" he said, glancing at the empty parking lot.

I shook my head. "It's nice weather. I prefer to walk. Besides, I'm near to here."

"I see, even this late at night you walk?" he questioned. "Don't you worry about safety?"

"Yep, and yep, but it's a pretty safe neighbourhood."

"So, where shall we go?"

I shrugged. "I don't know."

"Well, we could go to the park, or to the waterfront, but if there is another low-key place you like to hang out at, say the word. We'll go wherever you want."

For a moment, I thought about it. I'd been back in Eastport for two months, and the only places I'd visited were The Cooling Rack, my condo, the grocery store, and Brielle and Sawyer's. On my day off, I hadn't walked through the park or the waterfront. I let out a breath and thought for a moment.

"I guess we could go to Eastport Park." I smiled, pulling out two cookies and handing one to Asher.

"The park it is." He grabbed the cookie from me, shoving it into his mouth, and put the car into reverse.

A little while later, we were both walking barefoot in the sand, side by side. We sipped on our coffee as we walked.

"So how long have you been in Eastport?" I asked.

"Hmmm, almost a month," Asher replied, chuckling. "It's sort of what the doctor ordered."

I frowned. "Doctor?" Was he sick?

"Yeah, I just got out of a pretty nasty relationship and needed to get myself back on my path, clear my head, and take control of things again."

I looked out over the water, my own memories of divorce flooding my mind. "Those are the same things that brought me here to Eastport as well. That and the fact that I'd lost my job, and my best friend needed a manager to help at The Cooling Rack."

"So you too, huh? Was it a nasty divorce?"

"Are there other kinds?" I replied, looking out over the water.

"I guess not. How long were you guys married?"

"Five years. Seemed as soon as we signed our marriage certificate the troubles began."

"Any kids?" he questioned.

Sadness flooded me. That question would haunt me for the rest of my life. I swallowed hard, smiled, and shook my head. Somehow, I needed to be okay with never being able to have children, and I would have been, but Miles had made me feel so damn awful about it, it had made it harder to accept. "No, none."

"Well, that is probably better. It could have made things really bad."

"Oh, it did. Even not having them."

"What do you mean?"

"That's why we got divorced. Miles wanted them so bad and…"

"And you didn't?" Asher said, slowly walking forward.

I said nothing. I didn't want to rehash the entire experience. Instead, I cleared my throat, took a sip of my coffee, and asked, "It wasn't that simple. What about you?"

"No, no kids."

We both grew quiet, then almost as if we were both thinking the same thing, we stopped walking and looked at one another.

"Just to reiterate, I'm not looking for anything long term," we said in unison.

We laughed. Everything felt lighter. It was if someone had lifted a weight off both our chests. We began laughing again as we looked at one another. I looked down to the ground as Asher cleared his throat. "Well, now that we have gotten that out of the way…"

"Yeah." I softly smiled at him.

"Care to continue our walk?"

I didn't answer. Instead, I just nodded, and we began walking, sipping the last of our coffees and eating the last of our cookies, until we'd circled back to the car. He opened my door for me and waited while I climbed into the front seat, and then he made his way around to the driver's side.

"Bella, not to rehash the subject, but I just want you to know I'm just looking for a friend, someone to hang out with, to pass the time with. The last few months have been hard on me, most of my friends sided with her, so it's like I'm starting all over again." he said, firing up the engine.

It was as if he had read my mind. "I'd like that," I replied.

"Good, me too," he said, placing his large, warm hand on mine.

Asher was a good-looking man, and from what I remembered, he'd been good-looking in high school too. As we drove, I studied his chiseled features, perhaps a little too long and hard for someone who wasn't looking for anything more than friendship. He finally pulled into the parking lot of The Cooling Rack and turned to look at me.

"If you'd like, I'll take you home, or I can leave you here, so you can walk. I don't want to push you to give me your address."

I thought for a moment, glancing down. It was a little late, even though this part of the neighbourhood was safe. "You can take me home. You seem like a trustworthy guy." I winked. "I just live over on Eastport Park Drive."

"It's amazing how you forget an area you once knew so well," Asher said as he plugged the address into his GPS and followed the directions and turned onto my street, which from there I gave him directions to the condo. He pulled up in front of the big white building and put the car in park.

"There you go, Bella," he said, his large hand resting on the gearshift. "Safe and sound. I hope you had a good time."

"Thank you. I did. Will I see you sometime soon?"

"I think you might." He winked. "I'm sort of addicted to the coffee at The Cooling Rack." He chuckled.

I smiled. "Until next time then." And with that, I got out of the car and walked to the main door, glancing over my shoulder many times to see Asher still sitting in his car at the end of the walkway, waiting and watching to make sure I got inside.

One Week Later

IT HAD BEEN one week since the night Asher and I had gone out after work. Part of me was upset that I hadn't attempted to exchange phone numbers. He'd seemed like a nice guy, and I was excited to have hopefully made another friend, aside from Brielle and Sawyer. Yet I still hadn't mentioned a word about that night, or about Asher, to Brielle.

I let out a sigh and finished placing our order for our supplies when Brielle walked into the office.

"Bella, what are you doing on Sunday?" she questioned.

"Hmmm, let me check my calendar… Oh wait, that's right, no plans!" I laughed.

"Sawyer and I would like to have you for dinner on Sunday."

I shrugged. If I knew Brielle, this was another attempt at unsuccessfully matching me with yet another doctor from Sawyer's work. "No, wait, I have to work. Did you forget?"

"Of course not, silly. You'll finish before dinner," she said, making a silly face at me. "I'm the boss, remember!" She laughed, flinging her purse onto the desk and flopping into the chair in the corner. "I'll just schedule someone else to close."

She was being too accommodating just for me to come and have dinner with them. Something was up. I looked over at Brielle. "Uh-huh, who am I meeting this week?" I asked, letting out a deep sigh.

"Okay…okay. If you must know, he is a cardiologist. Very good-looking, highly successful, and very single," Brielle replied, smiling at me with excitement.

"Brielle, please, I am not ready for a relationship. I don't know how many more times I need to say it. I said it after the brain surgeon, after the psychiatrist, and after the endocrinologist you guys thought would be perfect for me."

"I know, you keep saying that. You just need to be open to the possibilities of a new relationship. We just want to see you happy."

"I am happy. Thrilled. I'd be even happier if you'd stop trying to fix me up with every single guy you know. I am happy just focusing on this job, and I've been focusing on decorating my place and committing to my yoga practice. For once, I'm focusing on me, and it feels fantastic."

"I agree. You have been doing all those things, but you need some spice in your life too," she said, pulling up a chair and sitting down beside me.

I let out a breath and looked at my best friend. "Spice can come when I'm ready for it. Honestly, I just want to focus on me. It's what I desperately need right now, Brie. Before I let someone else in, I need to focus on myself and get my life in order." I was practically begging my best friend to stop trying to set me up with people. I needed to just focus on the things that were important to me. It was something I'd never done before.

Just then a knock came to the door, and we both looked over to see Tomi, one of the staff, leaning against the doorframe. "Sorry to interrupt, but, Bella, someone is here to see you."

"Did they say who it was?"

Tomi smiled. "It's a guy, says that you'll know who it is." She smiled.

Brielle looked at me with surprise on her face. "Well, well, keeping something from your best friend, are you?" She laughed, getting all giddy with excitement, grabbing me and shaking me. "You little liar." She laughed again.

"My God, Brie, I'm not keeping anything from you at all. Now, if you'll calm down and excuse me…" I said, getting up.

"Not a chance. No way are you keeping this from me," she said, getting up and following me through the kitchen.

I glanced through the hole in the door to see Asher standing off to the side, hands in his pockets. He couldn't have appeared at a worse time I thought to myself. He was wearing perfectly fitted jeans and a white ribbed-knit sweater that hugged him in all the right spots. He looked amazing. I licked my lips and then glanced at

Brielle and gave her the same look she'd shared with me so many times over the years.

"Uh-huh. Not hiding anything hmmm…" Brielle giggled.

"I'm not," I replied.

"Okay, okay, fine. Go." She laughed.

I pushed the door open and stepped out behind the counter just as Asher turned around.

"Hey," I whispered, making my way over to him.

"Hey. I was hoping you'd be here. I had to go out of town for a few days, but I wanted to stop in and see you before I made my way home. I was hoping you might like to go out for dinner sometime this week."

I bit my bottom lip while thinking of any reason I could to get out of dinner. I even went to the extent of pulling my phone out of my back pocket and scrolling through my very empty, non-existent social calendar while my mind raced with any reason I couldn't go.

"It's not a date, if that is what you are thinking." He'd read my mind. He cleared his throat and placed his hand on my arm, pulling me aside. "Listen, I could really use a night out to take my mind off of some things, and since you are the only person I know here, I thought I'd ask you."

I met his eyes and could see the look of someone who really needed a friend. "Sure, what night?"

"Tomorrow?"

"Tomorrow works," I said. "What time?"

"How about I pick you up at seven?"

I thought for a moment, and then nodded. "Seven it is."

"Great." He rubbed his hands together and smiled. "Oh, do you like seafood? I've had a craving for it since I came to Eastport."

I nodded. "Love it."

"Okay, I'll see you tomorrow night."

Asher didn't give me a minute to protest or change my mind because he was already in his car and heading out of the parking lot by the time I realized what it was I'd just agreed to. As I shoved my phone back into my pants pocket, I realized I couldn't even text him to cancel because, once again, I hadn't gotten his number. *I really needed to get his number.*

I let out a sigh and made my way back to the office. The kitchen door had just swung shut behind me when I heard Brielle.

"Well? What was that all about?" she grilled as I walked through the door and back to our shared office.

"Nothing, just a friendly conversation."

Brielle stood there, a knowing look on her face. "Whatever, not with a hottie like that. I can guarantee it wasn't just a friendly conversation. Are you seeing him?"

I shook my head and laughed. "Brielle, not being

ready for a relationship isn't just an answer I give you to stop fixing me up with people. It was also the answer I gave him. He's just a friend," I said.

"A friend?" Brielle was quiet for a moment. Then she looked at me. "Please, Bella, don't disappoint me."

"Yes, he's a friend. If you must know, we went to high school together. He was actually one of guys who played on the high school football team with Miles."

"Oh." I could hear the disappointment in her voice as she flopped back down into her chair.

"Yes, oh." I giggled, turning my attention back to what I'd been working on.

ASHER

I JUST HUNG up the phone after confirming reservations for two at The Harbourview Restaurant and returned to the bathroom where I started the shower. I'd just finished my workout for the day, and I had a little less than two hours to get ready before I picked up Bella.

I quickly showered, dried, and then wrapped the white towel around my waist. I shaved, then splashed some cologne on my neck. Then I wandered over to the closet, sifting through the hanging clothes, until I found my favorite pair of dark-blue jeans and crew neck.

I glanced at my reflection in the mirror before grabbing my jacket off the back of the chair. I made my way to my car and sped off toward the local flower shop.

I felt it was necessary to take her flowers; I had told myself many times in my head this wasn't a date, but my mother had taught me early in life that women like flowers, so I'd grabbed a bouquet of light-pink carnations, the same colour her cheeks went as she blushed. Armed with flowers, I pulled up outside of her building.

As I sat there waiting for her to come down, I kept looking to the bouquet. I was about to get out and dump them in the garbage bin when I saw her step out of the building. I could barely take my eyes off her. She walked toward the car, dressed in snug-fitting jeans and a light-pink sweater under a beige jacket. Her dark hair was wavy and soft and bounced lightly at her shoulders as she walked. I quickly got out of the of the car and walked around to her side, the flowers behind my back.

"You look great," I said, not wanting to come on too strong, but not wanting her to think I hadn't noticed.

"Thank you, as do you," she said, smiling at me.

I opened the passenger's side door and waited while she climbed into the car, then I handed her the bouquet. "For you."

"Oh…" she said with a look of surprise. "They're, um… they're beautiful," she said, seeming confused.

"Yeah, after I bought them, I wondered why I had. See, it's just my mother always told me that girls like flowers, and well…you are a girl," I explained, nerves fluttering through me.

"I am and I do," she said, smiling, bringing the flowers to her nose to smell them. "Thank you, they are beautiful. They are also very unexpected, but beautiful," she said, glancing up at me.

I swallowed hard, shut the door, and made my way around to the driver's side door, taking a deep breath before I climbed back into the car. "Hope you're hungry."

"I am. Where are we headed?"

"Well, I thought we'd go to The Harbourview."

"Oh. Okay," she said, looking out the window and not meeting my gaze.

I glanced over. I could tell she was uncomfortable. Was it me, the flowers, had I overstepped the 'friends' thing? "Is something wrong with that restaurant? I just looked up 'local seafood restaurant' on the computer, so if it's no good, I'd rather know now. Nothing worse than horrible seafood."

She shook her head, but I still wasn't convinced. "No, it's nothing. The Harbourview has got fantastic food."

"Then what is it, because that's not a face of someone who likes food in a restaurant and is happy to be going to it."

She shifted uncomfortably in her seat and looked over at me. "Really, it's nothing, really. The flowers are really pretty. Thank you," she said, pulling her seat belt across her.

I wasn't sure I believed her, but I'd also learned from

my previous relationship that dwelling on things wasn't healthy, nor was it smart. It was a surefire way to end up in an argument, even with a friend. Instead, I pulled away from the curb and headed toward the restaurant's, determined to make this a night of fun for both of us.

"So, what is your choice?" I questioned, looking over the menu just as our drinks arrived at the table.

"Hmm, I thought that the Lobster Bisque looks good, but then, so does the Lobster Tagliatelle. What about you?"

"Funny, I was looking at the Tagliatelle or the Grilled Atlantic Salmon."

"Oh, I missed the salmon," she said, smiling over at me then looking back down at her menu as she picked up her wine and took a sip.

"So, what are you doing to heal yourself?" I questioned. "You told me you were focusing on that."

"Well, aside from working, I have been putting a lot of focus on me. I have been setting up my new place, spending time with Brielle, my best friend, and her husband, Sawyer, and Emma, their little girl. I've been doing yoga, and recently I started a meditation group at the yoga studio. Honestly, I'm focusing on me and the things I want to do. I didn't get to do many of those things while I was married."

"That's good. How are you liking meditation?"

"Um, well, I have done it twice, and honestly, I'm not sure I get it. Silencing the mind isn't as easy as one would think, but I'm trying. I find I get a lot out of yoga, more so than in meditation."

"Yoga is fantastic! I actually used to practice at a local studio before I moved here. It was always what I needed to clear my mind after a tough day."

"What about you?" she asked, sipping her wine again.

"The same as you. Just focusing on myself. I took some time off from work to clear my head, and I've started running again and hitting the gym. There is something very healing about running on the beach in the early morning, watching the sunrise. Have you ever tried it?" I smiled, passing the bread basket that had been placed on our table.

"Thank you," she said, reaching in and grabbing a piece and placing it on the small bread plate beside her. "I used to run in high school but stopped when I went to college, then got married, and it was just another thing I allowed my life to take over."

"I understand. Well, perhaps you could join me sometime?"

"I'll think about it." She picked up her bread and tore a little piece off, shoving it into her mouth and looking around like she was trying to avoid being seen.

"So, I couldn't help but notice you looked a little upset in the car. This wasn't a terrible choice, was it?"

She looked over at me, then shook her head. "No, not at all. I've heard the food is fantastic here."

"Bella? Bella, is that you?" a woman's voice called out.

I looked in the direction the voice came from, and suddenly a woman appeared. "Bella, it is you!"

"Oh, hey," she said unenthusiastically before glancing over at me.

"How are things? I hope you're okay? God, I could kill my brother for what he did to you," the woman said as she stood at the side of our table, giving me the occasional glance.

"Yeah, well, it's over now. I'm fine."

I could see the tension in her shoulders as the woman looked between her and me and then back to her as if questioning what it was she was doing here with me. The conversation had literally stalled, so I jumped in.

"Hi, I'm Asher, a good friend of Bella's," I said, shoving my hand out toward this woman.

"Hi. Stacey. So, you say you're a good friend of Bella's?" she said, glancing my way. "Perhaps I'm not so angry with my brother after all. Perhaps I should be angry at you, Bella, for cheating on my brother. Anyway, I'll talk to you later," she said, taking off in the direction she came.

Bella smiled at me uncomfortably and shrugged. "That was Mile's sister. She works here and apparently, she hasn't changed one bit. She used to spread rumors about me in highschool, and she apparently going to do the same now."

"Why didn't you say something? We could have gone somewhere else!"

"I didn't want to do that. I hoped she wasn't working tonight, and at first, I thought I was safe, but then I caught sight of her. She has a hard time minding her own business, as you can see. Plus, all that talk about how she hates her brother for what he did to me is a lie. However, now it looks like she'll have a real hate on for me," Bella said, taking another bite of her bread.

"Don't worry about it. People love to talk. It says way more about them than it does about you." I winked. I'd learned that over the past six months as rumours flew around about me.

Bella smiled at me. "Yeah, and she loves to start them. I can almost hear her now."

"So, let her. I used to tell people when they'd approach me with the latest rumour they'd heard to add to that rumour whatever the hell they wanted. That would just make them stand and stare at me, wondering if I were serious." I chuckled.

"I bet. So, you had someone like that in your life too, then?"

"Oh, try about ten of them. All my ex's friends. I do not know what she told them, but the things I heard just blew my mind."

Bella let out a little giggle. "I'm sorry that happened to you."

"And I am sorry I chose the restaurant your sister-in-law worked at."

Dinner finally came, and the rest of the meal passed, drinks flowed, and so did conversation. We avoided our past issues as a topic of discussion and talked about our hobbies and things we were interested in. Turned out we had more than a few things in common, and before we knew it, we had an entire list of events and things to do throughout the summer. When the server set the bill down on the edge of the table, we both reached for it, but I grabbed it first.

"Asher, please, let me see it."

I opened the billfold and shook my head. "No, I got it," I said, pulling out my credit card, placing it on top of the bill.

"No, that isn't fair. I'd like to pay my share."

Asher looked at me and smiled. "How about you get it next time?" I said, winking at her.

I was surprised she didn't fight me. Instead, she just agreed. As soon as I paid the bill, we walked out of the restaurant together and climbed into my car.

"Thank you," I said, before starting the engine.

"For?"

"For joining me, taking my mind off of things, and for being my friend."

"You are welcome," she replied. "And thank you for dinner and for teaching me to learn that it's okay to let people talk." She giggled, placing her hand on top of mine. "It means a lot," she said in a hushed whisper.

"You're welcome."

Our eyes locked and silence fell between us. We sat there staring at one another, neither saying a word. I could have gotten lost in her eyes if I allowed myself, but I finally tore mine away from hers and cleared my throat. "We should exchange numbers. Maybe I can convince you to come for a run with me one day this week," I said, reaching into my pocket to pull out my phone.

She reached into her purse, pulling her phone from inside, and smiled. "I think that is a good idea, and perhaps I could convince you to come and join me for some yoga."

"No convincing needed. I'll be there. Just let me know when," I said.

We switched phones and entered our own information into the contacts area and switched back, then I started the engine and drove to her condo. We said our good-byes, and I waited while she walked up to the door. Once she was inside, I was about to pull away from the curb when my phone vibrated to let me know I had a message. I reached for it, looking at the screen to see Bella had already sent a message. I clicked it open and read it.

> BELLA: Thank you for a wonderful evening. Looking forward to the next ;)

I smiled. I had a feeling this was the beginning of a wonderful new friendship.

BELLA

One week Later

I DROPPED my yoga mat inside the door and kicked off my sneakers. I'd taken a yoga class down in the park this morning. It had been a gorgeous day, and yoga had become my favorite way to spend a Saturday morning. I went into the kitchen and turned the kettle on, looking forward to my cup of chamomile tea, when the phone rang.

"Hello," I said, without checking my caller ID.

"Bella, it's Miles."

Irritated, I made a mental note to make sure next time I checked to see who was calling before answering. "What do you need?" I asked, feeling the irritation climb into my body.

"I've got some mail for you here at the house. Thought I'd let you know and find out where to send it."

I knew Sawyer was going on a medical retreat next week and had asked him to stop and pick up some things I'd left behind. "I'll have Sawyer pick them up when he is in town next week, okay?"

"Okay then. I also heard from my sister. She said she saw you the other night with some guy? What's going on?"

I remembered Asher's words from that night. *People will talk; let them. It says more about them than it does you.* No matter how true those words may have been, it still didn't stop me from being bothered.

"She said it appeared you were on a date."

I softly smiled to myself. "Of course, it did."

"Is it true?"

"Miles, it will be whatever your sister said it was."

"Bella, what is that supposed to mean?" I could hear the irritation line his voice.

"Exactly what I said. My word certainly will change no one's mind. Never did. However, I wanted to let you know Asher says hello."

The line was quiet for a moment. "Asher? As in Asher Harrison?" he asked, his voice cracking like he was still going through puberty. "You were on a date with Asher Harrison?"

"Yes. Now, I have to go. I will give Sawyer your address." I didn't wait for a good-bye. Instead, I hung up. I did not know what had possessed me to lie to Miles, telling him it was Asher I had been out with. It certainly wasn't to make him jealous, or perhaps it was. Perhaps I'd done it to give him a taste of his own medicine after the five years of abuse I'd dealt with. It felt good to kind of stick something to him. Either way, I went back to making my tea and started cutting up some cucumber for a light snack.

I'd just sat down when I heard a knock at the door. I was on my way to answer it when I heard a familiar voice call out, "Come on, woman, open up."

I laughed and opened the door. "Come on in." I giggled. "Want a tea?" I questioned, looking at a frazzled Brielle.

"Oh, yes, please. I have an hour to myself. Sawyer and Emma are napping."

I closed the door and went to the kitchen, pouring Brielle a tea and carried it into the living room, placing it in front of her.

"Thanks. It's been a long morning," she said, releasing a yawn. Her hair was everywhere, and she looked exhausted, quite a difference from how she appeared at work every day.

"Of course. Oh, before I forget, can Sawyer pop by Miles' place and get some mail of mine and a few other things that he has of mine next week before he returns from his conference?"

"Sure, I'll let him know. So, tell me, how was dinner the other night?"

I'd made the mistake of asking Brielle to help me get ready for dinner the other night with Asher. She had been good about it, until she wanted to look at my old year-books to see what he had looked like then. I'd dug them out of a bin in the closet, and while I was busy getting ready, she'd flipped through the pages, glancing at images of a young Asher. I figured the first chance she would have, she would ask me all about it, and I was right.

"It was nice. We had dinner at The Harbourview. Although I ran into Stacey. Of course, she had to stuff her nose into everything. Plus, she told Miles. I'm not sure if he called just now to tell me about the mail or to find out if what she had told him was true."

"What did you say?"

I giggled. "I told him Asher said hello."

"You didn't."

"Yep, I did. Just thought I'd try to give him a taste of what my last five years were like, although I doubt it affected him any. Although, I know there were times in highschool that he thought Asher was trying to steal me from him. Oh and I heard through the grapevine that his new girlfriend is pregnant, and they are planning their wedding."

"Oh God, already? Did he even give himself a chance to get over you?" Brielle questioned.

"He was over me before he'd even contacted a lawyer. I'm sure of that. It's honestly not an enormous surprise."

"Guess I should tell you that Sheila was in the diner the other day, too," Brielle replied.

"What for? She never comes in there."

"Oh, she told me she was meeting a friend there. However, no one showed up, and after an hour, she left. I'm guessing she was there to see you, or perhaps see if Asher and you showed up together."

Didn't she have anything better to do with her time? I rolled my eyes and giggled.

"Apparently not. Knowing Miles, he put her up to it. Now he knows the truth, or part of the truth." I giggled.

"Anyway, enough about those two! When are you seeing Mr. Gorgeous again?" Brielle questioned.

I rolled my eyes at my friend and sighed. "Look, we are just friends, nothing more. Now please, stop with that. He is good-looking, but honestly, Brie, I'm not looking for anything."

"You say that a lot," Brielle cried, letting out a sigh. "The least you could do is humour me. Honestly. Make up something," she said, laughing.

I picked up my tea and took a sip, then looked to my best friend and started laughing. "You are so impossible."

Just then, my phone vibrated against the table. Brielle leaned forward in time to see Asher's name flash on the screen. She looked at me and lifted her eyebrows.

"Just friends, huh? Does he know that?"

I knew Brielle was just trying to get under my skin, and it was working. "I really like Asher, and if things were different…" I could feel my cheeks heating at my realization.

"If things were different… what?" Brielle said, sitting forward on the couch, waiting for me to continue.

I let out a sigh. "Well, perhaps if things were different, I'd consider dating him." I shrugged.

Brielle looked at me, a mischievous smile on her face.

"What?"

"How do we get you ready?" She giggled. "He may be just too good for you to pass up."

Just then, a knock came to the door. I shook my head and got up. I opened the door to see a dishevelled Sawyer standing there holding a crying Emma. "Bella, please tell me Brie is here."

"Yes, come on in."

"What's wrong?" she called from the living room.

"I have to go to work. There's an emergency, and

they've called me in," Sawyer said, handing Emma over to me. I watched as he made his way over to Brielle, bent down, and gave her a kiss good-bye, then he made his way over to me again and kissed Emma, then kissed me on the cheek.

"Guess we are on our own for dinner, eh, Emma," Brielle said as I placed Emma on her lap.

"You guys can always have dinner with me tonight," I said, thinking about what I could make that was easy.

"Sounds perfect," Brie said as she bounced Emma on her lap making her laugh.

BRIELLE AND EMMA left shortly after nine. After taking a hot bath, I crawled into bed. I'd just begun reading the book I was in the middle of when my phone vibrated against my nightstand. I reached for the phone and smiled when I saw Asher's name on my screen.

ASHER: Ignoring me, are you?

BELLA: Depends, who's spreading rumours now lol

ASHER: Me ;P

I couldn't help but laugh.

ASHER: What are you doing?

I quickly snapped a picture of my book on top of my flannel-clad legs and sent it off.

ASHER: Ohhh baby. Stop sending dirty pictures.

BELLA: :O You wish!

ASHER: How did you guess ;)

I rolled my eyes and laughed.

ASHER: What are you doing tomorrow?

I glanced to my calendar. Again, it was empty. I really needed to fill it up. I couldn't even use work as an excuse since Brielle had given me a week off since I'd need to cover for her for two weeks later in the summer.

BELLA: Not a lot, see it's empty :(

I quickly attached a screenshot of my calendar for him to see. I waited as those three dots appeared bouncing around excitedly.

ASHER: Fear not! Meet me at the beach for 8.

BELLA: Eight! In the morning?

ASHER: Yep, 8 in the morning. We'll go for a run then have breakfast afterward, then we will head off to an antique market I found up the coast.

I smiled as I read his message. It sounded like a lovely day, and part of me was excited, but the other part was hesitant.

ASHER: Don't overthink it. Just say you'll join me.

I tapped the screen of my phone while biting my lip, trying to decide if I should say yes or no. I was afraid that perhaps I'd been giving him the wrong signals. God, I hoped I wasn't.

ASHER: You're overthinking

BELLA: No I'm not!

ASHER: Then what is taking you so long?

BELLA: You're impossible! I'll see you at 8 ;)

ASHER: ;) I look forward to it.

ASHER

I'D LISTENED to her laugh all day long, and I still wasn't tired of hearing that sound. We approached the door to her condo, and she dug around in her purse, looking for the keys as the smell of pizza drove us crazy.

"I'm starving. That smells so good, and I… seriously… why can't I find my keys?" she cried, now furiously digging deeper into her purse.

"Well, we could always just park ourselves on the floor here and eat the pizza!" I said, glancing around as the smell of pepperoni made my mouth water.

She let out a laugh and shook her head. "You're ridiculous! Actually, look, we're saved from hallway pizza!" she said, pulling her keys from her purse and holding them in the air.

I chuckled as I followed her into her condo. "Go on

in. We can eat in the living room. I'll just grab some plates and glasses."

I carried the pizza into the living room and set the box down on the small coffee table in front of the couch. Her place was beautifully decorated, and I smiled as I glanced at the small bookshelf in the corner. I took a quick glance at some titles and noticed we both had many of Wayne Dyer's books. He had become one of my favourites since my relationship took a dive. I then turned my attention to the floor-to-ceiling window and wandered over to see that her place looked out over the water. There was even a small bistro table and chairs on the balcony.

"We could always eat out on the balcony," I suggested, just as Bella stepped into the living room. "Watch the sunset."

"Whatever you would like. I figured you'd just like to relax and watch Netflix or something."

"Well, I'm shocked," I said, trying hard to hide the smile on my lips.

"Why? What's wrong? Did they get our order wrong?"

"No, but I wonder, are you suggesting that we… Netflix and chill?" I said, still trying not to laugh.

I watched as her cheeks went to my favourite shade of pink and a smile came to her lips. "Oh God… I did, didn't I," she said, burying her face into her hands.

"You did." I smiled, walking over to her.

She stepped into me and buried her face into my chest, wrapping her arms around my waist as she laughed. "My God, I can't believe what I did."

Instinctively, I wrapped my arms around her, hugging her close to me. She smelled heavenly, and we stood there, her holding me and me holding her.

The day had gone so smoothly. Better than I had thought it would. We'd gone on our run, then headed to a small breakfast diner. We drove up the coast, listening to music, and had spent the day walking through the large antique market I'd found online. The pizza and a movie were an impromptu suggested by her.

I felt her arms slowly slide from my waist, and so I too let her go. She took a seat on the edge of the couch and flipped open the pizza box. She held out a plate to me, which I took and sat down next to her.

"We can eat outside if you'd like," she said, pulling a slice of pizza from the box and placing it on her plate.

I shook my head, leaning back on the couch. It had been a long day. We'd had a lot of sun and fresh air and no doubt she was as tired as I. "Nah, let's kick back, relax, find a movie."

She smiled and leaned back against the couch, taking a bite of her pizza. "Sounds like a good idea."

Two hours later, she was curled into my side, a blanket over her legs as we watched a movie. She'd chosen a thriller, and from the looks of things, it hadn't been a wise choice. She seemed petrified.

"Oh God… why do I watch these?" she cried as she snuggled closer to me and hid her eyes behind her fingers.

I couldn't help but chuckle. She was so damn cute. "It's not that bad," I said, putting my arm around her and pulling her close to me.

"It is! And why are you laughing at me?" she questioned, gripping my shirt.

"I'm not laughing at you," I said, grabbing her side causing her to laugh. "Okay, perhaps I'm laughing at you."

"Oh God, don't do that. I'm so ticklish," she said, grabbing my hand.

"Oh… are you now?" I grabbed her side once again as she laughed hard, forgetting about the movie.

"Yes, please…stop…" she said, laughing hard as I continued tickling her.

She grabbed my hand. "Please, Asher," she pleaded, out of breath, continuing to laugh, "Please, stop."

"Okay… okay…" I said, holding my hands up as if I were innocent. I pulled her into me. "Now, behave yourself. Let's watch the rest of the movie."

W HEN THE CREDITS ROLLED, I felt Bella stretch. I rubbed her arm just as she sat up. She let out a yawn and stretched again.

"Did you fall asleep?" I questioned, stretching myself.

"Perhaps." She smiled, grabbing our plates and glasses, then heading toward the kitchen. "You are very warm, and I was very comfortable."

"I see. I'm warm and comfortable?"

I followed her to the kitchen and stood in the doorway, watching as she slipped everything into her dishwasher.

"You are." She shrugged and giggled, turning to me and wrapping herself around me again.

I really liked this girl, and I knew I needed to get out of here before I made a mistake and kissed her. Her lips had been on my mind all night, and I'd almost kissed her once before while tickling her. "Well, I should get going," I said, glancing at my watch to see that it was almost midnight.

She nodded. "I guess morning does come early."

I turned and made my way to the door, sliding on my

shoes. I wished I wasn't in the position I was, just having had my heart broken. I wished I'd met her under better circumstances and that I was ready to move forward into another relationship. Only when I looked over to see her standing against the wall, watching me, I was sure I saw a hint of want in her eyes.

"Thank you for today and tonight."

"Of course," I said, making my way over to her and placing my hand against the wall above her head. "I had a wonderful time." I looked down into her eyes, brushing a strand of hair out of the way.

She looked up at me. "Call me?" she questioned. "I'm off this week."

God, it didn't matter how much I knew I shouldn't kiss her, how much I wasn't ready. All I could think about was what her lips would feel like against mine. This wasn't the first time this thought had passed through my mind today. I'd thought about it this morning over breakfast. Then on the way up the coast. Then many times as we got close enough in the antique mall, and throughout the movie. Yet I hadn't done it. I'd restrained myself. Even when she'd slipped her hand slowly into mine, I'd held back.

"I think I can do that," I whispered. "Of course, you can always call me as well."

She nodded and bit her bottom lip as she stared into my eyes.

Her eyes said everything I needed to know. I could feel the push and pull between us. It hadn't been my imagination; it had gotten progressively stronger all day, and now it was so strong I couldn't fight it any longer. The room grew quiet, the noise from the TV falling away, and I swallowed hard. I leaned in slowly, bringing my lips to hers, grazing them.

My body instantly lit up as her lips met mine. The kiss started out slow, each of us unsure. I didn't move; I didn't want to scare her, but when I felt her left hand slide around my waist and the right rest against my chest, I claimed her mouth.

She let out a small moan and gripped the front of my shirt as I swept my tongue through her mouth. I pulled her tightly against me, kissing her harder when someone knocked on the door.

Our lips parted, and I brushed a loose strand of hair from her eyes as she looked up at me. "Want me to get that?" I asked quietly, silently praying she said no.

Another knock, this one a little more urgent. I looked down at her and she nodded her head.

I unlocked the door and pulled the door open to see a woman I vaguely recognized but couldn't place. She stood there in sweatpants and a sweatshirt. Her hair was an absolute mess, and she was holding a small, sleeping child.

"Oh. I'm…" She glanced at the number on the door. "Um, is Bella…"

I felt Bella's body press up against mine and her hand on my arm as she peeked her head around me. "Brie, is everything okay?" she questioned, alarm filling her voice.

"The alarm went off at The Cooling Rack, Sawyers at work and, well, I have to go. Can Emma stay here with you? I'm sorry to… um… ruin your evening," she said, glancing to me, then back to Bella.

"Of course, she can stay. You're not interrupting anything. Asher was just—"

"I was just on my way home. If you'd like, I can drive you over. I mean, that way you aren't heading there alone," I offered.

Brie looked at Bella and then at me. "That is very nice, but I'll be okay."

"You're sure? Really, it's no trouble."

"Yeah, Brie, you probably shouldn't go alone. Let Asher take you. Here, give me Emma," Bella said, stepping forward and taking the baby from her.

"Thank you."

Bella held on to Emma as I turned and glanced at her. "I'll talk to you tomorrow," I whispered, then leaned in and kissed her cheek.

"I look forward to it," Bella whispered, and then quietly closed her door.

BELLA

"HAVE YOU HEARD FROM HIM YET?" Brielle questioned.

Of all the times for her to knock on my door, it had to be when Asher had finally kissed me. Our first kiss had been interrupted by the only person who had tried so hard to get me on a date with someone. "No, not yet. He told me he had to go out of town."

I'd told Brielle nothing about what had happened before she opened the door, and I'd tried to play the kiss on the cheek as just a friendly good-bye. She was skeptical and had kept asking me all these questions.

"Well, hopefully, tonight then. You'll need to let me know." She giggled.

"I will. Listen, I've got to lock up. I'll call you a little later?"

"Sounds good."

When I hung up the phone, I went to the front of the store and locked the door. I'd just made it back into the office when my phone vibrated in my back pocket. I pulled it out and looked to see if Brielle was messaging me to tell me something she'd forgotten and was surprised to see Asher's name on my screen.

He'd told me he was going to be busy the past week and that he had to go out of town for the better part of it. He said he had some business ends to tie up, and he had to meet up with his ex to finish closing out their shared apartment lease.

I'd messaged him twice during that time, but he'd remained quiet. I figured perhaps everything had been too much for him and had decided to just leave him alone.

ASHER: Up for some drinks?

I smiled, looking around at what little I had left to do. It had been a long week, and I hadn't been able to forget that kiss he'd delivered the night Brie had appeared at my door. In fact, I'd woken up many times this week imagining his lips on mine. He was an amazing kisser.

BELLA: Love to.

I watched as those three little dots jumped around for what felt like forever.

ASHER: 205 Water Road

BELLA: Give me twenty minutes

ASHER: I'll be waiting.

I smiled and went about doing what needed to be done, and within five minutes, I was out in my car, heading toward Water Road.

I was just about to knock on the door when it opened and Asher stood before me, a welcoming smile on his face. "Hey."

I smiled and stepped into the front door. As he closed it, he turned and wrapped his arms around me. "Good to see you."

The scent of his cologne invaded my senses as I wrapped my arms around him. When I went to pull away, he leaned in and kissed my lips.

"Come, let's grab a drink and head out back," he said, gently placing his large hand on the small of my back and guiding me to the kitchen.

His backyard looked out over the water and was perfectly lit. "You set all this up?" I questioned.

"No, I'm just renting, remember? Apparently, the people I'm renting this place from normally only rent it out to tourists for weekends. I got very lucky. They had no reservations when I inquired, so I took it for the entire summer. It is beautiful, isn't it?"

"Yes, I'd love to own something like this one day. A small piece of heaven, my own little postage stamp, if you will."

"Same here. So, what is new? How have you been?"

"Not too much. I filled in for Brie today, open to close. I've actually been doing that for most of this week. Emma came down with the flu."

"Oh, well, why didn't you say anything? We could have done this another night," Asher said, sitting forward, a look of concern on his face.

I smiled, biting my bottom lip. "I could have, but I'm really not that tired," I said, drinking the last few drops of the gin and tonic Asher had made for me. "So, what about you? What have you been up to all week?"

Asher stretched, drinking back the last of his beer. "I was in negotiations. Two business contracts, both of which are almost completed."

"So, what is it you do?" I couldn't believe I'd never asked him before now.

"I'm a doctor. After my separation from my girlfriend, I decided that I no longer wanted to stay in the area, so I sold my practice and started looking for a new opportunity. One sort of fell on my lap, so once things have been finalized, I'll be setting down roots."

"That must take up a lot of your time Your practice?"

"A little, but I love what I do."

"That's good," I said, softly smiling, even though I was feeling a little defeated that perhaps our time was coming close to an end. Yet, it wasn't right to let it defeat me. We started out as friends, we'd kissed, we'd also agreed that neither of us was looking for anything. I'd told myself if something happened, it happened, and that this was part of my healing journey. Yet, after spending this time with him, kissing him, I couldn't help but feel that if things were different, I would've given us a chance.

"Then I had the joy of having to deal with my ex."

"How was that?"

He chuckled. "How is it when dealing with yours?"

"Yeah, no need to answer that question." I giggled.

"So, you never told me. How long are you in East-port for? Is it a permanent move or a temporary one?" he questioned.

"Well, right now, until the end of the summer. My old job might bring me back on board. At least that was what I was told."

"Then what?"

"Well, then I'd move back to Boston. Although I'm still not sure if that is what I want." I shrugged. "I guess I will figure that out when and if the opportunity presents itself." I smiled.

Asher nodded and looked up at the night sky. "It's beginning to cloud over. Looks like it may even rain."

I looked up to the sky to see a dark-grey cloud looming overhead. "Yep, those are definitely storm clouds," I agreed.

"Did you want to head in and catch a movie or something?"

I nodded at the same time I felt a drop of rain hit my arm. "That sounds like a good idea. I just felt a drop of rain."

"Alright, after you," he said, standing.

I bent down and grabbed my glass, then made my way to his back door and stepped inside and placed our glasses down on the counter.

In a matter of moments, we were on the couch, surfing through Netflix's suggestions, debating what to watch while munching on popcorn. We finally agreed on one selection we had passed up from the other night.

"Are you sure you have it in you to watch a thriller and then drive home alone?" He chuckled as the eerie music played during the credits.

"I hope so." I giggled.

Asher leaned back against the couch and placed his arm behind me just as I leaned back. The credits had barely finished when a loud crack of thunder erupted, shaking the windows, causing me to jump.

"Wow, that is some crazy-ass thunder," Asher said,

looking at me before pulling me close. "Are you okay? You must have jumped a mile."

Another rumble hit. I jumped again, and this time the TV went blank. He reached for the remote, pressing some buttons. "Damn, it looks like I've lost internet."

"We aren't having much luck tonight, are we?"

He shook his head and threw the remote down on the couch beside him, leaned back, and rubbed his hand over his face. Just then, another crack of thunder hit, and the room was plunged into darkness.

I shrugged. "I don't know… this is kind of nice," I said, running my hand over his hand.

His eyes met mine. There was nothing left to say between us. He slowly leaned forward, and once again the memory of that kiss came flooding back as his lips meant mine. Everything fell away in that moment.

Lying beside him on the couch, I allowed myself to get lost in his kiss and his touch. I could feel his arousal pressing into my leg, and each time his fingers grazed my bare skin, shock waves flew through my body. It had been so long since I'd been kissed and touched like this, I could barely contain myself. Every part of me was on fire.

"Want to go where we will be more comfortable?" he whispered in my ear before letting his lips dance down my neck.

I tilted my head back, my eyes closed. All I heard myself murmur was yes, as his hands gripped my hips.

He tore his lips from the spot on my neck and stood up. Taking hold of my hand, he gently pulled me through the dark living room and down the hall to his bedroom. He didn't give me time to think, almost as if he knew I'd change my mind.

Once in the room, he closed the door behind us and took hold of me. Placing me up against the door, he kissed me hard. I didn't hear the thunder, but when I opened my eyes, his small bedside lamp was on. He guided me to the bed and sat me down.

I watched as he pulled his shirt off over his head one-handed, exposing his muscular chest and very well-defined six-pack. His eyes were filled with want, and I bit my bottom lip as he took hold of my hands and pulled me to him, the feel of his warm skin comforting me.

My body tingled when his fingers grazed the skin on my sides as he slowly lifted my shirt off me. He dropped it to the floor, and I watched his eyes roam over my body. That was it, he didn't go for more. Instead, he pulled me into his arms, wrapped them around me, and kissed me hard.

I SLOWLY OPENED my eyes and stretched, my body hurting in places it hadn't been yesterday. I looked around the unfamiliar room, the events of last night coming to me. We'd started out slow, and soon we were both breathing hard and writhing against one another. I smiled at the memory and looked over to the other side of the bed, expecting to find Asher still asleep, but saw nothing but a pile of messed blankets. I sat up, listening hard. Nothing but silence surrounded me.

I swallowed hard. Had he left? Why would he leave me here in his house? That was when I heard a clatter of dishes and a muttered curse word.

I lay back in the bed just as the bedroom door opened and his deep voice greeted me. "Morning."

I stretched, sat up, and smiled as he carried a full tray toward me. The first thing I noticed was the small vase of flowers that sat on the tray. "Morning."

"Thought you might like some coffee and some food," he said, placing the tray down at the foot of the bed. He picked up one mug and brought it over to me.

"Thank you." I smiled, taking the mug from him and inhaling the scent of the hot coffee.

I watched as he grabbed his cup and sat down beside me. "So, is everything good?" he questioned. "Was last night okay for you?"

I nodded, taking a sip of the hot coffee.

"It was amazing for me as well."

I could feel the blush rising to my cheeks, Miles had never once asked me if the sex was okay, and he'd never told me if he liked it. "It was more than okay," I said, swallowing hard.

"You're sure?"

"Yeah. Are you sure it was okay for you?"

I watched as Asher nodded. "No, it was. I figured you might be a little wigged out this morning... you know... after the condom broke last night."

Instantly, my eyes fell to the mug in my hands, and I let out a breath. I hadn't told him anything about my divorce, simply that I was, in fact, divorced.

"Bella?" Asher said, bending to catch my eyes. "If it's bothering you, you can tell me."

I sniffled and rubbed my nose, trying hard not to let the past five years of my life come flooding forward. "No, but I can tell you, you don't need to worry about that, like, at all."

Asher looked at me. "You on the pill?" he questioned.

I shook my head.

He frowned. "Why is it that if you aren't on the pill then I don't need to worry?"

I blew out a breath. "I'm infertile." The words rolled off my tongue as if they meant nothing. "So, there's no need to worry about a silly condom breaking," I said, putting on a brave face and meeting his eyes.

He said nothing else. He just picked up the plate that was filled with fruit slices, setting it between us.

"Aren't you going to say anything?"

"There isn't anything to say. I understand. Remember, I'm a doctor. I just didn't want you to be freaking out and think that I didn't care, because I do," he whispered, then leaned forward and kissed me.

As we sat there, he changed the subject, talking about the next exciting adventure he wanted to go on this summer and how he was hoping I'd join him. I smiled and laughed, nodding at what he said, but somewhere deep inside, I couldn't help but wonder how it was he was so understanding about what I'd told him. Sure, he was a doctor, and of course, we were nothing to one another except friends, or now friends with benefits. Perhaps, it had lifted a weight off him as well, the fear of being stuck in some sort of relationship because of some accidental condom mishap.

As much as I worried over that little incident over the coming weeks, things didn't seem to change between us. We began spending more time together. Asher would come and wait at The Cooling Rack until my shift was over, and we'd head to the drive-in. We began spending weekends together instead of just evenings, and while I didn't want to admit it to myself, I knew I was beginning to fall in love with him.

ASHER

I'D NOTICED the first sign of fall this morning while I was on my jog, which meant summer was ending. I'd just finished setting up my office on the thirteenth floor of Eastport General. It had taken way longer to complete the business purchase. So long, in fact, I'd held off on renting this space, in case things didn't go through.

Once all of that had been completed, I reached out to the owners of the small home I'd been staying in. I was more than comfortable there and wanted to see if they would consider selling it. I guess my timing was right because they were more than happy to sit down and work out a deal, and after work today I was to swing by and sign the paperwork.

Now that everything had fallen into place with work, I had one last thing to figure out: Where I wanted to take things with Bella. We'd spent an amazing time together this summer, and now that I knew I'd be living here, it was time to talk to her about us. I wanted something more with her—a lot more. I had mentioned nothing to her yet because I wanted it to be a surprise that I was staying in Eastport. A day hadn't gone by that I hadn't seen her or thought of her since we'd had sex the first time. I was lucky to have her in my life, and I realized she was too good to lose. However, this past week, things seemed to have been off between us. She seemed distracted and distant, and no matter how many times I'd asked her, all she'd say was not to worry. I was worried. I wondered if her perhaps her boss had called and she was worried about telling me she was going back to her job. I couldn't worry about it any longer, so I'd booked us reservations at a steak house for dinner tonight. I picked up my phone and shot her a text.

ASHER: Dinner, tonight, 7pm?

BELLA: Can I call you?

I frowned as I watched those three little dots jump around, then disappear, then jump around again.

ASHER: Yes, of course.

Only when the phone didn't ring right away, I decided to just call her.

She answered the phone, all out of breath. "Hey." She sniffled.

"Hey, everything okay?"

"No, I'm sorry if I've been distracted this week. It's my mom. She's in the hospital. Stage four cancer. I have to go to Columbus and care for her. She needs help, and I'm the only one. I was just on the phone with the airport booking a flight. I did ask that they get me on an earlier one, but for now, I'll be leaving on Friday."

My heart sank for her. My heart sank for me because that meant she would be leaving. "How long will you be gone?" I questioned.

"I've given Brielle my notice. I do not know when I'll be back… or if." She sniffled. "I even gave up my condo. I've been staying with Brie and Sawyer."

The other end of the phone went silent. I swallowed hard. This wasn't how this was supposed to go, and hearing her say those words to me made my heart flip. "How is your mother?"

"Well, the chemo has stopped working. Doctors aren't very optimistic." She sniffled again.

I wanted to be there for her. I wanted her to know I'd be here always. It was on the tip of my tongue to tell her I'd find an oncologist here for her mother to see, but since I was new here, I really didn't know anyone at the hospital yet.

"I'm sorry. Is there anything I can do?"

"Do you have a magic wand that will help me find a job out in Columbus and—" I heard a sob catch in her throat and the phone went quiet. "I'll see you tonight at 7?"

"If you'd prefer not going, we can always—"

"No, I really could use the time out. I've been crying for hours. It will do me good. It will do me good to be with you. Besides, I asked the airport to get me on an earlier flight if they could."

"Okay, I'll see you at seven."

I shoved my phone into my pocket and finished unloading the last of my books into the bookshelves in my office. Then I turned and looked out the window, taking in the view and thinking about what Bella was going through.

"Oh, Asher," Maureen said, popping her head into my office.

I looked up at my new receptionist. "Yes?"

"Mrs. Becker called. She has an appointment with you on Tuesday. She was wondering if her blood work had come back. Apparently, Dr. Kavanaugh was supposed to call her with the results."

I hadn't even gone through the pending files yet. Maureen had been busy booking appointments for me for the last two days. All the pending files still sat in a box on the floor in the corner of my office. I'd planned to go through them over the weekend.

"Call her back and tell her that the results haven't been sent through to me yet, that I am working on it. Let her know we will discuss everything on Tuesday."

"And Mrs. Lynch?"

I chuckled. I finally felt like I was at home. I'd missed this. "Tell her the same." I smiled, walking over and grabbing the box of files from the floor. "I guess I'll just start going through them now."

"Looks like you have your work cut out for you," Maureen said, looking at the box full of files.

"Thanks, Maureen, and thank you for all the organizing you've been doing."

"Of course, Asher." She smiled.

I looked down at my cell phone to see a text had come in. It hadn't been there prior, and I opened the message. It was from Bella.

> BELLA: I just got off the phone with the airport, they got me on an earlier flight. Do you think you can drive me to the airport tomorrow morning?

I swallowed hard. Tears blurred my eyes. I really wasn't prepared for this to be our last night together.

ASHER: Of course, I can.

BELLA: Do you think we could pass on dinner, perhaps just eat something at your place? Emma's been crying for hours. My head is killing me.

ASHER: Anything you wish. ;)

BELLA: :)

I STRADDLED HER NAKED BODY, digging my hands into her shoulders. I added more oil to my hands and rubbed her upper back.

"Oh God, that feels good," she whispered.

"That's it, just relax." I continued running my hands over her back, digging into the tight muscles. "You are so beautiful," I said, bending down and kissing her shoulder before I lay beside her.

"I wish things were different," she said, a hint of a tear in the corner of her eye.

I wiped the moisture away. I didn't want her to cry.

Instead, I kissed her, my tongue washing through her mouth, hoping to distract her from those thoughts.

"Make love to me," she whispered. "Give me that just one time."

She looked up into my eyes. She didn't need to ask twice. She didn't need to ask me once. I kissed her as I climbed between her legs. She watched me as I gripped my cock in my hand and found her opening, sliding into her.

I went slowly, wanting her to feel my connection, my passion, my feelings for her. She dug her nails into my back as I pumped into her, slow and hard. A small moan escaping her lips with each pump.

"God, Bella, it feels so damn good."

She gripped my back as I slowed my pace a little. I stilled my hips and took a moment to suck on her perfect nipples. My cock throbbed inside of her as she tightened around me. I began pumping into her again, slowly at just the perfect angle.

"Asher… it feels… so… good. Don't stop doing that," she cried.

I continued at the same pace I was going before, even quickening it a little, then slowing down again. I could feel her fingers gripping into my back as she tightened around me.

"I can't hold back… Asher…"

"Don't hold back…"

Soon she was writhing below me, calling my name as I poured myself into her once again.

We showered together, meeting once again in the shower. She was like a drug that I knew I might not have again. My body, my soul, craved her, and I planned to take every opportunity I had until I could no longer have her again.

She was quiet as we dressed. I'd made us coffee and brought her a mug, and while she dried her hair, I stood in the bathroom door watching her. Every part of me wanted to take away the sadness in her eyes. I wanted to see her smile again.

Time passed faster than I'd wanted, and an hour later, we stood facing one another in the airport. I didn't want to say good-bye, yet I knew delaying it was only going to make it that much harder.

"Thank you for a truly amazing summer." She stepped into me, wrapping her arms around my neck and pressing her body against mine. "I don't want to say good-bye," she whispered, placing her nose in the crook of my neck.

"I don't either," I whispered back, pulling her tighter into me.

I kept my hold on her until I felt hers loosen. She looked up at me with sad eyes, even though she was smiling.

"You have my number if you need anything," I whispered to her.

She nodded. "I do. Thank you. Good luck with everything," she replied. "I hope everything works out for you and that you find the office of your dreams."

I still hadn't told her. I couldn't, not with everything she was dealing with. I feared she would look at it as a tactic to get her to return. I wanted the best for her, and if that meant going to Columbus and creating a life for herself, then so be it. We'd find our way back to one another if it was meant to be. However, when she looked at me this time, it made me feel guilty for not telling her. "And for you," I said.

She leaned in and gave me one last kiss, then turned and handed her boarding pass to the agent at the booth. I watched, and with one last wave, she was gone.

BELLA

I SAT in the hospital waiting room fishing for a magazine, any magazine I hadn't read yet. I'd been in Columbus for a month, and I'd spent every single bit of time in this hospital. Mom had been in a lot of pain today, and the doctors had finally given her some pain medication to help. She'd fallen into a deep sleep, but I still felt I needed to be here.

I got up, stretched, and wandered over to another table, searching through the magazines that lay there. None of them were new. I yawned and flopped back down in the chair I'd been sitting in and looked at my phone. It was a little past seven. I'd now been in the hospital for almost ten hours. I let out a breath and checked my messages. I'd had my phone on silent for most of the day, but there was nothing.

"Bella."

I turned to see my mother's doctor standing in the doorway. "Oh, hi, doctor."

"I'm surprised to see you still here."

I shrugged. "It doesn't feel right going home. She was so uncomfortable today."

The doctor made his way over and sat down beside me. "Bella, you need to get your rest. Your mother is resting comfortably, and she is in excellent hands. We will call if there are any changes."

I wiped the stray tear that fell down my cheek. "I guess I just don't want to be alone." I smiled, even though I wanted to cry my guts out. "At least here there is noise and the occasional staff member."

"I see. Is there anyone here that you can call? A friend perhaps."

I shook my head. "All my friends are back in East-port and Boston. I don't know anyone here. Only my mother."

A throat cleared behind us. I didn't bother to turn around; I figured it was the nurse or another doctor coming to speak with my mother's doctor.

"She doesn't have to be alone, at least for the night, anyway," I heard a familiar voice say.

I turned and looked, not believing my eyes. Asher stood in the waiting room, a concerned look on his face. I didn't hesitate; I jumped up out of the chair and ran over to him, throwing my arms around him.

"My God, what are you doing here?" I cried, hugging him as tight as I could.

"I'll leave you two alone. Take care of her tonight, would you?" the doctor said before leaving the room.

It felt like forever that we'd stood there holding one another. Then Asher guided me over to the chair and sat down.

"What are you doing here?" I questioned, wiping the tears off my cheeks.

"I'm here for a conference."

"Why didn't you tell me?"

"Well, I wasn't sure until yesterday that I could be here, to be honest. So, I decided that if I was able, I'd surprise you. I checked with admissions to see what floor your mom was on and came up. Have you eaten anything?"

I shook my head. I hadn't been taking care of myself at all. Most days I'd lived on a piece of toast or an apple.

"Well, how about you get your things and come stay with me for the night? I have a room at the Hyatt, just across the street."

I wrapped my arms around his neck, still not believing he was sitting in front of me. "I'm so glad you are here. I've missed you."

"I missed you as well. Come on, let's go get you something to eat."

WE'D ORDERED in room service and spent the evening lounging in bed watching television. It was a little past ten when the credits rolled on the show we were watching and he shut the TV off, reached up, and shut the light out. He put his arm under my neck and pulled me closer into him.

"Are you sure you're doing okay?" he whispered.

That had been what I was telling him through text. I didn't want him to worry about me. Only with him here now, it was a little hard to prove it. "Not really. It's hard. I'm lonely." I sniffled.

He was quiet for a moment. "I wish I could be here with you. So does Brie. She told me to tell you that. She also told me in an extremely firm text message to tell you not to call Miles."

I couldn't help but let out a laugh. "Why on earth would she think I'd call Miles?"

"I don't know. She seemed to think that you might, for some sort of comfort, I'm guessing."

"Oh my God, he'd be the last person I'd call for comfort. A wall would provide better comfort."

"I guess perhaps she's just concerned and, like me, wishes she could be here."

I grew quiet and snuggled against him. I wished nothing more than to have them both here as a support system; however, life had been testing me in a lot of ways over the past few years, and every time I faced those challenges alone.

"God, why would she think I'd call him," I repeated, rolling away from Asher. "Does she think I'm stupid or something? I mean, would you call your ex if you needed emotional comfort?"

"Not a chance in hell!" Asher chuckled, pulling me back into him.

"What happened between the two of you, anyways?" I questioned. We'd never really talked in depth about either of our situations.

"So many things."

I could see enough of his face from the moonlight that poured through the window that he didn't want to tell me any more than I wanted to tell him what had happened between Miles and myself. I didn't want him to be angry and to ruin the night, so instead I rolled onto my back. "Never mind, it's none of my business."

"Whoa, just a minute. I want to tell you. I just don't want you to think badly of me."

"Why would I think bad of you?"

"Because most women do after I tell them the story."

"There isn't any judgment here," I said, laying back on my side and facing him.

He nodded, then thought for a few minutes, as if trying to figure out the best way to tell me. Then he took in a deep breath and rested his hand on mine.

"Things between Sydney and I were going well. All things were going well. She'd just gotten a promotion, and my practice had been steadily growing since I'd opened it. We'd gotten engaged about six months earlier, and because we weren't able to get away to celebrate our engagement, I'd booked us a weekend away at a bed-and-breakfast for Valentine's Day. We both needed a break—from work, from wedding plans—and just be together. We found our relationship a bit strained, but nothing that was going to break us.

"Anyways, we got to the bed and breakfast, we spent the day out wandering this small town, had did some shopping and took in dinner and we returned to our room. She started talking about our future and how excited she was to start our life together, and then she brought up having my babies. We'd never discussed this before. In fact, she'd never even mentioned wanting children, and before I knew it, I was already living in a sprawling bungalow with a dog, three kids at my feet, and we weren't even married yet."

"So, it just freaked you out?"

"You could say that. Anyway, I guess she could tell from the look on my face that I wasn't sure about this, and she got upset. I tried to explain myself, but she wouldn't hear it, and she went to bed. The next morning, she was more quiet than usual, but she was speaking to me. When we returned from our weekend, she just seemed to act funny.

"This behaviour went on for weeks, so one night after a stressful day, I confronted her about it. She had somehow gotten it in her mind that I didn't want to have kids with her. That she was the problem. I tried to explain myself and tell her that her conversation had made me feel uncomfortable at that moment, since we were just starting our lives together and I wanted to be selfish to start. I wanted it to just be us. Only she just got angrier at that. Then about two months later, she brought the topic up again."

"What happened this time?"

"Well, I'd been dealing with some pretty heavy things at work. I'd just seen two women lose their first babies, and it absolutely devastated both couples. Plus, my sister had just had a miscarriage and was dealing with the emotional side of it, and her husband had become numb. She had no support. It was hard watching and dealing with this situation on a professional level, not to mention trying to be there for my sister.

"I'd just gotten off the phone with my sister one night when Sydney brought it up to me again. I lost my temper and told her I didn't want children and not to bother bringing it up to me again. She went to bed in tears, and the rest is history."

"Why would I judge you for that? Perhaps it was circumstances that made you feel that way."

Asher ran his hand over his face. "No, the more I've thought about it, the more I realized after seeing the things that I see daily and what I'd just seen with my patients and my sister, that my reaction was very truthful. I think ultimately that was what lead us to breaking up. She really wanted kids, and well, I wanted to focus on my career. Honestly, the more she talked about it, and the more time we spent with friends that had kids, the more I realized I didn't want any, and I didn't think it was fair to not tell her. Only when I sat down and told her, it was like I ended her world. We broke up shortly after that. That's why when you told me you couldn't have children, I really didn't find it that big of a deal. I know you thought I did, but I'm good with it."

"I guess it shocked me a little, especially after how Miles reacted to the entire situation," I whispered.

"Some people, Bella, are incapable of understanding. It's not your fault. It's not something you chose. There are many options out there for those who can't have children."

"I know."

He rolled onto his side and met my lips, pulling me tighter against him. "I'm sorry he treated you the way he did over something so insignificant."

I kissed his lips. His words, his understanding soothed a place in my soul that I needed at that moment. "I'm so glad you are here," I murmured, kissing him again.

"Me too. You're beautiful, Bella."

His kiss this time felt a little different; it was slower, and as his hand cupped my cheek and his other hand held me tight, I wished he'd never let me go.

"I wish you didn't have to leave already."

"Same. I wish I could stay here with you for a little while longer anyways. You seem calmer than you did when I arrived," Asher said, looking up at me as he threw the protein bar into his bag.

"I am. It's been nice having someone to have dinner with and to go to bed with, even if it was only for a couple of days."

He smiled. "Yes it was. It's been…lonely." He winked.

Lonely didn't even begin to cover it. The most comforting times I had this weekend was when I had been in his arms. They really were my favorite place to be, and I knew I needed to stop thinking that way, because in a few minutes he'd be on his way to his gate, and I'd be returning to my mother's empty, cold apartment.

"How was your mom today."

I shrugged. "Doctors aren't too optimistic. They are giving her four weeks at most," I said, wiping at my eyes.

"Bella, you know if you need me, you can message or call, right?"

When I didn't look at him and respond, he tucked his finger under my chin and raised my head until I was looking at him.

"You can call," he repeated.

"I know. Thank you."

Asher looked up at the departure board and saw his flight was on time and that they'd be boarding shortly. "I have to get going. Make sure you message me." He leaned in and kissed me.

"I will. Safe flight, okay."

"You be safe getting back to your mom's. I don't like the idea of you taking a cab through this city."

"I will."

He looked into my eyes, not saying anything, then

one more kiss and he turned and headed toward the agent at the desk. I stood there watching until he'd waved one final time and disappeared through a set of doors.

For some reason, I'd been waiting for thc bubble to pop while he'd been here. Once he was gone, I turned and made my way to the front door to hail a cab. Then it hit me. Somehow, this was all too good to be true. I didn't need to wait for the bubble to burst because it already had. I'd been pretending all this time that he was my boyfriend when, in fact, he was only my friend. Wherever it was that I settled, I'd be alone.

BELLA

Three Weeks Later

"I HAVE CHICKEN SOUP," Brielle said, coming into the living room at my mom's apartment. "You should have some. It will make you feel better." She placed the bowl down on the table in front of where I was laying. "Come on, sit up."

"I said I'm not hungry," I muttered, the smell of the soup making me feel nauseous.

"Bella, you've barely eaten anything in the past two, possibly three, days. You've been sick, and now you're hardly drinking anything. I've called Sawyer. He told me it's important that I get something into you before you dehydrate," Brie said, sitting down beside me.

Mom had passed away two weeks ago, exactly one week to the day that Asher had left. The end had been brutal to watch and, for her sake, I was glad it was over. She'd been in pain and had done nothing but cry since nothing would stop it. However, everything I had to do now, combined with the funeral, had been too much. I'd passed out the night of her funeral from stress and exhaustion. Thank goodness Brie had been here. She'd called an ambulance, and the doctor at the hospital would only discharge me if she planned to stay with me. The stress of it all, of everything, had been too much.

Then I'd never looked for another place. I'd been too busy looking after Mom, but now her landlord was being unreasonable. He refused to transfer her lease to me because I did not have a job. So now, on top of every-thing else, I had no place to live as of the end of the month, which was only in a few short days.

Brie had helped me clean up and pack most of the apartment, and I'd donated most of Mom's things to charity. They'd picked up the last of her things today, aside from the living room furniture and my bed and the few dishes I'd kept to get me through until I left. The rest of my things were back in Eastport. Sawyer and Brielle had rented a small storage unit for my things until I set down roots. Not that it mattered. I was still going to be homeless on Friday.

"God, get that soup away from me. I think I'm going to be sick again," I said, getting up and running to the bathroom, my hand over my mouth.

I slammed the door shut, locking it behind me, making it to the toilet just in time.

"Bella, are you okay?"

I lay on the floor in front of the toilet, clutching my stomach. "I'll be—" I heaved into the toilet once again, this time feeling as if my stomach were about to come out of my mouth. There was nothing left in me to throw up.

I was clammy and grabbed a cloth off the edge of the sink from the last time I'd been in here. I needed to wipe this clamminess off me.

"Bella, open the door," Brie cried as she pounded on the door, jiggling the handle.

The bathroom spun as I was about to stand. "I'm dizzy, Brie," I called out.

"Bella, open this door." I heard her jiggle the handle once again.

I slid across the floor and unlocked the door.

Brie shoved it and took one look at me. She bent down and took the cloth from me and ran it under the water. Ringing it out, she placed it on the back of my neck. "Bella, just breathe."

"I have a headache," I mumbled.

"Yes, no doubt. Now come on, let's get you up and get some soup into you," she said, placing her arm around my waist. "It will make you feel better. I promise."

I was so weak she practically carried me back to the living room, sitting me down on the couch. She sat down beside me and held on to the bowl, bringing a spoon full of the liquid to my mouth. I sipped on the salty chicken broth. At first, my stomach turned and my mouth watered, but that was only for a moment. After the second mouthful, I wanted more.

"Sweetie, you need to look after yourself. I know things have been tough," Brie said, putting the spoon back into the soup and bringing it to my mouth again. "I wish you had called me and taken me up on the offer to come and stay with you before your mom passed."

"I know, but you have enough on your plate with The Cooling Rack, Emma, and the baby on the way."

"Yes, and so do you, and you needed help. Never think you can't call us. If I couldn't have been here, Sawyer would have been. We love you, Bella."

Her words made me feel like I was a child. Then the thought of Friday creeped into my mind, and I imagined I'd be living on the side of a road somewhere. "What am I going to do? I don't have anywhere to go," I cried, tears welling into my eyes. "I have no job. I have no money."

"You know you always have somewhere to go."

"No, Brielle, I'm not imposing again."

"No, of course not. I was going to surprise you, but while I've been here, Sawyer has bccn working with the landlord. Apparently, the same apartment you had is still available, so he is getting your place back. We both agreed to pay for your rent until you get a few checks under your belt. Plus, I still need an assistant manager, so you still have a job."

Tears flooded my eyes. "Really?"

"Yes," Brie said, wrapping her arm around me and pulling me in for a hug. "However, you need to be strong for the trip back. I need you to share the driving time with me. You are coming back home to Eastport."

FRIDAY MORNING HAD COME. Brie and I had packed everything into my car. Since I'd had to leave Eastport so fast, Brie had kept my car and had driven it up when she came for the funeral. She had planned on taking a flight back, but since I was now going with her, we packed up the car.

"Are you still feeling nauseous?" Brie asked as she shoved the last box into the trunk of her car.

"Yeah. I feel stronger, though," I said, taking a drink of the electrolyte drink Sawyer had recommended.

"Good. Sawyer wanted to know if those were helping," she asked, nodding to the green fluid in the bottle I held in my hand.

I nodded. "I just wish they tasted better."

"Yeah, well, he drinks the green one all the time after his workouts. He said you would probably like the blue one better, but that was the only one I could get." She shrugged. "I figured it would be better than nothing. You ready to go?"

"Yes," I said, deciding against going up to the apartment one more time to do nothing but look at the empty rooms.

"You drive first," Brie said, handing me the keys and climbing into the passenger's seat.

Our plan was to drive halfway today, stop for the night at a hotel along the way, then finish the drive tomorrow. We'd stopped and gotten something for breakfast, and half an hour later, as we were driving on the interstate, I felt that familiar gush of saliva in my mouth. I tried to fight it, but the feeling got worse over time, so I pulled over to the side of the road.

"What's wrong?" Brie asked, pulling her head out of her phone.

"I'm gonna be sick again," I said, cutting the engine, ripping my seatbelt off, and shoving the door open.

I just made it to the front of the car and was sick. I leaned against the side of the car, just taking in the air, hoping and praying that some air would calm my stomach down. I could see Brie in the front seat on her phone, no doubt texting Sawyer. I rolled my eyes, wondering what other doctorly advice he had for me now. When I finally felt better, I climbed back into the driver's seat and put my seatbelt on. I was about to start the engine when Brie put her hand on mine.

"How long has this been going on?"

"What?"

"This being sick? How long?"

I shrugged. "I don't know, a couple of weeks maybe."

Brie looked out the window and nodded. "I was speaking with Sawyer just now. He, um, recommends that you take a pregnancy test."

"Is that supposed to be some sort of joke?" I said through blurry, tear-filled eyes. "Why would you even suggest that to me? You know the same as I do that Dr. Kavanaugh told me years ago I was infertile, that there was no way I would ever get pregnant."

Brie closed her eyes and rested her head against the seat. "Doctors can be wrong... Besides, I know that you and Asher...."

"That Asher and I what? That we slept together?"

Brie slowly nodded. "Yes, you didn't need to tell me that. I knew a long time ago, from the way you looked at him. Regardless, you don't have flu symptoms at all. Sawyer also doesn't think this is stress. I hate to admit it, but I agree with him."

"Brielle, I've had enough of this conversation. It's time to get back on the road."

"Bella…"

"No, please, don't," I said, fighting back tears. "I'm shocked you would even suggest that to me. You know how badly—" I stopped. There was no point in even continuing this conversation. She knew how badly I'd wanted a baby. She also knew how hard it had been for me to accept the fact that I would never have one.

I put the car into drive, checked my mirrors, and pulled out onto the road. The silence between us became so loud I turned the radio on. Soon, Brie kept her face down, typing away into her phone, no doubt telling Sawyer everything. He was probably on the phone to that psychiatrist they'd tried to set me up with when I'd first moved to Eastport, booking me in for an appointment instead of a date. I swallowed my hurt and my anger and kept my eyes on the road.

We'd switched up about halfway into the afternoon and finally stopped around eight at a small roadside motel. I would have been just as happy to continue driving through the night, but Brielle insisted I needed to sleep.

Two hours later, I was lying in bed watching TV when Brie came through the door with a bag of snacks. She smiled as she threw the bag down on the bottom of her bed and kicked her shoes off. Sitting down, she pulled out a bag of plain chips, tossing them onto the bed beside me, along with a bottle of soda.

"Thanks," I muttered.

"You're welcome."

I watched as she pulled out a bag of barbeque chips for herself, as well as a bottle of soda, then she carefully folded the bag around something else and set it behind her.

I frowned. "What else do you have in the bag?"

"Oh, just a box of condoms. We're out at home," she said, giving me an odd smile.

I looked at her and rolled my eyes. "I've seen condoms before, you know. You don't need to hide them as if they are a national treasure. Plus, I don't think they are really necessary at this point," I said, nodding to her small baby bump.

Her face went red, and she gave me an awkward smile. "So, when was the last time you spoke to Asher?"

I tore the bag of chips open and shrugged as I shoved one into my mouth. "I don't know. I guess it would have been right after my mom passed."

"You mean he hasn't messaged you at all?"

"No, he has." I hadn't told her about the weekend he'd been in Columbus. She didn't need to know about it, because I was certain I'd never hear the end about the pregnancy test.

"And…"

"And what?

"Are you two an item?"

I shook my head. "We agreed that neither of us were looking for anything. It was more of a healing journey. Honestly, it's exactly what I expected. That we'd keep in touch, as friends."

"So, he's the one who messaged you. Does that mean you haven't even tried to contact him?"

I shook my head. "I have, but honestly, there is no point. He was starting his new chapter, and I was starting mine. I need to get some rest." I folded the bag of chips closed, reached up and shut the light off and rolled over onto my side, facing away from Brie. After I set my alarm, I opened my text messages to see Asher's name. I clicked the messages open, reading the ones he'd sent.

ASHER: I hope everything is going okay. It's been a few days since I heard from you. When you get some time, message me. Thinking of you.

ASHER: Hey Bella, I'm sure you are busy with the funeral and everything. Please, when you get a free moment, message me, I want to talk to you about something.

ASHER: I'm getting the weird feeling that you don't want to talk to me. I hope that isn't the case. Please let me know how you are doing. I want you to know that I am here for you.

ASHER: Letting you know I'm thinking of you.

I blinked hard, clearing the tears from my eyes. He'd sent the last message this afternoon. The rest, I just hadn't had the energy to respond to. Plus, I was afraid of what it was he wanted to talk to me about. I had turned my entire world, as small as it was, upside down, and as much as it hurt me not to respond, I figured it was for the best. I couldn't take any more disappointment. After all, even though I was on my way back to Eastport, Asher had left. I now needed to focus on my path of starting our lives over.

THE SCENT of bacon and eggs woke me. I stretched, rolling over. Brie sat at the small table in our room, digging into a plastic container of food.

"Ah, you're awake. I went to the small diner across the street and brought back breakfast."

"What time is it?" I questioned, still noting it was dark outside.

"A little after five."

I'd set my alarm for six; I wasn't ready to get up yet. I just wanted to close my eyes and stay curled up under these blankets, but I knew I couldn't, so I kicked the covers off and made my way over to the table. I looked down at the food through the clear lid of the plastic container and opened it. The smell of steamed eggs wasn't very appealing.

The smell got worse as I dug the fork into the eggs. I sat back, trying to avoid the smell, and opened the lid on the paper cup that contained a coffee. I dumped two packets of sugar and two creamers into it and stirred it, then took a sip.

"You not hungry?" Brie questioned.

I shrugged and picked up a piece of bacon, taking a bite. Knowing she was watching me like a hawk, I took my fork and dug into the messy pile of scrambled eggs again. The second the eggs hit my tongue, my stomach turned. I tried to fight it by shoving another mouthful of eggs into my mouth, but that only made it worse. I spit the eggs back into the container and took off in a mad dash toward the bathroom.

A few minutes later, I stepped back into the room and looked at Brie, who sat there with a knowing look on her face. She said nothing. She just reached for the bag she had wrapped up last night and pulled out a pregnancy test. She stood up, walked over to me, and shoved it into my hand.

"I thought you said this was a box of condoms?"

"Well… I lied. Now, humour me, would you?" she said, nodding to the bathroom.

Minutes later, I sat there in disbelief as I looked down at both of the little white sticks, both showing the same result. Double pink lines stared back at me. I'd taken both. I figured the first one was faulty, but when the second one produced the same result, all I could do was stare. Brielle had been right.

"Well?" Brie called from the other side of the door. "You've been in there a long time. I can't take the suspense."

I tore my gaze away from those two white sticks and looked at myself in the mirror. *What mess had I gotten myself into?* I stormed out of the bathroom, shoving past Brie and heading for the door. I stepped outside and pulled the door closed behind me, taking in the fresh morning air. I walked over to the railing and leaned against it, looking out over the parking lot. My mind was racing with all kinds of thoughts.

"It's going to be okay, you know," Brie said, placing her hand on my shoulder.

I let out a little laugh. "Why is that? Because it worked out for you?"

Brie said nothing. I didn't want to hear it. I'd spent years trying to get pregnant with Miles, looking at the disappointment on his face every single time one of these tests came back negative. It had torn us apart.

My family doctor in Boston had sent me to Dr. Kavanaugh in Eastport, and he'd been the one who determined I was infertile. Miles at first refused to believe it, and every time we'd have sex, it was only to try once again to have the same outcome. Anger coursed through my body as I thought about his diagnosis. The depression I'd went through, all the hateful words Miles had said to me in the last two years of our marriage. The lack of love he'd given me had created a pit in me so deep, I feared it would be impossible for me to get out of. And for what? Now that I was almost out of it, I find out that none of it was true. Now I was pregnant, and Asher was the opposite of Miles; he didn't want to have children.

"Are you going to call Asher?"

I shook my head. "Nope. I'm going to call Dr. Kavanaugh."

Brie frowned. "Bella…"

"We should get going. It's getting late, and we can probably beat some of the traffic."

"Bella? Stop," Brie said, grabbing hold of my arm.

"What?"

"You should call and speak with Asher. Let him know."

"Brielle, I barely know! I don't know anything at this point. I barely know what I'm doing tomorrow."

"Bella…"

I looked at her and let out a sigh. "Why should I message him? So he can be cold and heartless? No thanks. I had one man treat me that way. I refuse to allow another."

"Whoa, when was he mean to you?"

He hadn't been mean yet, but I was certain that if he found out about this baby, that would change. I hadn't told Brielle about him not wanting kids, because that would mean I'd have to explain that he'd been in Columbus. Besides, once he'd explained it to me, it made me feel that someone could accept my situation.

"He hasn't been… yet."

Brie frowned. "What's going on, Bella? Asher seemed to really adore you. I can't imagine that he'd be mean to you in any way."

I looked at Brielle, considering what she was saying, but I also knew she was wrong. I let out a breath. "Yeah, well, that might be true, but I know if I tell him this, the Asher who adored me won't be the same one to respond."

BELLA

I'D BEEN BACK in Eastport for four days. Sawyer and Brie had made sure what little I'd had in the small storage facility in Eastport was delivered to my place on Monday.

I'd unpacked the last of the boxes last night after I'd gotten home from The Cooling Rack. It was a beautiful fall day, and I sat out on my balcony enjoying a warm cup of tea with some arrowroot cookies, while I waited for the dryer to finish.

I reached for my phone and looked up Dr. Kavanaugh's number, then hit the call button. After three rings, I heard a woman answer. "Hello."

"Hi, I need to book an appointment with Dr. Kavanaugh. It's Bella Langdon."

"One moment, please."

I sat listening to the god-awful jazz music that played on the other end of the line, and I took a bite of cookie, followed by a sip of tea.

"Ah, yes, Miss Langdon. Did you receive a letter in the mail?" the friendly voice asked.

I glanced at the stack of mail on the small table inside the living room. I hadn't looked at the stack of mail Brie and Sawyer had collected. "Ah, not that I know of."

"We mailed it to your address in Boston."

"No, I'm sorry. I've moved recently," I said, glancing at the pile of mail that Sawyer had brought back from Boston with him earlier in the summer. I'd glanced through it. Nothing seemed to be all that important, and I wondered if perhaps I'd missed it.

"Oh, okay then. Well, Dr. Kavanaugh has retired."

"Oh. I see. Well, I need a doctor. Is it possible that whoever took over could see me?"

"Please give me a moment."

Suddenly, that horrible music returned. As I sat there, I could feel the tension in my shoulders. I just so badly needed clarification, and I hoped they had transferred my entire file. I needed to know what had happened, or where the mistake was.

"Bella, I can see we have transferred your file to Dr. Alonzo Love. He actually has an opening Thursday morning at ten thirty. Can you tell me what this is regarding, so I have some information to mark down. Also, it will help me figure out if you need any blood work prior to the appointment."

"I'm pregnant," I blurted. No matter how many times I said it, the situation still didn't sound right.

She cleared her throat and said, "I see… but it states here that—"

"I know what it states, which is part of the problem," I bit out. I didn't need some receptionist to tell me what was written in my file.

"Miss Langdon, are you able to head down to the lab at Eastport General sometime today or tomorrow to have some blood work done? That way, we can have your results for the appointment."

"Yep."

"And do you know where our office is?"

I let out a sigh. "I'm guessing it's still in the same place."

"Actually, it's in the hospital, thirteenth floor. Just go to the main elevators and take it up to thirteen. You'll turn right and then make a left at the first corridor. The office is on the right-hand side."

"Okay."

"We will see you Thursday, Bella."

I REACHED OVER and picked up a magazine that lay on the table. It was the only magazine in the entire office that wasn't about parenting or pregnancy. I let out a sigh as I flipped it open and began looking at ideas on how to organize a kitchen. I was doing everything I could to distract myself from thinking about my blood work results.

I'd wanted to call all day yesterday to find out, yet I knew they probably wouldn't share those results with me over the phone. A door opened and out came a very pregnant woman, a smile on her face as she said good-bye to the nurse who'd walked her out. I placed the magazine down on the table and rubbed my hands together.

"Bella Langdon?" the nurse called.

I closed my eyes, took in a deep breath, and stood up.

"Hello, Bella, follow me, please."

I followed her down a hall where she stopped at the first door she came to and opened it up. "Take a seat. The doctor will be with you shortly," she said, placing my file in the hanging folder on the door.

As I sat there looking around, my eyes kept landing on my file that sat in the holder on the door. I could always just take a quick peek, I thought to myself. When I had just about built up the nerve, I heard a door open and the doctor appeared.

"Bella. I'm Dr. Alonzo Love." He opened the file and looked over a couple of things before he shut the door. He smiled at me and then sat down behind his computer. "So, what is bringing you in today?"

"Well…" I looked around the room and rubbed my hands together, trying to gather my thoughts. "Sorry, I'm a little nervous."

"No need to be. This is a safe space. Take your time." He smiled at me and sat back against the chair.

"A few years ago, I was having a hard time trying to conceive, and Dr. Kavanaugh diagnosed me as being infertile. It seems, though, that perhaps the diagnosis was incorrect, and well, after being intimate with someone recently, it seems I am pregnant."

"I see. So, what did Dr. Kavanaugh say the cause of the infertility was? Did he do any tests?" he said, glancing down to my file.

"From what I remember, he didn't say what the cause was. He did some blood work, other than that, nothing. My ex-husband and I at the time were trying to have children, and I just couldn't conceive."

"I see. Do you think the problem could have been him?"

"I don't know. He said it was all me." I shrugged.

"Who did? Dr. Kavanaugh?"

"No, my ex. He was irritated, perhaps disappointed, and he booked me in with my family doctor, who sent me to Dr. Kavanaugh. After the blood work that Dr. Kavanaugh ordered came back, he told me I couldn't have children."

"So, he did no other tests, no ovulation testing, no hormone testing, imaging tests?"

"No."

Dr. Love flipped through my file, studying my history, then he stopped to look at what I hoped was my most recent blood work report. "Well, Bella, I can tell you that your recent blood work came back, and you are pregnant."

"Hmm." I nodded my head. "I'm sorry, but I'm having a hard time understanding how that is possible."

The doctor sat back and clicked his pen. "Bella, would you say at the time of the diagnosis that you were highly stressed, perhaps a little anxious? That the situation you and your husband were facing was, perhaps, a little more than you could handle at the time?"

A lot anxious and extremely stressed was more like it. Miles wasn't patient or understanding. "Yes, it would be fair to say that."

"Were you at the time being treated for depression when this was going on?"

I nodded and picked at my fingernail as I sat there. "I

wasn't on depression medication, but my family doctor said he had noticed changes in me, and he was watching me for signs of depression."

"I see," Doctor Love said, clicking his pen. "Did you know that high periods of stress, anxiety, and depression can severely alter your ability to get pregnant? That it can take years for you to regulate your body again after the stress is gone?"

I shook my head. "I didn't."

"I take it Dr. Kavanaugh didn't mention any of these things to you?"

I shook my head. "He never even hinted at any of those questions."

"I see." Dr. Love made some notes. "How long has your ex been your ex?"

"We are closing in on a year now."

"And how have your stress levels been?"

"Good, aside from recently. My mom just passed away. But I spent most of the summer working with a friend of mine at her bakery and just focusing on myself. I met someone, but I was upfront and honest about what it was I wanted, which was only friendship. It just so happened that things went an unexpected way between us."

"There is nothing wrong with that. Also, self-care is an amazing way to heal. You need to more of that, especially right now, after all the stress of your mom. Which I'd like to say that I am sorry for your loss."

"Thank you."

"I want you to do more of the self-care. I also want to know how your relationship is now with the man you met."

I looked at the doctor, then down to my feet. "At the moment, I am not sure. He was just out of a terrible relationship as well. We both were on a healing path. At the end of the summer, my mom got sick, and I left Eastport. He'd already told me he was moving out of Eastport. We saw one another three weeks ago or so, and we have spoken through text."

"I see. Does he know about the baby?"

When I didn't answer him right away, he put his pen down and looked at me. "Bella? Does he know about the baby?"

I shook my head. "No. I haven't told him yet. Not sure I am going to."

"I see. Why is that? Do you not think he has a right to know?"

"He, um, he told me he doesn't want children."

Doctor Love nodded, then stood up from behind his desk and came around, leaning on the front of it. "Well, there's lots of time for you to tell him if you change your mind. I think the best thing is for you to take some time and think about it. Don't just decide not to tell him because he doesn't want children. His opinion may change."

"No, it won't."

"Bella there isn't a rush to decide. You have time. Now, I'd like to take your weight and blood-pressure. Then I will have you get changed into this robe for your physical exam."

Doctor Love assured me that everything was fine and booked me in for my next appointment. I left the office feeling better than I had when I arrived and headed to my car. As I climbed in, I placed my purse on the passenger's seat and dropped the appointment card in the cupholder. I did up my seatbelt and then looked down at the appointment card. The date for my next appointment was staring back at me. As I sat there, I realized I didn't know how I felt. I was angry; I was upset; I was excited. These feelings flooded my body. I knew I had the support of Brielle and Sawyer. However, their support didn't mean anywhere near what Asher's would have meant.

There was no point in dwelling on it. He'd only know if I told him, and right now I'd decided against that. I had a lot of things to get organized before I started back to work. I put the key into the ignition, turned on my favourite radio station, and pulled out of the lot, heading toward my condo.

ASHER

October

I DROPPED my keys into the dish I kept at the front door and kicked off my sneakers. I'd gotten up early this morning to go for a run. It was my first day off in two months, and as much as I missed my practice when I wasn't working, I hadn't realized how much I'd needed some time off. The last couple of months had been stressful.

It appeared Dr. Kavanaugh had been behind on many appointments, and it had been hell trying to catch up. Every single day, Marie had booked me solid with appointments. I was hoping things would be slow to start; however, I'd gone at warp speed every day with no signs of things slowing down. I'd been so overbooked that I ended up needing to find an OB/GYN to hire to help with the overflow, plus to help me with the intake of new patients. With that simple change, I'd finally been able to take a day off.

Stripping off my sweat filled T-shirt, I made my way to the bathroom and turned on the shower. I quickly checked my phone, hoping that perhaps Bella had left me a message, but once again, there was nothing. Despite all that had gone on in the last couple of months, work hadn't been the only thing to stress me out. It bothered me that I'd thought of Bella every single day since she'd left, with those thoughts getting stronger since I'd been in Columbus and spent the weekend with her.

She'd never know it, though. I'd messaged her a grand total of four times since I'd left. Four times, it was horrible for me to claim I cared for her. Anyone who looked at the situation would say I only wanted another romp in the sack. I didn't even know if the messages had gone through. For all I knew, she could have changed her number, especially if she'd stayed in Columbus. I'd been so busy with work, I hadn't even had time to stop over at The Cooling Rack. Even though I knew she wouldn't be there, I could have at least inquired with Brielle. Surely, she would have heard something.

I figured today was as good of a day as any to make

that change. I showered, quickly ate breakfast, and then made my way to The Cooling Rack. I had to go into town anyway, as I needed to do some errands.

I pulled into the parking lot. The place was a mess when I walked inside. Dirty dishes were on every table, and the two kids behind the counter didn't seem to care that people were waiting for a seat. Surely, Brielle wasn't here either, if this was the state of the place.

"Can I help you?" the kid behind the counter asked as the other grabbed a bus pan and headed out onto the floor, beginning to clear off the tables and wipe them down.

"Yeah, I'll take a large coffee, and I was wondering if Brielle was here?"

"She isn't here at the moment, but she should be back in shortly," the kid said, placing a paper cup on the counter.

"I think I'll take one of those blueberry scones as well. Also, please put my coffee into a mug. I'm going to just take a seat and wait for Brielle to come in."

The kid looked at me, rolled his eyes, and dumped my coffee into a mug. Then he grabbed a scone from the display case and dropped it onto a plate and put it on the counter.

I'd just sat down and bit into the scone when out of the corner of my eye I was sure I spotted Bella. I looked and, sure enough, walking beside Brielle was Bella.

Excitement built in me as I watched them approach the front of the building. I was about to get up and go greet them, but they walked right by the front door.

As they walked by the window, I took in her face. She looked upset, and she was talking frantically, her hands flying around as Brielle listened intently. I wanted to know what it was she was saying. They walked by and continued on their way to the side of the building. They must have been going in the back way, I thought to myself.

I took a sip of my coffee. I could wait, I thought. I had nowhere to be. Not today, anyway. I'd just finished my scone when Brielle stepped through the door. She spoke to the gentlemen who had served me. He said something to her, and her eyes met mine. I waved, only she didn't wave back. Instead, she said something else to the kid and then went back into the kitchen.

A few minutes later, she reappeared and made her way over to my table. "Hey, Asher. How are you? Benny said you wanted to see me."

"Hey, Brielle. Bella, she's back?" I questioned. I wasn't going to beat around the bush. I wanted to see her.

"She is. She's just in the back. I'm not sure if—"

Suddenly, she stopped speaking, and I followed her eyes over to the kitchen door to see Bella standing there, looking at both of us.

I couldn't tell from the look on her face if she was happy to see me or if she was going to run. Brielle said nothing; she just studied her for a moment. My stomach churned with excitement, and when I was sure she was going to back away and run, she surprised me by taking a step forward and making her way to the table.

"Hey, Asher." Her voice was soft, and I hadn't realized how much I'd missed hearing her say my name.

"Bella, you don't need—"

She looked at Brielle and smiled. "It's fine. I'm just going to talk to Asher for a few minutes, then we can have our meeting."

"You sure?" Brielle said, like a protective older sister.

"Yep." She smiled as she met my eyes. "It's fine."

"Okay, I'll have Benny bring over a hot tea and a refill for you, Asher," she said as she got up from where she'd been sitting and made her way behind the counter.

Once the tea and coffee had been delivered at the table, Bella smiled at me. "What are you doing in Eastport?"

I'd hated myself for not telling her before she'd left. After she'd gone, I hated myself, and I couldn't even explain how I felt for not telling her after I'd left her in Columbus. "I hadn't wanted to say anything until I knew for sure everything was a done deal. The night I'd planned to tell you was the night you told me about your mom. It wasn't really a time for celebrating. You were leaving. I was going to tell you in Columbus, and once I saw how upset you were I, once again, waited. That's what I wanted to talk to you about when I'd messaged you. I wanted to tell you I stayed in Eastport, and I opened up a practice here. I hoped that may make you come back."

"Oh. Congratulations. I'm happy for you," she answered. I could see she was uncomfortable, and she sat there running her finger around the rim of the mug that sat in front of her. I was quiet. She had something on her mind. I could see it.

"I wanted to respond to you. To your messages," she whispered.

"Why didn't you?" I questioned.

"It… it was just too hard. You were too far away. It was so hard dealing with my mom, and I knew if I had messaged you, I'd want you to be with me."

Now I felt even worse for not picking up the phone. There had been so many times over the last couple of weeks I'd wanted to call. Each time I'd pick up the phone and dialled, I'd hung up before it had gone through.

"Instead, at night, I'd lay in bed, reading over your messages, then fall into a fit of tears. I figured you'd left Eastport, anyway. Once Mom passed and everything was over, I quickly realized I'd moved there and hadn't even looked for a job. My mom was behind on her rent, and while the landlord was kind enough to allow me to stay there once she passed, he wasn't as willing to work with me. He'd given me time to find a new place to live, but once the first of the month rolled around, he'd asked that I be gone. I had Brielle come and stay with me for a while, to help me pack things up, and she was the one who convinced me to return to Eastport."

"Bella, I'm so sorry. Fuck, I knew I should have called you."

"It's okay," she said, placing her hand on mine. "No doubt you were busy with things here. The last thing you needed to be dealing with was my issues." She shrugged.

"I'm sorry about your mom," I said, taking her hand in mine.

She looked at me and nodded. "Thank you."

"Are you back for good?" I questioned. "Or are you planning just to stay here until something better comes along?"

She nodded. "I'm back for good. Brielle offered me my job back, and Sawyer was able to get my condo back. I took it. What about you? Where are you living?"

"Well, at first, I was going to find a place, but the people who I was renting from ended up selling me the place instead."

"I'm happy for you that things have fallen into place," she said, growing quiet.

She was talking, and I didn't want her to stop. I also didn't want to stop talking. I wanted her to know I was still here, and I wanted her to know I wanted to carry on things from where we left off. She needed to know that she could still trust in me. I cleared my throat. "I'd still like us to be friends."

She nodded, a look of concern on her face.

"Well, perhaps more than friends. I'd like us to try…" I swallowed hard. "I'd really like us to continue from where we left off."

Her eyes met mine. She said nothing; she just sat there looking at me. I grew scared that she was about to turn me down.

Then Brielle popped her head over the back of Bella's seat and smiled. "Perfect. She'd love to. She'd also like to know if you would like to join Sawyer and I for dinner this weekend?"

I glanced at Bella, who closed her eyes and clenched her jaw. I cleared my throat. "Um, I…"

Bella looked at me, then she shook her head. "Brielle, please." Then she turned to me.

"You don't have to," she said, shaking her head.

"Dinner sounds good. What time?" I asked, ignoring what Bella had said.

"Say eight next Friday?"

"Eight on Friday. I'd be happy to join you," I said.

For whatever reason, Bella didn't look happy. Whatever was bothering her, I knew she was doing her best to hide it.

"Eight on Friday," she said, more to herself than to anyone else. "I really should get to work." She slid out of the booth and stood up.

"I'll message you later?" I questioned.

"Sure… whatever you'd like," she replied, then took both mugs and my plate and made her way over to the counter where she placed them down and grabbed a cloth.

I slid out of the booth and made my way to the door, turning to look at her one more time before I left. She was wiping down tables, a sad look still on her face. I hoped it was only because of her mom and that she was happy to be back. I guessed I'd find out soon enough.

BELLA

———

I LAY in bed Thursday night reading my latest library pick as the TV droned on in the background. Tomorrow night was weighing on my mind as I barely focused on the words. I dropped the book down on the bed beside me and stared up at the ceiling. I'd read the same paragraph three times and still hadn't been able to follow the story. Why had I agreed to dinner this weekend? I should have said no immediately. I didn't want Brielle to put pressure on us. What had I been thinking?

I reached for the glass of water I had beside the bed and took a sip. It was almost one in the morning. Doctor Love had told me he wanted me to get extra rest, which meant going to bed early. I'd been exhausted lately, more than normal, and when I'd shared my concerns with him, he'd popped me on a prenatal vitamin and told me to be in bed by eleven, and earlier on the nights where I had to work earlier the next morning. So far, it wasn't working.

I reached up and turned the light off, hoping that by some miracle laying in the darkness may help me relax enough to fall asleep. Asher had texted me earlier, but I hadn't replied. That too was weighing on my mind.

I reached for my phone. Perhaps if I messaged him now, that would clear enough of my mind to allow for some sleep. He'd be asleep now anyway, I thought to myself, so there wouldn't be a chance he'd message me back until morning.

I skimmed his message again.

ASHER: I was wondering if you wanted to get out for a coffee?

I tapped the edge of my phone and then typed.

BELLA: Sorry I just saw this now. I went to the library, and then to the craft store, my phone was in my purse with the ringer off. Raincheck? Say tomorrow night?

After hitting send, I put the phone down on the table and flipped through the TV channels. I'd just found a movie to watch when my phone vibrated against the table, causing me to jump.

As I picked it up, I frowned as I saw a message from

Asher. What the hell was he doing up? I opened the phone.

ASHER: No worries. What are you still doing up this late?

BELLA: I should ask you the same? Those three little dots bounced around furiously, matching my heartbeat.

ASHER: Just finished up at the hospital. It was a good thing I was here because I needed help distracting my thoughts from thinking of a certain someone.

I smiled as those three dots bounced around again.

ASHER: Now why are you still awake?

BELLA: Can't sleep.

ASHER: I see…does the doctor need to prescribe something? ;)

I felt my cheeks get warm at his text. I knew I was blushing, and my centre throbbed as I thought about what it was he would prescribe.

BELLA: Perhaps ;)

I sat staring at my phone. Why had I just typed that? It was almost as if I were a glutton for punishment. As I lay there waiting for his reply, I could have kicked myself, and the longer it took for him to respond, the more I'd wished I could actually do just that. After a full minute, those three little dots began bouncing again.

ASHER: Since we both can't sleep do you feel like company?

I bit my bottom lip. We hadn't been alone since those nights in Columbus. The memory of them had sat in the front of my mind ever since. How he'd comforted me, how he held me before, during, and after sex. I'd grown to love being held by him, and for the past week, ever since seeing him at the diner, I'd been dying to feel that again. I'd have died to have had him hold me when my mother passed, but that had been impossible. Now, with a pregnancy looming over my head, I felt I needed him more than ever, and yet I was afraid to tell him for fear he said good-bye.

BELLA: Sure come over

That was all I texted, then immediately I wanted to kick myself again.

ASHER: On my way

I kicked the blankets off me and made my way out into the hallway. The crib Brielle and Sawyer had gotten me earlier this week was leaning against the wall, still in the box. I walked over and tried to move it, but it was too heavy to even drag into the small spare bedroom that would end up being the nursery. Panic filled me. Sawyer was supposed to have come back tonight and move it into the room for me, but he'd had an emergency and wasn't able to, and now I knew Asher would ask questions.

I gave it another try, moving it only an inch. "Shit," I muttered to myself. I thought about getting my phone and just telling Asher I was tired when I heard a quiet knock on the door.

I took a couple of steps and spotted the small bag of baby clothes I'd also purchased laying on the floor. I picked them up and threw them into the spare room before making my way to the door.

"Hey," he said, smiling.

I stepped to the side and let him in, taking his coat and hanging it on the small hooks just inside the door. I shut and locked the door and turned to see him toe his shoes off. He was barely in the door and the scent of his cologne was driving me mad.

We stood in the entryway, looking at one another. Then he stepped toward me, placing his arms around my waist, and pulled me against him for a hug. He was so warm, I could feel his heat through my thin silk pajamas. I buried my face into the crook of his neck as he hugged me tight. God, I'd missed how his body felt against mine. I hadn't really realized it until now. As I stood there, in his arms, our bodies pressed against one another, I knew in a matter of moments I would want more. I'd want to feel his lips on mine and his hands exploring my body until I could no longer stand it. I was about to step away when our eyes locked.

There was no time to stop and rationally think about what I was doing, because my lips were already against his. The kiss broke, both of us breathing hard. We finally pulled away from one another. Then he blew out a deep breath.

"I need to calm down. I didn't just come here for this. I don't want you to think that," he said in a quiet voice as he ran his fingers through his thick, dark hair.

He looked around my dark apartment. "I thought you said you were up when you messaged me?"

"I was, but I was in bed watching TV." I giggled. "Come." I placed my hand in his, hit the light in the hall-way, and pulled him down the hall and into my bedroom, shutting the door behind us.

I crawled into bed and watched while he removed his shirt and unbuttoned his jeans. Then he crawled into bed, under the covers, and pulled me into him.

"You know, I thought a lot about you while you were gone. I thought more about us after I left Columbus too."

"You did?"

"I did. I meant what I said earlier this week as well. That I wanted us to continue from where we left things off."

"What does that mean for you?" I questioned.

"I really like you, Bella. We said we were only going to do the friendship thing, but I want more. I want you, and I want to see if we can give a relationship a try."

I was quiet. My head spun. I wanted that so bad. "I don't know," I whispered.

"What don't you know?"

"I don't know if that—if we, are a good idea," I said, swallowing hard.

Asher met my eyes. "Don't say that."

"I can't help it. I'm afraid."

Asher pulled me into him. "Tell me, what would make you less afraid."

Thousands of thoughts flew around my head, while only one of them came forward. The fact that in a few short weeks he'd notice a baby bump.

"You can tell me, you know. Is it something from your past relationship?"

Yep, he'd figured it out. The two men were exact opposites.

"I'm not Miles. I'm not the type to run from problems and place blame where it shouldn't be placed."

"How did you know that he did that?"

"I grew up with him, remember. We may not talk now, but he never changed. He was like that as a kid, he was that way in high school, so I'm sure he's that way now."

"Yes, he is," I whispered.

"You know, I've made mistakes in my past, done things that I wasn't proud of, but with each mistake, I learned to grow. You don't need to worry about me doing those things."

I let out a breath. "I know."

"How about we give it a trial run. Why don't we, after dinner tomorrow night, spend the weekend together. I have the weekend off and so do you. We can stay at my place, go shop, make dinner, watch movies. Just be together?"

"I'd love that," I whispered as he kissed my neck again.

"If that weekend goes well, I know that there's a musical festival coming up. Some of our favorite bands are playing, and I was thinking of getting us tickets. We could get a hotel, spend the weekend away."

"That sounds like fun. I'd love that," I replied, wondering how long it would be before I'd start showing.

I let out a yawn, and Asher reached around behind him and shut the TV off, then pulled the covers up around us and pulled me into him. I closed my eyes and allowed the heat of his body to relax me.

"You need to get some rest," he said as he held me in his arms, stroking my hair.

"You too. I'm just happy you are here with me," I murmured into his chest.

"Same, baby, same."

A bit later, I rolled onto my opposite side and swallowed hard, trying to rid my throat of the large lump that sat in the centre of it. I'd just gotten comfortable when I felt Asher slide his arm under my neck and felt him press his body against my back, his other hand running around my waist, landing on my abdomen. On our baby. He kissed my neck.

"Good night, sweetheart," he whispered. In a matter of moments, I lay there fighting the burning sensation behind my eyes, while he drifted off into a deep sleep. Here he was planning our future, and I was hiding something from him that would surely end it.

Asher had been asleep for a couple of hours; I was still awake. I'd been getting that nauseous feeling again and knew it was only going to be a matter of time before I needed to be sick. I slipped out from under the covers, careful not to disturb him. The last thing I wanted was for him to get up with me and wonder what the problem was. I pulled the door shut and bolted to the bathroom.

I'd just taken a cloth and wet it down, patting my face, when I thought I'd heard a noise. I listened hard. Whatever it was I'd heard stopped. I hung the cloth up over the edge of the tub and made my way out to the kitchen to make a hot cup of tea.

Thoughts of telling Asher about the baby were still running through my mind. Actually, they'd gotten worse once I knew he wanted to take things further with me. I knew that nothing good would come from me holding on to this information. I should have immediately come clean, and I never should have agreed to the weekend with him. Yet, I wanted to be with him. It was almost as if he were a drug, and I was being pushed by an unseen force toward him. I let out a sigh and carried my tea into the living room, grabbing my cell phone as I went.

I needed to unload some pressure, and the one part of this weekend that was stressing me out the most was having dinner with Brielle and Sawyer. I knew she wanted what was best for me, yet I was afraid that she might spill the beans about me being pregnant.

I sat down on the couch, pulling the blanket that lay across the back of it over me. After grabbing my phone, I sent a message to Brielle to cancel dinner. There was no reason for us to have dinner tonight. As soon as I sent the text, my phone vibrated. I should have known she'd be up and getting ready for work now.

BRIELLE: What do you mean you're cancelling?

BELLA: Just what I said.

BRIELLE: What happened?

I tapped my phone. I didn't want to tell her he'd spent the night. I also didn't want to tell her that a few moments ago I'd decided that after the weekend I was going to tell him I no longer wanted to see him. Yet, as if someone else had my phone, that was exactly what I'd typed.

BRIELLE: WHAT? He's there now? Girl, you are in a pretty messed-up situation! What do you mean after this weekend you're going to break things off? What is going on in that head of yours? It's pregnancy hormones, isn't it?

BELLA: Yes, it's a fucked-up situation. Yet, if you knew what I know, you'd do the same thing. So, let me have my weekend with him and let me say good-bye in my own way.

I dropped the phone beside me and placed my head in my hands. I wanted to cry. Losing him was the last thing I wanted. I sat like that for a few minutes, until I heard the bedroom door open. I grabbed my mug and leaned back against the couch, curling my feet underneath me, pretending as if nothing were wrong.

"Morning." A very sexy, sleepy-looking Asher emerged from the hallway.

"Morning. Want a tea? The kettle should still be hot."

He made his way over to me and knelt in front of me, taking the mug from my hands. He looked into my eyes and smiled. "I have to get going. I have appointments this morning, but I'm looking forward to dinner tonight and spending time with you."

"Oh, about that. Brielle had to cancel. She isn't feeling well. Baby things." I shrugged.

"Oh, is that why you're up? Is she okay? Do you need to go in for her?"

"Yeah, unfortunately, I do. I told her we'd reschedule."

"Oh, okay. Well then, I guess I will pick you up tonight for our weekend."

I smiled, placed my hand on his cheek, and leaned forward, meeting his lips. "Can't wait."

Once he stood, I got up off the couch and followed him to the door. He turned and kissed me good-bye, then opened the door and took off down the hall.

I made my way back to the couch and grabbed my phone. There was a pile of missed messages.

BRIELLE: I wish you'd come to your senses

BRIELLE: It's not fair to him what you are doing

BRIELLE: It's not fair to yourself either

BRIELLE: You are so damn stubborn

BRIELLE: He isn't Miles! I wished you'd of kicked that asshat to the curb years ago! Just like I told you!

BRIELLE: My god! I can't believe you are just going to spend the weekend with him and get that much closer to him just to end things.

BRIELLE: For the love of god woman! Now you aren't answering me either.

BRIELLE: UGH!!!! You're impossible!

I thought for a moment. She was right. Everything she was saying was right! I blew out a breath, and then I responded to her.

> BELLA: I know what I am doing. I am giving my heart a chance to say goodbye. I really like him and wish things were way different, but they aren't. I'll message you later.

I placed my phone down on the table and sat back with my tea. The instant it vibrated against the tabletop, I reached over and hit the power button. I needed time to digest what it was I was doing, and I didn't need to hear it from Brielle. I knew what I was doing was wrong, and I already felt guilty about it.

BELLA

It was Saturday night. The weekend had seemed to fly by in a flash. We'd spent Friday night sharing a wonderful dinner in the moonlight in his backyard, followed by two movies that neither of us barely watched. This morning we got up, went for a yoga session, and then spent the day up the coast at the fall fair. Afterward, we made our way back to Eastport, stopping at a local bookstore for a coffee and some browsing. We returned to his place where we cooked dinner together.

Now we lay on our backs looking up at the night sky. We'd made our way down to the beach, where we'd spread out a big blanket, threw two pillows down, and once we were comfortable, he covered us with another blanket. We'd been out here for a couple of hours now, watching a meteor shower.

"Did you see that one?" I cried. "It was so bright."

"I did. Probably the best one of the night," he said, pulling me tighter against him. It was early October, and it was colder than usual. The wind had picked up, and I shivered a little.

"You cold?" he asked

"Hmm, maybe a little."

He tightened his arm around me. "Want to lie on my other side? I'll block some of the wind."

"Do you mind?"

He shook his head and held on to me as I straddled his lap. He gripped my hips, stopping me. "This is something I might like to try," he said, holding me there and smiling up at me.

I laughed as my cheeks heated. "Might be able to be arranged," I said, bending down and meeting his lips.

I pulled my other leg over him and lay down on the other side of him. He was right; it was warmer, and I snuggled against him as he pulled the blanket up around my neck. "That better?"

"Much," I whispered, breathing in his scent.

He rolled onto his side and met my eyes. I could feel the intensity of his stare. "What is it?" I questioned.

"Nothing. Just, I've really enjoyed our time together this weekend."

"Same here."

He met my lips and kissed me hard, just as another gust of wind blew. I shivered as we parted, and Asher looked down at me. "Want to head back inside?"

I could tell from the look in his eyes that he had other things on his mind that he'd rather be doing, and that they'd best be done inside and not on a beach, so we gathered all the blankets and made our way back to the house.

In a matter of minutes of being inside, he grabbed me and carried me down the hall to his bedroom. Placing me gently on the edge of the bed, he pushed me back and stood over me. He leaned down and kissed me hard. Then he stared down at me as he undid the buttons of my shirt, opening them one by one. His eyes fell to my breasts when he opened the clasp of my bra and he leaned down, tenderly kissing them. I closed my eyes as his fingers grazed the skin of my stomach and stopped at the button on my jeans. He flicked the button open and slid his hand into my pants, running his fingers between my legs.

Just lying in his arms outside had turned me on, and I was slightly embarrassed by how wet I was. Yet Asher licked his lips as he slid my pants off my body. He parted my legs and buried his face between them. I wanted to tell him to stop, but he gripped the waist of my panties and ripped at the lacy side, pulling them off me, then buried his face between my legs. My fingers instantly gripped his hair as my head fell back.

The feeling of his tongue on me was so strong that I felt like I could let go. I bit my bottom lip to keep from screaming when he stopped. Opening my eyes, I wondered what was going on. I looked to see that he stood before me, looking down at me. He'd removed his shirt and pants, and he stood there with his hand over his hardened cock, straining against his boxers. I pushed myself up and went to move his hand, but he stopped me.

"Lay back. Just let me look at you," he said, gripping his cock.

A little self-conscious, I laid back on the bed and met his eyes.

"Fuck, you're beautiful," he gritted.

I lay back there waiting for him to join me. I kept my eyes on his hand. He noticed, and pulled himself out of his boxers and began stroking himself. "You like that?" he questioned.

"Very much," I whispered as I concentrated on his hand and watched what he liked.

"Touch yourself?" he whispered. "I want to watch."

I'd done nothing like this before, and my heart raced as I shyly placed my hand over my breast, the other moving down toward my centre.

"That's it." He groaned. "Run your fingers between

your legs." His voice was strained as he told me what he wanted.

I opened my eyes and watched as he gripped his hard cock in his hand, stroking himself at a slow pace as I ran my fingers through my wet centre.

My fingers circled the small bundle of nerves, a small moan escaped my lips. Instantly, I felt the bed dip and his large hand gripped mine and placed it on his cock. He placed his hand where mine had been and continued circling the little bud. The more he continued, the hotter my body got, even more so than I already had been. His cock slid through my fingers and my thumb spread that small bead of pre-cum over the head. He groaned and slid one and then two fingers inside of me, gently fucking me.

He met my mouth while he pumped his fingers into me. Our lips parted. I continued stroking him while he pulled his fingers from me, leaving a void I wanted to have filled again. He pulled my hand away from his cock and quickly moved between my legs and gripped my hips, lining himself up at my entrance.

Our eyes locked as he slid into me, slowly inching his way in until he was buried deep inside of me. The void that had been begging to be filled was now content. He held himself there for a moment, deep inside of me, barely moving his hips, then began moving in slow, deep bursts. I'd felt nothing this good before.

As he continued, I closed my eyes and held his hands. I could feel the threat of my orgasm ready to come on already. I didn't want this to end. He must have sensed it because he stopped moving and pulled out of me, then slid himself right back in. He did this move a few times, stopping and kissing me before he slammed himself back into me.

"Oh God, Asher. Do that again…please," I begged.

"Come for me, Bella," he said, breathing heavily while repeating the same thing over and over. "Come hard."

He found the swollen little bud and began stroking his thumb over it as he pumped in and out of me, faster but just as deep.

I gripped the blankets and cried out as he continued stroking me. I clenched tightly around him, feeling my body let go.

"That's it, baby. Let go." He groaned as he continued thrusting deep and fast into me, until his body tensed and he let go, collapsing onto me.

We lay in bed wrapped in one another in the wee hours of Sunday morning. I was exhausted. We hadn't only had sex once but twice, and only a few minutes ago, the third time ended. Only something had changed. It was slower, more sensual, and when it was over, he'd pulled me into his arms and held me in a way he hadn't before. Everything from the way he'd looked at me, the way he'd touched me, to the way he'd kissed me had changed.

I lay with my eyes closed, feeling his light breath against my shoulder. He was wrapped around me in a protective embrace that I loved. I swallowed hard as I thought back to how things were even different from Thursday night. As the weekend passed, I'd noticed many little things had changed. Conversations flowed way easier between us, and all those accidental touches felt normal but still sent waves through me. Our hands lingered longer on each other, and we fell into sync with one another. Everything was different with Asher than it had ever been with Miles.

I was certain Asher was asleep, and I let out a ragged breath. Anxiety had filled me, and it felt like I had an elephant sitting on my chest just thinking about what tomorrow night would be like when I told him I couldn't do this anymore. I shifted my body a little, trying to get comfortable.

"What's wrong?" he whispered and pulled me tighter into him.

"Nothing. I… I just a bad dream," I replied, rubbing his muscular forearm. I wasn't lying. This entire situation was a nightmare.

"Can't have that," he whispered, his lips kissing my bare shoulder, up my neck to my ear. I rolled a little onto my back, where I met his mouth.

He kissed me slow, and as our lips parted, he met my eyes. "Can I tell you something?"

I nodded.

"I think I'm falling in love with you." He met my lips again, kissing me deeper, his tongue washing through my mouth.

I was screwed.

BELLA

"Brie, I have to go to my doctor's appointment at one today," I said as Brielle walked into the office where I was working on the upcoming schedule.

"No problem. Will you be coming back afterward?"

"I dunno. What's this appointment like?" I asked, looking at her growing belly.

"Ah, let me think. It should just be an ultrasound. You should be fine. Did you want me to go with you? I mean, I could," she said, glancing around at the mess on her desk.

"No, I was just wondering."

"Well, it's totally up to you. See what time your appointment ends, and if you don't feel like coming back, then it's not a big deal. You were in early today anyway. I don't think we are going to be that busy tonight."

"Okay, thanks."

"I noticed Asher was here last night when I left."

"Yeah, he came by to see me. I hope it's okay that I took my dinner hour with him?"

Brie frowned. "I thought you were going to end things with him?"

She was right. I was supposed to end things with him three weeks ago. Only I hadn't been able to. Every single time I'd gathered the courage, I fell in love with him a little more. My heart was content and happy, something it hadn't been in years.

I shrugged. "I was, but…"

"But what?" Brie stood there looking at me, her hand on her hip, waiting for me to respond.

Suddenly, Sawyer appeared in the doorway. In one hand, he held what was surely Brie's lunch and her laptop bag.

"You forgot these in the car." He smiled, stepping in and placing them down on the floor beside the desk. I watched as he placed his hand on her belly, leaned in, and kissed her. "I'll pick you up after work, okay, baby? Take it easy today," he said, kissing her again before even noticing I was in the room.

"Hey, Bella. How you feeling?"

"Good, Sawyer, thanks for asking." I smiled, watching as he kissed her again.

"How's the morning sickness?"

"It's changed to mid-afternoon." I giggled, and Sawyer laughed, patting my shoulder before he left.

Brielle shifted a few things around on her desk, making room for her laptop.

"That's what I want."

"What?" Brie asked, looking at me over her shoulder.

"That. I want that. You and Sawyer have what I want. That is something I want with Asher. That's why I haven't told him yet. I mean, look at the two of you."

Brie sat down and slid her chair over to me. "If you want what we have, then you need to tell him. But know that things weren't always this way between us. It took a long while for him to trust me again. I mean, I robbed Sawyer of experiencing all the baby things with Emma. The only memories he has of her were from the time he met her to now. I was wrong about doing that. You're wrong to do this to him."

"I know."

"I just don't understand what the big deal is?"

"Brie, he told me he doesn't want children."

"When did he say that?"

"He told me back before I knew I was pregnant. Well, before I knew anyway. He thinks I can't have children, and he was relieved. He didn't even falter when I told him."

Brielle looked at me, her arms crossed over her chest. "Bella, I don't know what to tell you. You can't keep doing this to him, or yourself. You are going to end up hurt if you don't figure things out."

"I'd planned on doing it. I just… I couldn't."

"Why not?"

"Because I'm in love with him."

The room grew quiet. Brielle stood there looking at me, while I just wanted to crawl under the desk and hide.

"I don't know what to tell you. Just tell him soon or I can guarantee he's going to find out. Eventually, you're gonna pop, and…."

"I know…I know…I'll tell him this weekend. We are going to a music festival up the coast. When he drops me off on Sunday, I'll do it."

I sat in the waiting room reading a magazine that I'd found lying on the table. I glanced down at my watch. It was already half an hour past my appointment time. I frowned, wondering what was taking so long. I threw the magazine down and picked up another one when I heard my name called.

A nurse stood inside the door that led to the waiting room. I smiled, placed the magazine back on the table, and followed her down the hall. I followed her into an exam room, where I saw a gown on the end of the table.

"Sorry, Bella, Doctor Love had an emergency delivery, which is taking longer than expected. He asked me to do your ultrasound. He's hoping by that time he'll be back up to finish your appointment."

"Oh, well, I can always come back another day if it's more convenient."

"Nope, no need. These things sometimes happen. We will get everything taken care of. So, please, get undressed. You may leave your undergarments on, gown open at the front. I'll be back in a few minutes." She smiled as she pulled the door closed, leaving me in the empty room.

I placed my things on the chair in the corner and began getting undressed. I was feeling nervous about this appointment, and I wished I'd taken Brielle up on her offer to come with me today. It would have helped to calm me down a little to have her here, I thought to myself.

Once I had the gown on, I pulled it closed at the front and hopped up onto the end of the table and sat there waiting. Finally, I heard a soft knock on the door and it opened an inch.

"Alright, Bella, all ready?" the nurse asked, taking a peek into the room. Once she saw me sitting there, she closed the door behind her. Then she pulled the curtain closed around the table.

She adjusted the table a bit. "Alright just lean back here," she said, standing beside me while I shifted myself and rested my back against the cold paper-covered table.

I watched as she walked around and turned on the monitor, then she grabbed a tube of jelly. "This may be a little cold," she said, removing the sides of my gown off my belly and squirting some gel onto my skin.

"Oh God, doesn't this stuff come warmed up?" I said, giggling.

"I know. It's a shocker." She smiled. "Now just relax."

She sat down on the chair and grabbed a wand, rolling it over my abdomen. "You may be uncomfortable with the pressure, but this shouldn't take too long."

I watched as she rolled the wand around my abdomen while looking at the screen. After a few seconds, I began leaning forward, trying to see the screen. When she noticed, she smiled. "There isn't a lot to see right now," she said and turned the monitor a little toward me. "Do you have any other children?"

"No, this is my first," I said, still watching the screen for anything I might see.

"Ah, now I know why you're so keen on seeing what is going on." She studied the screen intently, moving the wand around a little, and then smiled. "And there you are," she quietly said.

"Where?"

She pointed to this little odd shape on the screen. "Right there."

I frowned. "That's it?"

"That's it!" She smiled. "Don't worry, most first-time parents say the same thing. It's like a little kidney bean, isn't it?"

I nodded, still watching the screen. "That's what has been responsible for my morning sickness?"

"That's it! Amazing that something that tiny can do that to us, isn't it?"

I nodded, watching as she marked a few things down on the paper in front of her. Then she took a paper towel and cleaned the wand off and passed me a pile of them.

"Alright, my dear, once you get dressed, you can head through the side door into Doctor Love's office. I'm just going to get this image printed off and a report ready for him, and hopefully, fingers crossed, he should be here in about twenty minutes."

"Thank you," I said.

Once she was gone, I did as I was told, cleaning

myself up, then getting dressed, and then I made my way into his office. I took a seat on the comfortable-looking couch in his office and pulled my phone from my pocket.

There was a message from Asher. I smiled as I read it.

ASHER: Will be a little late tonight picking you up. Work issues. I should be there by seven thirty. We'll get dinner to go, then head up to the hotel. ;)

BRIELLE: Sounds good, take your time ;)

ASHER

I stood in line for a coffee in the hospital cafeteria when my phone vibrated in my pocket. Today of all days, one of Alonzo's patients had to go into labour. She'd had a high-risk pregnancy as it was, and both Alonzo and I had been glad he was here to deal with it. I'd seen her once during her second trimester, and she'd been a basket case, worried that Alonzo was going to abandon her. My phone vibrated again, and I pulled it out, looking at the screen.

> BELLA: Sounds good, take your time ;)

I quickly sent another message.

ASHER: This is what my career is like.
I hope you can take it

I watched as the three little dots bounced up and down.

BELLA: I know, Brielle complains all the time about Sawyer, at least I can now relate :D

I let out a laugh.

ASHER: Hope you don't complain about me.

BELLA: Not yet, you've only made me wait twice. Although one more time that will give me rights to start lol

I smiled. God, I loved her.

ASHER: You all ready for the weekend?

BELLA: all packed and ready when you are.

ASHER: Bags in the car. Good thing I packed last night.

BELLA: Looking forward to it. See you tonight. Hope your day goes by fast.

I pocketed my phone just as I got to the counter. I ordered my coffee and a muffin and headed back upstairs. It would have been nice to get out of the office for a bit and head to The Cooling Rack for lunch, but this would have to do. I'd just walked through the doors of the office. The waiting was room full. Marie waved, catching my attention. I shut the outside door and made my way over to her desk.

"Asher, Alonzo is stuck downstairs. Apparently, some complications arose, and he's had to do a C-section. I've rescheduled most of his appointments the second I found out. However, there is one patient here that is waiting for him in his office."

"Okay, no big deal. I can take care of it," I said, glancing down at my watch.

"It shouldn't take you long. It's an eight-week ultrasound. Everything is already done. You just need to go over the results."

"Sure, no problem. These are actually a favourite of mine. However, I'll need you to cancel my six o'clock then. Try to reschedule for Monday."

"Ah, yes, you have that festival this weekend, don't you?"

"Yep, and now I don't feel so bad asking Alonzo to watch over my three ladies who may go into labour this weekend, knowing he will probably be here anyway." I chuckled.

"That's okay. He'll get you back next weekend," Marie said, smiling. "I'll get that appointment rescheduled. I can also reschedule your five thirty if you like."

I thought for a moment. "Please do. That will help a bit, just in case I run over with the rest of the appointments this afternoon."

I headed on down the hall, carrying my hot coffee into my office. I took a few sips, a couple bites of the sandwich I'd been working on for most of the afternoon, and then headed toward Alonzo's office, pulling the file out of the file hanger and opening it to glance and make sure the results were there. Sure enough, the page was on top, and I opened the office door.

"Hello, sorry about the wait. Doctor Love had an emergency and unfortunately can't make it. I'm Doctor Harrison and I'll…"

As I turned around, I stopped dead in my tracks as I laid eyes on my next patient. Bella stood in front of me, the look on her face matching mine. With our eyes locked, it was all I could do to stand there as shock flooded my body. Neither of us moved. In fact, I wasn't even sure if I was still breathing. My hands shook as I tilted the file to see the name of the patient, and sure enough, Bella Langdon was neatly typed on the nameplate.

The silence in the room was deafening. I could barely take it. I looked at her; she looked at me; I felt completely blindsided. "Is this some sort of joke?" I asked.

She didn't move; she just stood there.

"What kind of sick joke is this, Bella?" I asked again, raising my voice.

"It's not a joke," she whispered, her voice barely audible.

"You're here for an eight-week ultrasound? You're pregnant?"

She barely nodded her head, but she did, in fact, nod.

"I take it… fuck me… that it's mine, unless there are other things you aren't telling me?"

She nodded her head as her bottom lip trembled.

The room spun as I stood there. I needed to sit down, but that would mean I'd want to entertain a conversation with her and really all I wanted was to run from this room. Instead of responding, I turned and left. I shut the door behind me and made my way into my office where I took a seat. I just needed to breathe, I thought to myself as I studied the wall.

After I'd taken a few deep breaths, and once the room finally stopped spinning and I didn't feel as if I would faint away, I got up. Leaving the file on my desk, I made my way back toward Alonzo's office, opened the door, and slipped inside to find Bella sitting on the edge of the couch, her face in her hands.

"How long have you known?" I demanded, trying to keep my voice down.

She shrugged. "About six weeks."

"So you've known since before you came back to Eastport?" I bit out as I paced back and forth.

She slowly nodded her head.

"So, was it all a lie?"

"What?"

"Was it all a lie? The 'I can't get pregnant' part. Was it all a lie?"

"What? No…"

"'Cause it seems to me that it might have been."

She let out a cry. "No, Asher, I wasn't lying," she said, standing up and taking a step toward me.

"Don't come near me," I spat as I listened to her sobs.

Bella stopped in her tracks, tears streaming down her face.

"Why didn't you just tell me?"

She looked at me, shifted from one foot to the other. "Because you told me you didn't want kids, that you hated them. Which honestly makes zero sense to me when you are a pediatrician."

"Whoa, who said I was a pediatrician? This is my office. Doctor Love is my employee. I'm an OB/GYN, Bella. What reason would there be for me to be here if I were a pediatrician?"

Bella shrugged. "I don't know. You could work with Doctor Love."

I ignored that statement. "Oh, and I don't hate kids."

"Then why don't you want them?"

I ran my hand over my face. "I never said I never wanted them. I said I didn't want them with the woman in my previous relationship. There were many, many things wrong with that entire situation. For starters, she constantly lied to me. Lied about little things and then about bigger things when the truth would have been sufficient. I can't even begin to tell you how many things were wrong with that relationship, and there appears to be just as many things wrong with this one."

"Asher...I..."

"You what? Not being able to get pregnant is what you lied about. Then you failed to tell me you were. How do I know anything that has gone on between us and said during our time together hasn't been one big lie?"

Bella stood there, tears rolling down her cheeks as she listened. Soon, loud, guttural sobs fell from her.

"Yeah, that's exactly it. I don't know what the truth is any more than you do."

"Asher, none of it was a lie," she cried.

"Yeah, whatever you say," I said, moving toward the door.

"It's not like you were completely honest with me either," Bella said.

"What do you mean by that?"

"You never told me you were an OB/GYN. You also never told me you were opening a practice right here in the hospital, either."

"No, I didn't. You are correct. However, I didn't really think that my specialty really mattered all that much. It wasn't like I would not tell you either. When I wanted to tell you about this office, your mother got sick. You had to leave, but I did eventually tell you. Perhaps not when I should have, but I told you. If you wanted to know my specialty, all you needed to do was ask. It's not a state secret."

"You're no different from me."

Anger flooded through me. She was trying to place me on the same horse she was on. There was no way she was going to do that to me. I grabbed the handle of the door and pulled it open, ready to walk out and close the door on this part of my life. It was going to kill me to do it, but I'd do it.

"Asher… please wait…"

I stopped. My heart was racing when I turned around to face her. "Bella, I loved you. I allowed myself to open my heart once again, and as stupid as it was, I fell in love with you. Everything we had, all of this has been shot to hell now, don't you think?"

"No, we can work through this," she cried.

"I can't. I don't think I can trust you. I'm sorry." I

said nothing more. I just stood there, staring at her, watching her cry. Then I shook my head. "It's over. I hope you enjoy your weekend. I sure as hell know I won't be enjoying mine."

I ripped the door open and pulled it shut behind me and went into my office. The patients could wait. I needed a minute. I needed an hour. Hell, I needed a long fucking time to get over this. I shut the door and leaned up against the wall, focusing on calming myself down. I didn't care how long she stayed in there. I just couldn't be there with her any longer. I walked over and sunk into my office chair, turning my attention to my next patient file. I had to get through the rest of my day, and the only way I was going to do it was to focus on my next task.

BELLA

My eyes puffy, my cheeks still tear-stained, I pulled a tissue from the box on Doctor Love's desk. Asher's words had torn my heart out. I'd been sitting here for twenty minutes, shocked to the core. I still wasn't sure what I'd been expecting him to say. I blew my nose, then grabbed two more tissues from the box that sat on Doctor Love's desk and dabbed my eyes. I needed to get out of this office.

I picked up my purse and walked to the door. The last thing I wanted was to run into Asher in the hallway. I took in a breath and pulled the door open enough to look out into the hallway. I glanced across the hall. The name-plate on the door read Asher Harrison. The door was tightly closed. I looked down the hall. The door to the waiting area seemed far away, yet this was probably my only chance.

I took off down the hall to the waiting room, and when I opened the door and stepped out of the hallway, everyone's eyes turned to me. They all stared. I was sure I was a sight with my puffy eyes and tear-stained face. Regardless, I gathered the courage and stepped into the room and headed for the door.

"Bella, before you go, we should book your next appointment in," the nurse behind the desk called out without looking up.

I swallowed hard. I turned my back toward her. "I'll call," I mumbled and stumbled out the door into the hallway of the thirteenth floor. I hit the button for the elevator and stood there, my vision blurring with fresh tears as memories from only a few minutes ago flooded my mind. Then I heard two voices and glanced down the hall to see Doctor Love rounding the corner with a nurse. I didn't want him to see me like this. It would lead to too many questions, ones I didn't want to answer right now. Instead of waiting for the elevator, I took off heading to the stairwell.

It took forever for me to walk down all those stairs and get outside to my car. Once I was seated behind the wheel, the tears flowed. I sat there sobbing into my hands. The look on his face sat in the forefront of my mind. Then his words—his harsh words—came into my head. Everything was a mess, and I had myself, and only myself, to thank for it.

My phone lay on centre console of the car, right where I'd thrown it, and there it vibrated. I glanced at it to see a message from Brielle. She was probably wondering where I was. I picked up the phone without reading it and turned it off, throwing it into my purse. I just wanted to be left alone.

Six hours later, I lay on my couch, wrapped in a blanket, absolutely exhausted from the events that had transpired through today. I stared at the television, barely hearing anything that was being said. I hadn't eaten; I wasn't hungry, and yet my stomach grumbled, telling me it wanted food.

I sat up and headed to the kitchen. After putting the kettle on, I put two pieces of bread in the toaster. I was supposed to have left with Asher for the weekend hours ago. He'd probably gone anyway, I thought to myself as I filled my mug with hot water and buttered my toast.

I woke early the next morning, my head still pounding, and jumped into the shower. I was exhausted, and my body ached from a terrible night's sleep. I'd finally turned my phone on before bed, hoping for a message from Asher, and each time I'd woken during the night, I'd checked to find nothing.

I'd gotten dressed and headed to the kitchen. I opened the fridge to get an apple, only to find out it was empty. Since I knew we were going away this weekend, I didn't do my regular grocery shop on Thursday. I let out a sigh. I'd have to get groceries. As much as I didn't want to leave, I figured that the fresh air would be good for me. I slipped my shoes on and grabbed my purse and keys.

I'd gotten the few things I needed from the store and then made my way over to The Cooling Rack. The fresh air had done me good, and now I needed my best friend. The parking lot was busy, but I found a spot. When I walked through the door, I could see from the look on her face that she was shocked to find me here after I took the weekend off to go away with Asher. I didn't need to say anything; she took one look at me and immediately wrapped me in her arms and directed me to this table where I currently sat.

She'd gone back to the counter and said something to the new hire behind the counter. Then she made her way over to the table carrying two blueberry muffins.

"They are bringing over two teas. I got you chamomile," she said, sliding the muffin in front of me.

"Thank you," I mumbled, breaking apart the muffin and taking a bite.

"We can go into the office if you'd prefer. More private. It's pretty busy here today," she said, glancing around at the full tables and the line of doctors that waited at the counter.

I shook my head. "No, it's fine. Hopefully, being in front of people will keep me from crying." I sadly smiled. "You were right. I should have told him," I muttered.

"What happened?" she questioned.

I took a minute and then looked at her with tears in my eyes. "It was awful. I went for my appointment with Doctor Love and, well, he had an emergency to tend to. I guess they passed me off to the next doctor, who was Asher."

Brielle's eyes shot up from her muffin and landed on mine. "What? When did this happen?"

Ignoring her question, I blurted, "He found out because I was standing in front of him waiting for my ultrasound results. I wanted to die."

"Oh, Bella." Brielle went to get up and move over beside me, but I stopped her.

"You'll make me cry…" I said, holding my hands out in front of myself. "It was awful. *He*, was awful."

"What did he say?"

My lip trembled, and I took a sip of tea to try and stop it. "He wanted to know why I just didn't tell him."

"And did you?"

I nodded. "Only he got angrier. It wasn't that he

didn't want children at all. It was… that he didn't want them with her."

Brielle sat there waiting for me to continue, but when I didn't, she leaned forward. "I see it's rather a good mess you've gotten into isn't it."

I nodded, picking up my mug again. I took a sip and then told her the entire story, and how things had been left: with me standing alone in the office crying my eyes out. When I finished, she sat there, tears in her eyes as she studied me.

"What am I going to do?" I questioned.

"I don't know. Perhaps give it a few days, then try to talk to him," she suggested. "Sometimes, in the heat of the moment, people say things they don't mean. I mean, think about how you might feel if the shoe were on the other foot?"

I looked over at my best friend. *That was her advice! Give him a few days? Think about how I'd feel if the shoe were on the other foot.*

"Brielle, seriously."

"Yes, seriously. You've jumped to conclusions this entire time, you've lied to him—well, maybe not lied, but told untruths."

"That's what he said," I muttered.

"So, give him a few days."

"My God, that is the most awful advice anyone has ever given me."

"Why?"

"What do you mean, why? He said I was a liar, that everything we had was based on a lie. Do you really think he'd entertain a conversation with me?"

"I don't know, he might. If he's the man I think he is, he will. But I know for the sake of that baby, you need to try."

ASHER

I'D BURIED myself in work since Friday. Finding out that Bella was pregnant had shocked me. Work had been the only way to escape the way I felt. I'd been blindsided. I was angry, and I'd acted out of that shock and anger. I'd been so mad I'd jumped to a conclusion that hadn't made me feel any better, despite thinking that was what I wanted. On top of all that, I was hurt. Over the course of our relationship, I'd always told her she could come to me with anything.

I'd worked the rest of that day on Friday and then left the office. I'd gone home and sulked around the house for the better part of Friday night and Saturday, but I needed to pull myself out of the funk I was in. I couldn't possibly see patients on Monday in this mood.

I'd sat down behind my desk with a hot cup of coffee

and switched my little radio on. I grabbed the file that lay on my desk for my first patient on Monday, looking over her test results, and made some notes to discuss some things with her. Then I moved onto the next. As I placed the last file Marie had left for me, I noticed one last file sitting on my desk. Bella's name stared me in the face.

I set it off to the side, but curiosity got the best of me. I flipped the file open and while I knew it was wrong to look over Alonzo's patient files, I did it anyways. I went right back to the beginning, looking over past blood work and diagnosis. She hadn't been lying; Kavanaugh had diagnosed her as infertile. The old bastard hadn't even done his due diligence and ran the proper tests. It didn't come as a shock to me. I'd found it in some of my own patient files.

I continued, flipping through notes from her appointment with Alonzo, and then to her blood work results. I ran my hand over my face and then flipped to the ultrasound image. I stared at that little bean, while in my head I replayed the entire event over and over in my mind, realizing that my reaction to the situation was just as bad, if not worse than her not telling me. She was probably afraid to say anything to me after what I'd told her. She was probably shocked to find out that what she'd come to believe over the past five years hadn't been true.

Bottom line was, I'd been a complete dick. I flipped the report over and saw that the baby, our baby... my baby, would be born somewhere within the first two weeks of June. I flipped her file closed and leaned back in my chair. I'd royally fucked up. I picked up my phone. Tapping the side, I opened a new message to Bella, then decided against it. She deserved an apology, face-to-face, not a fucking text message.

When I climbed into my car, I checked the time. It was a little after five. Bella normally closed The Cooling Rack tonight. I decided I'd go there first. As I made my way there, I played in my mind what it was I'd say to her.

I'd start by apologizing and take it from there. Only when I pulled into the parking lot, I didn't see her car. Regardless, I cut the engine and headed inside to find Brielle standing behind the counter dealing with a customer. The look on her face said everything I needed to know. She knew.

I waited, and once she was done, she turned her back on me and began filling the counter.

"Brielle, is Bella here?" I asked.

She ignored me, continuing to fill the counter.

"Brielle?"

She popped her head up to the top of the counter and glared at me. "No, Asher, she isn't here."

"Do you know where she is?"

She laughed. "You think I'm going to tell you after what happened?"

I shrugged, hoping she would.

"If you think I am, you're wrong. She is fucking heartbroken. One bastard in her life was enough. I will not stand by and watch another one treat her the same way."

"Look, not that I need to explain myself to you, but I think you're being a little harsh, don't you?"

"Not really."

I gave up and turned and headed for the door. "If you won't tell me where she is, I'll find her on my own," I said as I stopped at the door.

I made my way back to my car and climbed in. I wasn't giving up. I looked up the number for the local florist and ordered two dozen white roses, then headed off to pick them up.

With flowers in hand, I took the elevator to her floor and walked down the hall. I stopped to catch my breath and then knocked on the door. When she didn't answer, I knocked again, this time calling her name. Still no answer. I felt my phone vibrate in my pocket and switched the flowers to the other arm, while pulling my phone out to see it was the hospital. One of my patients had gone into labour and was on the way. "Fuck," I muttered, shoving my phone back into my pocket.

I knocked one more time, harder, and called her name a little louder. Again nothing. There was nothing I could do. I had to go. I placed the vase on the floor outside of her door and took off down the hall, making my way back to the hospital.

I ended up at the hospital for the better part of the night. Just as I was leaving, one of Doctor Love's patients came in. A young single mother had gone into labour. She was scared and alone and became even more afraid when I notified her I was the OB/GYN on call for the weekend. I'd spent some time with her, calming her down. When I asked about the father, she told me he wanted nothing to do with her. She admitted she was terrified to be facing all of this alone. People said I had a great bedside manner, that I knew exactly what to say, but Alonzo was the one who was perfect with these situations. I silently cursed him for not being here while I tried to say something to comfort her.

I went through the motions that night, while listening to her cries. Her words had ripped at my heart, because all I kept thinking about was Bella. She felt the same way as this young girl did—scared, alone and unsupported. I imagined this being Bella's situation, and that was the last thing I wanted for her. Hell, I didn't want this for anyone.

Before I left the hospital, I popped in to check on her. She lay there, holding her baby, whispering to her. I smiled. "How are we doing?" I asked, checking over her chart.

"Okay. Tired."

"Did you decide on a name?" I questioned.

"I think I'm going to call him Asher." She smiled, looking down at her baby. "I want to be reminded of how much you helped me tonight."

"Well, it's my job." I winked. "I've delivered lots of babies."

"Not for that. For your words, your kindness and your patience. Also, for not judging me."

I placed her file back in the holder at the bottom of her bed and nodded. "Good luck. Doctor Love will check in with you next week. Get some rest."

I stood there as she went back to talking to her baby and I walked to the door. I paused just before opening the door and turned back. "Oh, Crystal."

"Yeah."

"Thank you."

"For?" she asked, looking at me.

"For helping me." I pulled the door open and walked out into the hall. Taking my jacket off, I headed toward the parking lot.

BELLA

I WENT to step out into the hall to head to my yoga class and almost tripped on the vase of white roses that sat just outside my door. I looked up and down the hall expecting to see the person who'd dropped them there, but there was no one. I looked back down to the flowers then bent down and picked them up.

I carried them into the kitchen and placed them on the counter. They were stunning, I thought to myself and leaned in and placed my nose on top of one rose, inhaling. Then I noticed the white card stuck inside, my name written on the small envelope. I pulled the envelope out of the flowers and opened it, removing the small card from inside.

The only thing written on the card was Asher's name. The other side of the card was blank as I flipped it over. I softly smiled. This was exactly him, but if he thought flowers were going to fix this, he was wrong. I shoved the card in the small envelope and threw it down on the counter.

I headed to the door, grabbing my mat and small bag on the way. I looked back at the roses, thinking about calling Asher but decided against it. I had a yoga class to get to.

The music played on as the class went into a few moments of silence. I lay on my mat at the end of class, in a corpse pose with my eyes closed, inhaling and exhaling as guided by the yogi. For the first time, I'd done exactly as instructed and could bring my mind to a clear state, letting go of everything.

"Now, slowly sit up and come into easy pose, bringing your hands to your heart's centre. Everything I need is within my reach. I am exactly where I am supposed to be," she said quietly. "The light in me honors the divine and beautiful light in each one of you. I wish you peace, love, and light, and may the rest of your week be as beautiful as you are. Thank you for joining me today."

The rest of the class began gathering their things, but I lay back on my mat again, just soaking in all the calmness I felt here. Yoga was exactly what I needed, I thought to myself. When the last person left the room, I rolled into a sitting position and began gathering my things, shoving them into my bag.

On my way home, I stopped at the grocery store and made my way over to the produce section. I shoved three apples and two oranges into a bag and threw them into my grocery basket, moving on over to the salads. I placed my basket on the floor between my feet and had just picked up two pre-made salads, trying to decide between them, when I heard a familiar voice.

"You'll like the one in your left hand better."

I spun to see Asher standing there holding a basket full of produce. He smiled. "How you doing?" he questioned.

"I've been better." I shrugged, turning my attention back to the salads in my hand.

"If you choose the one in your right hand, you'll have to pick out all the sliced olives," he said, stepping closer. My body immediately responded to the warmth his body was giving off.

I nodded and placed the other salad into my basket before putting the other back.

"Did you get my flowers?" he questioned.

"I did, but, Asher, flowers aren't going to fix this," I said quietly, fighting back tears as the memory of what he'd said came flooding back.

"I know that. I didn't think they would. You were supposed to be home when I brought them to you."

I had been home. I'd put my headphones in and hid in my bedroom, because when I'd heard his voice at the door, I knew I wasn't ready to face him. I'd have crumbled, and that was something I had promised not only myself but Brielle I wouldn't do.

He bent down and picked my basket up off the floor. Then he leaned into me and whispered, "Meet me in your car. I'll take care of these."

His breath tickled my neck, chills running through my body, and the scent of his cologne was enough to drive me mad. I nodded and turned, leaving the grocery store. No matter how much I wanted to push him away, I couldn't. One look in his eyes was all it took.

As I walked to the car, I thought about the other two times I'd seen him this week. First out for a run Sunday morning in the park, then at The Cooling Rack when Brielle ripped him a new ass, which right after that I'd rushed home after seeing the pain in his eyes. I'd spent that night in tears, and now today.

I had been in the car about five minutes when Asher appeared, walking across the parking lot and opening my back door. He placed the bags in the back seat and climbed into the front passenger's seat. He'd barely gotten the door closed when I turned to him.

"I swear to you, I didn't lie about anything. It was all true. I was just afraid that if you found out you'd push me away."

"I know," he said.

"I swear, the diagnosis was real. I spent the last five years of my life living with that diagnosis over my head."

"I know."

"You aren't the only one in shock here, you know. I had finally accepted it and had moved on. Then you happened, and now…this."

"I know it all."

I'd finally stopped for a moment and heard what Asher had said for the third time. I looked at him, while the words sunk into my head. "You know?" I questioned.

"I know. I know it all. After you left, I continued with my day. It was the only thing I could do. I had patients waiting. I also didn't want to accept what it was I'd just found out. When I got home, the full magnitude of what had happened sent me into spiral I couldn't control. I spent the night moping around the house, Saturday as well. When Sunday came, I left for my morning run and headed to the office to get my head back in the game. I literally let go of my last career, virtually giving up. I wasn't about to do that with this one. As I was going through patient files, focusing on my upcoming week, I found yours."

"And…"

"Don't kill me. I shouldn't have done it, I know, but I read it."

"I see."

"I quickly learned that Kavanaugh had diagnosed you as you said, but I also noticed his lack of testing. He'd not only done it to you, but I've found things in other client files that weren't necessarily done correctly. Anyway, I read through it all, and I did it with a lump in my throat and pain in my chest as my heart crumbled once again into a million pieces. I'd made assumptions based on anger and shock. I want you to know I was wrong in doing that."

"Yes, you were."

Asher took a minute. "I was also wrong to treat you the way I did. I was shocked and upset that you didn't feel comfortable enough to come to me. Most of all, as I read through everything, I realized what I'd thrown away was something I wanted, and I wanted it more than anything in my life."

"What's that?" I questioned.

Asher looked down at his hands, then looked back up at me and met my eyes. "You."

A tear slid down my cheek, and I wanted to kick myself for allowing it to happen while he was sitting right here. I was supposed to be being strong, and instead I was unraveling.

"I wanted you, and everything that comes along with you, Bella. If I'd only taken a minute to step back, take a breath, and approach this with some form of rationale then we wouldn't be in this position." He swallowed hard. "I'm so fucking sorry I hurt you, and while I can't take back what's been done, I can go forward and prove to you I'm a much better man than that," he finished, his voice shaking.

Our eyes locked. I wanted to be in his arms so bad it hurt. Tears rolled down my cheeks. I hadn't wanted to cry in front of him, and yet here I was, sitting in my car, in a grocery store parking lot, a sobbing, crying mess.

He reached over and cupped my cheek, wiping the tears away. "Shall we try again?"

ASHER

I opened my locker and pulled out a clean pair of scrubs. I stripped off the dirty ones and threw them into the hamper at the end of the aisle. I glanced to the clock on the wall. It was almost two. I threw on the pants and reached into my jeans pocket, pulling out my phone. Sure enough, I had two missed messages.

BELLA: I'm here.

BELLA: I hope you're going to make the appointment in time.

I threw my shirt over my head, locked my locker, and

rushed out of the change room heading toward the elevator. The second I'd hit the button, I messaged her.

ASHER: On my way.

Bella and I had worked every single day on our relationship over the past six weeks. She even admitted to me after we'd gotten back together that she'd asked Sawyer to set her up with a psychologist to work through the trauma her ex had caused. I could tell she'd been nervous when she told me, but I listened with patience and understanding, letting her know that there was nothing wrong with that. I'd even attended a couple of her sessions with her.

The door to my office waiting room was open, and I saw Bella sitting in the corner. She waved and placed the magazine she'd been reading down. I walked over and sat down beside her, kissing her cheek. "How you doing?"

"Okay." She smiled, taking hold of my hand. "How was your morning?"

"Crazy busy. I almost didn't think I was going to get here in time," I said. "I even put on clean scrubs for the occasion." I winked at her.

Bella laughed. "I'm kind of glad you did. It may traumatize me seeing you covered in all the... Oh God, just the thought of it is going to make me sick," she said, sitting forward and covering her mouth.

"Just breathe," I said, rubbing her back.

A few moments later, we made our way down the hall to one of the exam rooms. I waited outside while Bella changed, and when she called to me, I stepped inside. She sat at the end of the table, her socked feet dangling as she held her gown closed. I walked over to her and kissed the side of her neck.

"None of that now."

"None of what?"

"Patient/doctor shenanigans." She giggled.

I laughed. "In order for that, you'd have to be my patient. You chose my colleague." I tsked.

A knock on the door caused us both to jump a little, and in walked Alonzo. "Hey, guys," he said, washing his hands in the small sink. "How are we today?"

"A little tired," Asher said.

Alonzo looked at Bella and then at me. "Asher, I meant Bella."

The three of us laughed.

"I'm good. Feeling good," she said.

"Well then, let's get to it, shall we?" Alonzo took a seat beside the table, while I adjusted the back of the table and guided Bella to lie back. Alonzo squirted some of the jelly onto Bella's barely-there baby bump.

"God, I hate that part. It's so cold," she said, taking my hand.

I placed one elbow on the back of the table and stood beside her, my hand over hers, as I watched the screen as Alonzo moved the wand around. Then he stopped. "Before I continue, I just want to make sure you both want to know what the sex is."

Bella looked up at me, and I to her, both of us saying yes at the same time.

"Okay, just wanted to be certain. I know one of you knows how to read these." He chuckled. "Wanted to make sure it was going to be fair to everyone," he said, winking at Bella.

I felt her grip on my hand as he moved the wand around a little more, no doubt applying a little pressure. "Okay, well, everything is looking good. I am almost certain that it's a girl."

Bella looked up at me, her eyes shining with tears. I leaned down and kissed her forehead while Alonzo passed her a small towel.

"I'm just going to give you guys a few moments," he said, quietly getting up from the stool and leaving the room.

"Are you happy?" Bella asked once the door was closed.

I smiled at her, nodded my head, bent down, and met her lips. "Very," I whispered. "What about you?"

"Very… and nervous."

"No need to be. I'm here," I said, wrapping my arms around her. "I'm not going anywhere. I'm here."

Want more Asher and Bella?
GRAB THE BONUS SCENE

To get your FREE bonus scene visit
https://geni.us/DoctorRightBonusScene

DOCTOR FROST

His name suits him well and he hates Christmas. Bottom line, Doctor Frost is a grumpy jerk.

I'm sure he has his reasons. We all do. Yet I won't be his punching bag in what you could call a rather combative relationship.

The day his daughter shows up crying I take pity on him and step in to offer some womanly advice. That's when I find out the reason for his horrible demeanor, and my heart goes out to him.

I didn't expect that information to change things. Soon I find myself looking at him a little differently. We start talking, and I start getting to know his kids, and soon I'm doing more than just dreaming of tasting his lips.

Just as things begin to take a turn, a rival nurse has other plans. She is willing to do whatever it takes to keep us apart.
Only she doesn't know who she is up against. I'm feisty and Doctor Frost is grumpy and together we will fight for what we both want this Christmas.

DALTON

NOVEMBER

Rain hit my office window, the steady tap annoying me, pulling my focus away from the report I was working on. It had been a long day and combined with the steady giggling from the girls out at the front desk, I was growing more annoyed by the minute. What did they think this was, a playground?

I let out a sigh, flipped to the next screen, and went to write more of my report when I got to one section of my notes and couldn't read them. I frowned as I stared at the messy handwriting. I'd asked my nurses to add this part when I was on my way out of an appointment. They should have better penmanship than this. My writing was one thing, but this was inexcusable.

When another round of laughter erupted through my

wall, I got up from behind the desk and took off out my door and around to the front desk.

Charlotte took half a glance in my direction, stopped laughing, and focused on whatever it was she was supposed to be working on, but when I set my sights on Amelia, she sat there looking up at me with a huge grin on her face.

It was always the same with her, and it had been that way since she'd started working for me. She was always certain that people could be cured. It was exhausting when I knew that wasn't the case. I looked at Charlotte and then over to that grin again.

"Last I checked, it's only two. There are three more hours before you're finished today, which means you should do the work that needs to be done and not be goofing off. This office should be silent," I said, slamming the patient file I had questions about down on the counter in front of Amelia.

Charlotte jumped, but Amelia sat there giving me that look. She cleared her throat, rested her chin on her hand, and met my eyes.

"We are just creating a healthy work environment," she bit back. "Everyone knows laughter is good for the soul. Something you should do a little more of."

My jaw clenched as I placed my hand on the desktop and opened the file I'd brought out. Then I met her eyes. "Are you saying this isn't a healthy work environment?"

She'd been a thorn in my side ever since she'd started working for me. She was always cheerful, always bubbly, something that any doctor in this hospital would probably love to have. She was also attractive and beautiful as hell, but she was also always talking back and put a lot of effort into making my life hell. It was exhausting and, as of late, had been irritating me more than ever.

"Is there something you needed? If not, I'd like to go back to laughing and having fun while we finish out our day." She rested her chin on her hand, giving me that adorable grin I absolutely hated.

I shoved the file at her as I stared down into those big cinnamon eyes. "Page three…halfway down there is some sort of scribble. Can you tell me what you wrote there?" I questioned, remembering that it was her working with me that day.

She smiled at me, slowly taking the file while looking me directly in the eyes. "Sure thing, Doctor Frost!"

She opened the file, flipped to the third page, and ran her finger down the page, stopping at the scribble mark. She studied it for a moment as I watched her, then frowned and swallowed hard before looking back at me. Did she not know what it said, either?

"Well?" I grunted.

"This mark here?" she asked.

"Yes, Amelia, that mark right there."

"Geez, I'd love to help you out, but I don't have a clue what it is. Besides, that is your handwriting," she said, pressing her lips together as she closed the file and placed it back on the counter in front of me.

I looked at her, at those beautiful cinnamon eyes, growing more irritated by the second as she looked up at me while the phone rang. Charlotte quickly grabbed it, whispering as I locked eyes with Amelia.

"And you know, you really ought to say please when you ask someone to help you with something. Just adds, oh...I don't know, a touch of something to the question." She shrugged.

I felt as if my head were going to explode. She'd been on me about that recently whenever I'd given her direct orders on anything. She reminded me every single time, just like now, that I should say please and thank you.

"Amelia..." I barked, only to be stopped by Charlotte quietly clearing her throat.

"Doctor Frost?" she said, her voice squeaking.

I turned my attention toward her, waiting for her to speak.

"What?" I barked when she didn't immediately start talking.

"One of your patients would like to see you..." she said, her voice cracking. "She's up on floor fifteen, room 223."

I glanced at my watch and then let out a sigh. I'd already done my rounds for today. I'd had all the patient interaction I'd wanted. I was about to tell her to put it off until tomorrow when I saw Amclia looking at me.

"Fine. Pull the file, Amelia. Let's go."

Only she didn't move. She just sat there, giving me that same smug smile she'd given me for the past few minutes.

"NOW!" I barked, causing her to jump for the first time. Poor Charlotte almost dropped the phone and had to take a drink before she answered the line and let them know we were on our way.

I didn't wait for another word. I took off out of my office and made my way toward the elevator, quickly pressing the call button, hoping I could get up there before she arrived, but just as the doors opened, Amelia appeared at my side. We both loaded into the elevator and stood in silence as we waited to get to the fifteenth floor.

We made our way to the unit the patient was in, and I quickly exchanged information with the doctors and nurses on duty before I decided if I actually needed to see the patient or just change her treatment plan. At least they'd called me to get my opinion before doing anything. Once I'd gotten the information I needed, I made my decision and looked over at Amelia, who waited patiently by my side, pen at the ready to make any notes.

"Go tell Mrs. Jackson I'm switching her off the medication that is making her sick to a new one," I muttered, while writing down the name of the new medication in the chart for the nurses.

When I handed the clipboard back to the nurse and turned toward Amelia, she was staring at me.

"What is it?" I questioned.

"Does that mean you aren't going to come in and talk to her?" she questioned. "She specifically asked to see you. She probably has questions."

I averted my eyes. I swore if she started, I was going to explode. I let out the breath I was holding and then looked back at her and nodded over to the right. I took a few steps and waited until she made her way over to me.

"Amelia, there is no need for me to go in and speak with her. You can take care of this."

"Doctor Frost, that woman has been your patient since she got sick. You really should—"

"Amelia, worry about yourself and what I just told you to do. Now, go and speak with her."

"Seriously? She's dying, Dalton." Amelia frowned, looking up at me.

As I studied her, I noticed her eyes getting watery. "I know, it's you that normally doesn't acknowledge that."

Amelia looked at me. I was certain I saw a hint of a

tear in her eyes, but she swallowed hard and straightened her back. "Dalton…"

"Amelia, don't make the patient wait any longer. I have to go. I have work to do and test results to go over. I need to prepare for the day tomorrow, and so do you. It's best you take care of this patient now, rather than later." Without waiting for her to respond, I turned and went to take a step when I heard Amelia clear her throat.

"I can't believe you! Are you serious? You really won't speak with her?"

I looked over my shoulder at her, at the disappointment and anger on her face. "Yes, Amelia, believe it," I said, taking another couple of steps away from her.

"What about please? What if I ask you to please speak with her?" she begged.

I didn't have time for games. Ignoring her, I made my way to the elevator where I hit the call button and waited. While I waited, I glanced over my shoulder to see if she'd done what I'd asked. Instead, I saw her wipe at her eyes and then glare at me.

The elevator doors opened, and I stepped inside, turning to see her still standing there, the look in her eyes now one of disappointment. I didn't care, though; I hit the button for my fifth-floor office and watched as the doors closed.

It was a little after seven when I shut the light off in my office and pulled the door closed. The office was dark aside from the small overhead lights at the check-in counter, which normally stayed on until the last person left, which was normally me.

I reached to turn them off when I heard something hit the floor. I glanced around the corner to see Amelia bent down on one knee, picking up a stack of files, stacking them once again into a neat pile.

"What are you still doing here?"

She jumped and dropped the stacked files off her knee as she looked over her shoulder at me.

"Oh my god, you scared me. I thought you left hours ago," she muttered, picking up the files and stacking them again.

"You didn't answer me," I barked.

She didn't say anything as I waited, and then she let out a sigh.

"You didn't answer me either. If you need to know, I'm here because Mrs. Jackson had questions and concerns, so I stayed with her for over an hour and a half, doing my best to answer them. I then had to finish up my work for today and prep for tomorrow, which was what I was doing until you made me drop the patient files."

Why had she been with the patient that long when all she needed to do was give her a simple answer?

"What questions did she have?"

Amelia huffed and looked over toward me as she stood up. "If you wanted to know, you should have gone to see her," she barked.

"Well, if you needed help, you should have called me."

Ignoring me, she grabbed the rest of the files and put them in a messy pile as she muttered something under her breath.

"What was that?" I questioned, my voice taking on a stern tone.

She let out a sigh and shook her head.

"What did you say, Amelia?"

She stood up and turned toward me. "I said, lots of good that would do. You couldn't even take five minutes to come in and see her, as if I was going to call you."

"Amelia, you've worked with me for what, a year? You should know I don't hold the hands of my patients. Now, if they have a concern, of course, it's my job to answer them, but…"

"That's just it. It is your job, not mine. You should have been there to listen to her. Instead, you couldn't or wouldn't. I'm not sure which it was because you claimed you had work to do. So, why on earth would I call you and bother you? I took the time, answering questions I'm not even sure I gave the correct answers to, even though I had work to do as well, which is why I am still here."

"Amelia, that's enough. I don't like your tone."

"You know, last I checked, you are a doctor, and you are supposed to have some sort of bedside manner. Instead, all I've seen is a cold-hearted man who treats patients as objects instead of showing compassion to the emotional, scared people they become when they are ill. It's disgusting."

If ever I'd felt irritated, it was now, right at this moment. She'd overstepped. I had a fucking heart, and I showed compassion, and I had a fucking great bedside manner. All she needed to do was look at the awards I'd gotten in the last year. I was about to speak, but she held out her hand, stopping me.

"Dalton, I don't want to hear it. All you do is stomp around, yell out orders as if we are some sort of waitstaff instead of colleagues. We can't laugh, we can't have fun. You know the other day Mrs. Linton even commented how different this office had become, and she'd only been in here to pick up her prescription. I don't know who the hell ever pissed you off that bad, to make you into this sort of person. Life in this office is a living hell sometimes, but I can't imagine what home must be like for you. Honestly, I feel sorry for your significant other, if this is what she has to deal with day in and day out."

Amelia, red-faced and out of breath slammed the stack of files down on the desk. She bent over, grabbed her purse from the drawer, and then went for her coat, but the phone rang. Not thinking, she grabbed the receiver and in an almost unrecognizable voice from the last few moments sang, "Hello…"

She didn't look at me. Instead, she shoved the phone out in front of her.

"We don't answer calls after the office is closed. Now, take a message and I'll call them back in the morning," I barked.

"It's your daughter. Do you want to take it, or would you like me to tell her what a grump you are?" she questioned, looking me directly in the eye.

I was seething with anger as I ripped the phone from her hand. "Hello."

"Dad…sorry to call you at work. Mrs. Jenkins wanted to know what to prepare for supper tonight. You left nothing on the sheet."

I looked up to see Amelia staring at me with hateful eyes. I'd definitely have to deal with her, but right now, I needed to get home to the kids. Her words, which were way out of line, had struck a chord, one I didn't even remember having. Had I really become that bad?

Okay, perhaps I'd grown a little cold here at work,

but she had no right to attack my personal life the way she had. That was far over the bounds of a professional relationship.

"Tell Mrs. Jenkins I'll be bringing home dinner. I should be there in…oh, thirty minutes," I said, glancing at my watch and then back at Amelia. "See you soon," I said, and then held the receiver out in front of me for Amelia to take.

She hesitantly grabbed the receiver from my hand, hanging it up. I was going to say something to her, reprimand her for answering the phone, but decided against it. Instead, I turned and made my way to my office and stopped at the door. I didn't need to look back, I knew she was staring at me. I could feel her eyes boring into the back of my head.

"Oh, Amelia. Take tomorrow off. I'll see you back here on Wednesday. Then I will figure out what the punishment shall be for talking back to your boss."

I didn't give her time to respond; I pushed the door open and walked out of the office, doing my best to calm down before heading home to my kids.

AMELIA

I sat inside The Cooling Rack, waiting for Charlotte to meet me after her shift. It was probably a good thing he'd forced me to take the day off today, to give me time to cool down. If only it had worked. I was still angry over everything that had happened yesterday but was now starting to feel sick.

To top it off, I woke up with a horrible headache, teetering on the edge of a migraine and probably would have either called in or went home sick anyway. Or it could have ended up way worse. Perhaps, I would have told him off again and would have found myself jobless, or maybe he'd already decided my fate, and I didn't know I was jobless. I already knew that option wasn't off the table. I'd been pretty horrible to him, and even though I regretted some of the things I'd said, I knew in my mind he'd deserved it.

I'd worked for Doctor Frost, or Dalton as most co-workers referred to him, for almost a year, and he'd been an asshole since day one. I'd hoped that over time there would have been something, some sort of gentler, softer side to him, but there was nothing. He was nothing but short, snippy, and rude to everyone who crossed his path, but it seemed he was worse with me. I swore the only reason he kept his job was because his patients loved him. Even when I'd sat with Mrs. Jackson, she couldn't say a bad thing about him, which blew my mind.

Staff differed from patients. They all had the same feelings toward him I did. At least that was what they told me. I'd brought him up to Connie, the head RN in the hospital. She worked in the emergency department and there had been a couple of times I'd helped out there after a run-in with him. She'd listen and sympathize but then would be different to him in person.

It always blew my mind how no one stood up to him, either. He'd bark orders at them, and they would just do as they were told. Only when it came to me, he was way worse. I would not cower from him like the rest of them, which was why I'd blown up at him. It honestly hadn't surprised me I'd finally lost control over myself when he wouldn't come and speak with that sweet woman who spent over an hour crying on my shoulder. In my mind, it wouldn't hurt the man to show some sort of compassion once in a while.

"My god, what did you do?" Charlotte whispered under her breath as she slid into the seat across from me.

"What? Why?" I questioned, wondering if maybe he had changed overnight and became human.

She blew out the breath she was holding and looked over at me. "That man was more than unbearable today. If you think he's cranky on a normal day…" She looked up at me, her eyes wide. "He was hellish today. So, whatever you said to him last night pissed him off."

I looked down at the menu in front of me, still trying to decide what it was I wanted to order as I thought about everything I'd said to him last night. Thank God Charlotte hadn't been there to witness it.

"I stood up to him. It wasn't anything that didn't need to be said, except, well, except for the fact I may have overstepped with my words when it came to his personal life. But, honestly, Charlotte, the man deserved it."

"You what? You mean you actually talked back to Doctor Frost? Like while you were working, and you brought his personal life into it?" she questioned, her eyes widening with disbelief.

I nodded.

"What did he say?"

"He said nothing. The man was actually speechless

for once, and you should have seen the look on his face. It was like he didn't care at all about what I was saying."

"I bet he did."

"I'm telling you, it fell on deaf ears."

"Maybe at the moment, but not afterward. I think whatever you said stirred something inside of him. I've never seen him act the way he did today. He was worse than ever. He even lost it with Sawyer and Connie."

Here I'd hoped what I said would have struck a chord and turned him into the opposite of what he was. Instead, from the sounds of it, I'd made it worse.

"I probably should have kept my mouth shut, but honestly, when he wouldn't go see Mrs. Jackson, I guess that was my breaking point. Honestly, that wasn't really the last straw, it was the fact that she had nothing bad to say about him at all. She sat there thanking him for changing the one medication, praising him for being an amazing doctor. The woman is dying, she was upset and scared and had a pile of questions. Her doctor refused to see her, and here she is upset as hell, of course, thanking a man who couldn't care less. It just pissed me off."

Charlotte nodded in understanding. Then looked up at me. "Are you afraid of facing him tomorrow?"

I shook my head. What was there to be afraid of? He's a grumpy, uncaring asshole. I only called it like it was.

"No. I'm sure he'll be his usual charming self toward me tomorrow, like always."

I could see all the questions lining her eyes, maybe even a hint of worry. She looked at me and bit her bottom lip.

"What is it?"

She let out a sigh. "Aren't you afraid he may fire you?"

I thought for a moment and then shook my head. "No, I think if he were going to do that, he would have done it last night after I told him I questioned how his significant other could stand to be around him."

"Amelia, you didn't." Charlotte looked at me with horrified eyes.

"Damn right I did. Like I said, I lost it. I couldn't take his lack of caring any longer." I shrugged, just as my cell phone vibrated against the table. I glanced down to see an email from Doctor Frost requesting my presence at a meeting tomorrow. I shoved my phone over to Charlotte and showed her the email. She bit her bottom lip as she read the message and then looked up at me, concern flooding her face.

"Well, all I can say is good luck with that tomorrow."

I'D SHOWN up to work early because of the meeting. Instead of finding Dalton in his office, it was empty. I figured he was running late, and instead of dwelling on it, I went about my morning calling his patients to schedule their upcoming appointments.

Dalton still hadn't arrived by ten thirty, which I thought was odd, but again I wasn't going to worry about it. Instead, I grabbed my things and was about to head down on my break when the phone rang. It was Sawyer, one of the head ER doctors, requesting my help in the emergency room, which I happily volunteered for. If it meant getting out of this meeting with Mr. Grumpy, I was in.

I stopped and grabbed a coffee and bagel and then made my way over to the emergency room. The ER was crazy and looked like a bomb had gone off inside, which wasn't out of the ordinary. I placed my things behind the nurses' station, and that was when I saw Dalton. He was dealing with a patient over in the corner.

I sat down and took a bite of my bagel, waiting for Connie to give me some instruction. Not only was

Connie my direct boss, but she was also Eastport General's gossip queen.

"Thanks for coming down. It must be nice to be recognized around here," she said, smiling as she sat down beside me.

"What do you mean?" I questioned.

"Well, I shouldn't tell you, but Dalton requested you."

"What?" I frowned.

She was about to say something when another ambulance pulled up to the bay doors just as Dalton appeared with some files, which he put on the desk. He looked at me as the EMTs brought a man in on a stretcher.

"Stabbing…" the one EMT mumbled to Dalton as they took him over toward an empty room.

"Amelia, looks like it's you and me. Let's go," he muttered.

Those are the nicest words the man has ever said to me, I thought to myself as I looked over at Connie, wondering what she'd meant, when I heard Dalton clear his throat.

"Coming."

I got up from my chair as two other nurses came rushing over to help us. It was touch-and-go for a while. The patient had lost a lot of blood, but we finally got him stabilized. Once our job was done, I stepped out of the room, closing the curtain and pulling my gloves off, dumping them into the trash while the other two nurses worked on finishing up the stitches.

I took my blood-covered gown off and dumped it into the laundry and then made my way over to the sink and began washing my hands when I heard someone clear their throat behind me. Glancing over my shoulder, I saw Sawyer standing there.

"Sorry, I'll be just a moment," I said, rinsing the soap from my hands.

"Amelia, you can head down on your break now. Janice just got in," Sawyer said, coming up beside me and shoving his hands under the warm water.

"Thanks." I smiled. "What a day. I'm beat, and I still have another, what, four hours?" I giggled.

"All part of the job. Keeps us young." He chuckled. "Brielle said you came into The Cooling Rack yesterday. She said it was nice to see you."

"Yeah, I had coffee with Charlotte. I was hoping she'd have Emma, but no luck. She doing well?"

"Yeah, she's getting so big. We'll have to have you over for dinner soon."

"I'd love that! Well, I guess I'll see you in an hour." I smiled and made my way down the hall toward the exit doors.

"Thanks for coming down last second. We appreciate it."

"No problem." I waved. "Glad I could help. It feels great to save lives."

I was just about to push the doors open to exit the emergency area when I heard my name called. Figuring it was Sawyer again, I stopped and turned, only to see Dalton following me.

"Wait up a moment," he said again.

Unsure what to expect, I just stood there waiting until he caught up with me. He'd missed our meeting, so he couldn't be pissed with me. He never thanked me for helping, which would have been nice after that last patient, but he said nothing. He just looked at me.

"Aren't you going to say anything? Thank me for an outstanding job?" I questioned, probably pushing my luck.

His eyes locked with mine. He just glared. Then he pushed the door open and took off in front of me.

"Yeah, you're welcome!" I shouted after him.

I stood there wishing that the things I'd said to him the other night would have resonated with him, but they apparently hadn't. Charlotte was right, he had become worse. At least, before he'd tell me I had to do a better job.

I was just about to push the doors open when Connie came out of the supply room with a handful of stuff.

"Connie, what did you mean earlier, that it must be nice to be recognized?" I questioned.

Connie stopped and smiled. "Well, by Dalton, of course."

"Huh?"

"He was the one who told Sawyer to call you. Said he wanted to work with one of the best nurses in the hospital. I just thought it must be nice to be thought of that way. I'll have to put that in your file."

I could have fainted right on the spot. Dalton had spoken about me that way? There was no way in hell he actually said those words after the way I'd spoken to him.

"What's your secret? It would be nice if some of the other nurses were looked upon that way with the other doctors."

I swallowed hard and smiled, trying to come up with something other than to tell your boss off because that was what I'd done, and it had somehow earned me respect. It wasn't an appropriate answer to tell your direct boss though.

I swallowed hard. "Ah, just tell them to be a good team player. It took a long while to get noticed," I said, smiling. "I'm gonna grab some food. See you soon." I needed to get out of there before I did faint.

"Dalton, welcome home," Mrs. Jenkins said as I walked through the door. Christmas music played, and the smell of dinner caused my stomach to grumble.

She began shoving the kids' shoes into the closet, then made her way into the living room tidying up where Tommy had clearly been playing with some toys after school.

"Good evening, Betty. How are you and the kids?" I questioned, hanging my coat in the closet, then taking off my shoes.

"Oh, I'm good and, of course, they're fine. Claire is doing her homework in the kitchen, and Tommy is upstairs working on his project. Neither of them wanted to eat their vegetables tonight. Apparently, Tommy no longer likes carrots and Claire no longer wants to eat corn, but that is how it goes."

Mrs. Jenkins had worked for us since Claire was born. When Kenzie passed, she stepped up and began working for us full time, helping me raise the kids and allowing me to continue my practice. She was part of the family.

I smiled. "That figures, last week, that was all they wanted." I chuckled as I placed my laptop bag down on the floor inside the doorway.

"How was your day at the hospital?"

"Hectic. Sorry I couldn't make it back in time for dinner, which smells delicious, by the way." I glanced at my watch, cringing. "Again, I'm sorry. I know you like to be home with your son by now."

"Dalton, it's nothing to worry about. After all these years, I know things get out of control at the hospital."

She continued to run around, picking up the toys Tommy had left, and then was about to head on down the hall toward the kitchen when I stopped her.

"Betty, you've done enough for today," I said.

"Nonsense. I was just going to plate your dinner, throw in a load of laundry, and do the dishes. Then I'll be on my way."

"No. I've kept you long enough today. You head on home. I can take care of those things. Plus, I know your son isn't here all the time and that you want to spend some time with your own grandkids."

"I know, but you and your children need me, too."

"I know. In all seriousness, you go. I'll drop the kids off at school in the morning and we will see you tomorrow night." I smiled.

"You're sure?" she asked, looking around at the mess that was still left to clean up. "There is still a lot to do."

"I'm positive." I smiled.

I waited at the door and helped her with her coat and then wished her a good night. Once I knew she was in her car and had backed out of the driveway, I made my way down to the kitchen, where I found Claire sitting at the table, agonizing over her homework.

"Hey there, sweetheart. How was school?" I questioned, plating up my dinner from the leftovers in the pan on the stove, popping it into the microwave to reheat it.

"Fine," she muttered.

"Only fine?" I chuckled.

I watched as she stared at her notebook, chewing on the end of her pencil like she was working on the hardest question in the world.

"What is it?" I questioned, just as the microwave beeped. "Do you need some help?"

"Oh no, I'm okay," she said, still staring at the paper in front of her.

"Okay then."

I grabbed my plate and carried it over to the table where I sat down and cut into chicken and popped a piece into my mouth.

"Dad…can I ask you something?"

"Of course. Anything."

As she smiled up at me, all I could see was my wife. God, she looked just like Kenzie, and the older she got, the more the resemblance stood out. She had her hair and her eyes, even her smile was the same. Some days, it was hard to look at her without remembering everything about my wife, not that she was ever far from my mind.

"Well…there is this dance at school…"

"Ah, yes, I saw that permission form on the fridge door. The Christmas dance, right?" I questioned.

"Yes, you said I could go."

"Yes, and I signed the form. You took it into school, right? Or do I need to talk to your teacher?"

She nodded. "No, I took it in."

"Good." I turned my attention back to my plate. "So, what is this question you want to ask me?"

"Dad, I was wondering, would it be okay if I got my hair done for that? I've been saving my allowance, but I am short," she asked, looking up at me with hope in her eyes.

I looked at her, at her beautiful brown hair that had natural copper highlights, exactly like her mother, and cleared my throat.

"What did you want to do to your hair?"

She looked up at me and shrugged. "I just wanted to get it cut a little."

Relief flooded me. I was hoping she didn't want to colour it like some girls in her grade. Her hair was far too beautiful to change, and I'd have had a hard time agreeing to that.

"I think that could be done, and you keep your allowance." I winked.

"Thanks, Dad." Clair smiled and went back to her homework just as Tommy came into the kitchen, pulling the juice carton from the fridge with his small hands.

"What you doing there, sport?" I asked, watching him struggle to reach the table.

"I want some juice." He shrugged before making his way over to the cupboard to grab his cup off the counter.

He placed the cup down and was about to open the carton of juice, only I stopped him and did it for him, pouring him half a glass, then placing his glass in front of the empty chair.

"Thanks, Dad."

He sat down on the chair beside me while I continued to eat my dinner and Clair worked on her homework. I smiled as both my kids sat with me. We'd all gone through a hard change after losing Kenzie. She was taken so suddenly, and it had changed all of us. We'd all struggled to find a new dynamic, making our smaller family life work. It was hard, stressful, and I worried how not having a other might affect Clair and Tommy in the future. I did my best to be there for both of them, but I barely understood my own feelings.

"How would you guys like to hit the Christmas market on the weekend with Mrs. Jenkins?" I questioned.

Claire's eyes lit up. The Christmas market was something she'd always done with her mother and since she'd passed, I'd avoided the topic. Honestly, it had been hell even thinking of this time of year, since Kenzie had died so close to her favourite holiday.

"YES!!!!" she screamed, her eyes lighting up! "I can't wait!"

"What about you, sport?"

Tommy nodded as he drank his juice.

"Okay, it's a date. Get your homework done." I winked as I took the last couple bites of my chicken, sat back, and watched my kids.

"ALRIGHT, GUYS, OUT YOU GO," I said, pulling up in front of the school, waiting while the kids gathered their things before getting out of the car.

"Tommy, you have your lunch, right?" I questioned, looking in the rear-view mirror at my son.

"He better. I put it in his bag this morning," Claire said, grabbing her schoolbag and throwing it over her shoulder, then looking over at her younger brother as he grinned up at her. "I swear, if you took it out of there, you're on your own," Claire said.

"Tommy, stop bugging your sister and check your bag, please. Last thing I need is a phone call from the school saying I didn't send a lunch."

"I got it," Tommy shouted as he looked inside his bag and zipped it back up.

"What about you?" I questioned, glancing at my watch to see I still had lots of time before I needed to be at the office.

"Lunch money," Claire said, holding up the twenty dollars I'd given her this morning.

"Spend it wisely." I winked. "Not on fries and junk."

"Dad, can't you just let me enjoy junk for once with my friends instead of shoving healthy food down my throat?" Claire said, rolling her eyes.

"Fine, but only today." I chuckled as she shut the door and then turned and smiled my way. Watching until I knew they were both safe inside, I pulled away from the sidewalk and toward work.

I stopped on my way at The Cooling Rack for a coffee and just as I pulled into the hospital parking lot, rain started coming down. I looked up at the sky, hoping that snow was in the forecast for the Christmas market, or I knew Claire and Tommy would be disappointed.

With hot coffee in my hand, I made my way toward the hospital. I was just about to the employee entrance when Amelia came rushing around the corner, almost banging the coffee from my hand.

"Whoa," I said, pulling my coffee into the air, "slow down there."

"Sorry about that," she muttered as she looked up from her phone. Those pretty cinnamon eyes of hers met mine.

When she wasn't opening her mouth and giving me a snarky attitude all day, she reminded me of Kenzie. I held the door open for her and waited for her to step inside.

She looked up at me with shock, then stepped through the door, shifting her purse to the other hand as she turned and smiled up at me.

"Thank you, Dalton."

Even the way she said my name reminded me of my late wife. There was nothing I could do. I had to walk away. So, ignoring her, I pulled open the next door and once again waited until she walked through, then turned to make my way down a different hallway. I didn't believe in following my nurses to the office, anyway; I preferred to make my way into my office on my own.

"That would be when you're supposed to say you are welcome!" Sshe yelled in my direction.

I held my hand up and waved without looking back. As I continued down the hall, I finally heard her stomp her foot on the floor and let out a huff. That was when I turned to see her march on down the hall the way she'd been going, and I smiled to myself.

There were times I loved seeing her get all riled up. Somehow, it added enjoyment to my day. Like I said, she was a pretty woman, and for whatever reason, getting under her skin was something I looked forward to. I wasn't sure if it was the fact that she even acted like my precious Kenzie when she'd get upset with me or if it was because there was no one in this entire hospital in the past three years that had ever thought to stand up to me. I was hoping it was the latter, and not the fact that I was certain I was crushing on my nurse.

My head pounded as I made my way to the cafeteria. The lights flickered as another crack of thunder and flash of lightning boomed across the sky.

"Ugh, isn't it supposed to be snowing?" I whined, coming up beside Charlotte, who had come in today to do some volunteer work for the staff Christmas party.

"You are in luck. It's in the forecast. Supposed to drop a couple inches by Friday, then it will finally look like Christmas." She smiled, looking at me. "Another headache?"

"Yeah, I already took some headache medicine, but I'm thinking this one just might be the beginnings of a migraine setting in."

"Hopefully not. How's Dalton today?"

I rolled my eyes. "God, he's impossible. Maybe worse than he was yesterday in the emergency room. Honestly, I don't know how much more of him I can take. He's just so…toxic. Did you know he is the only doctor in the entire hospital who hasn't decorated his office for Christmas? I noticed that this morning when I came in. I feel bad for our patients. Honestly, I'm tempted to bring in some decorations for the desk. You should do the same."

She smiled. "I worked for someone like that at the last hospital I was at. It's draining, that is for sure, especially at this time of the year."

"He's just so doom and gloom all the time. Doesn't he know this is supposed to be the most wonderful time of the year? He should be singing 'Jingle Bells' and smiling all the time. If not for his own peace of mind and mental health, then for the health and well-being of our patients. Thank God I have you to laugh with."

"I know. At least we make our own fun." She laughed.

I grabbed an apple and placed it on my tray, then an egg salad sandwich and a chocolate bar, followed by a soda.

"Although, we should remember that the holidays aren't the same for everyone, but I agree the office could use a little holiday spirit," she said, eyeing the food on my tray. "I haven't seen you ingest that much sugar in a while, especially with a headache."

I was normally a healthy eater, but today I was craving junk food. Dalton had tested my patience in more ways than one. Not only was I irritated, but it felt like someone was squeezing my head in a vise, and it didn't help that I was feeling highly emotional because most of the time my food choices reflected that.

"Yeah, I know. I shouldn't, but I can't help it." I shrugged. "Not today."

"Try to put a smile on that beautiful face." She giggled. "I know…it's that bad."

"I am," I said as we both laughed at her last comment, as I looked down at my sugar loaded tray.

We stepped up to the register, and we both paid, then we said our goodbyes and I went and sat down at an empty table in the cafeteria's corner. I needed to unwind and try to get rid of this headache before I went back to deal with my grump of a boss.

I cracked open my soda, took a bite of my sandwich, and began checking emails when I heard a high-pitched scream. I glanced up to see a young girl standing in the centre of the cafeteria, her hair an absolute disaster, her cheeks red and tear stained.

I frowned, wondering what was going on, and almost immediately I had my answer when she stepped to the side and I saw none other than Dalton sitting at the table.

No doubt he was the cause of why she was acting this way.

I rolled my eyes. Dalton was everywhere I was, even in the breakroom. I watched from a distance as the young girl stomped her foot and pointed to her head and started crying. I'd had enough.

Dalton looked panicked as he looked around the room. He didn't know what to do, and if people weren't staring, I'd have probably just sat there and watched everything unfold. I was interested to see how the man who caused chaos in my life daily would handle the chaos this young girl was causing him. However, when she screamed again, my head almost exploded, so instead of just sitting there and watching, I got up from my seat and made my way over to where he sat, trying to calm the girl down with no luck.

"Dalton, I couldn't help but overhear…is there anything I can do to help?" I questioned, looking down at the young girl's tear-filled eyes.

One look at her told me she must be his daughter, and one look from him told me I was interrupting this special father-daughter bonding moment.

"Not now, Amelia," he barked, then focused his attention on his daughter.

"Claire, I don't know what you want me to do about this," he said back to the young girl who broke down into tears again.

Ignoring his orders like I normally did, I knelt down beside her and turned her toward me before she let out another one of those nails-on-the-chalkboard screeching screams.

"What's wrong, sweetheart?" I questioned, looking up into her tear-filled eyes.

She looked at her father first and then at me. Wiping her eyes, she let out a sigh.

"I wanted to get my hair done at the same place my friend went to, but Dad chose the place instead and look at what they did. It's a disaster. I have a dance tonight, and I can't go like this. The kids will make fun of me. It's never gonna look right, and it's all his fault."

I glanced over at Dalton, who was watching me. He looked angry that I'd disobeyed him, but he clearly did not know how to fix this issue.

"I don't think your dad did this," I said, meeting his eyes.

He shrugged at me.

"He picked the salon." She sobbed.

I held my hand out toward him, hopefully signalling him to not say anything, as Claire wrapped her arms around me and cried against me.

"It's okay," I said, turning my attention back to her. "I could help you if you like. We could head over to the washroom. I have some things in my locker that I can use to fix your hair," I said.

She lifted her head, and those tear-filled eyes stared back at me. "Really?"

I nodded. "Yep, we can get you looking perfect in no time." I smiled.

"Can I, Dad?" she asked. "Please?"

Dalton just glared at me, not saying anything.

"Come, sweetheart," I said, gently placing my arm around her and guiding her toward the locker room. I knew if I gave Dalton time to answer, she'd more than likely have a meltdown. I knew how the man worked. He took pleasure in saying no.

"Amelia, she'll be fine. She's overreacting," I heard Dalton say as we walked away.

I ignored him as I heard him call my name again. We continued on to the locker room, where I helped her climb up on the counter before getting my things from my locker. I quickly started working on her hair. Twenty minutes later, I had her cute new hairstyle brushed out and styled.

"Wow!" she said excitedly as she hopped off the counter and glanced at herself in the mirror.

"You like?" I questioned.

"Very much. Thank you, Amelia," she said, wrapping her arms around my waist. "You should be a hair-dresser!"

"You are welcome. Now for one finishing touch. How about a spritz of hairspray?"

The young girl looked up at me. "I'd like that, doubt my dad will."

I smiled and carefully sprayed her hair with a couple of spritzes. A part of me cheered inside, knowing that Dalton would probably hate it.

"There you go." I smiled before carefully putting my things back into the small bag I carried them in for emergencies.

The young girl studied herself in the mirror and then turned to me. "Thank you, Amelia."

"You are welcome, Claire. Now, how about we head back to where your father is and you can show him?"

"How did you do this?" she questioned, while I quickly washed my hands.

"Ah, just things you learn as a girl." I smiled. "You will learn eventually as well."

Sadness fell over her face as Claire looked in the mirror. "Oh," she whispered.

"What is it?"

"Did you learn those things from your mom?"

I smiled and nodded. "I did."

It was then I noticed her eyes watered. "Oh. I wish I had a mom to teach me those things."

A wave of guilt and shock rolled through me at the same time as I looked down at this little girl, who finally looked up at me and smiled. Was Dalton divorced? Was their mother not a part of their lives? Did she run out on her children? Then I thought back to the other night, at the words I spewed at Dalton, and I swallowed hard, for once feeling guilty at how horrible I'd been in that moment.

"Well, Claire, if you ever need anything, I'd be happy to help you. I work with your dad, so you can always reach me at the office." I winked.

I opened the door and held it while Claire ran out and right over to Dalton, who was standing across the hall from the women's locker room. He took a couple of moments with Claire, hugged her, and watched as she ran off toward an older woman who stood there with a young boy.

I smiled as I watched their exchange and then turned to head back to the cafeteria and finish my lunch just as Dalton locked eyes with me. The look in his eyes differed this time from how he normally looked at me. It was softer, lighter, almost as if he were smiling.

I gave him what I was sure was a confused smile. It was almost as if there was now a human component to him for the first time since I'd met him, and I was really unsure how to take it. As we stood there looking at one another, I almost felt as if he were looking into my soul. I swallowed hard, nodded, and walked back to the cafeteria when I heard him call my name.

I stopped and glanced over my shoulder at him.

"Amelia, I just want to say, thank you."

Shock at his words ran through me.

Without another word, he opened the door to the stairwell and was gone. I stood there, not sure what to do or how to accept what had just happened. In those mere seconds, for the first time, I finally glimpsed a completely different man.

DALTON

I STARED at the wall in front of me, the tip of my pen resting on my lip. I'd not been able to get this afternoon out of my head. Watching Amelia deal with Claire had done something to me.

When she'd first approached us, I wanted her to leave, but then watching her actually care enough to help my daughter opened something inside of me I hadn't felt in a while. I already knew she had a compassionate side, and she already reminded me so much of my Kenzie, and that action right there had only added to it.

After all, it was me and my child, and Amelia hated me with a passion and would do anything and everything to irritate. After she told me off the other night, I figured she'd apologize and beg for my forgiveness because she is always all about please and thank you and I'm sorry, but she still hadn't apologized. Her words that night had hit me, and they'd hit me hard. I hadn't realized how distant I'd become with my patients, my staff and coworkers, and even with my own kids. I really didn't know how to deal with anything anymore.

I made my way through the cafeteria line, picking up a few items and placing them on the tray, then I made my way up to the cashier and quickly paid for them, asking for everything to be put in a bag.

I walked through the hospital, over to the emergency department, and ran right into Sawyer.

"Hey, Dalton, what's up? Figured you'd be home by now." He glaced at the bag I carried.

"I would be, but I had to deliver this first. Is Amelia here still?" I questioned. "She, um, she forgot this in the office, and I wanted to bring it to her before I locked the door," I lied.

"Yep, she's behind the desk, or at least was when I was down there."

"Thanks, have a good night."

Sawyer looked at me with a confused expression. "Ah, you too, Dalton."

After returning from lunch, Amelia worked in the office for about half an hour before coming to my office and knocking on the door. When I looked up, she notified me she was planning to finish out her shift today in the emergency department if I didn't need her for anything. It had come as a surprise. She'd been one of the most steady and loyal employees I'd had, only ever taking a shift in another department when they were overrun. Otherwise, she'd find things to do in my office.

I'd granted her permission, but only because I figured the department was slammed and Sawyer had asked her to help like he normally did. Only it was quiet.

I rounded the corner and saw her sitting typing away on the computer. I walked over and placed the bag of food on the desk beside her. Getting her dinner was the least I could do for helping with Claire.

Startled, Amelia looked up at me.

"What is that??" she questioned, glancing at the bag and back to me.

"Well, you were kind enough to help Claire this morning during your break, and it's getting close to dinnertime. I thought you might be hungry, so I grabbed you something to eat for your last break. Just sort of payback." I shrugged.

"I didn't do it for you, or for compensation," she said, letting out a huff before slamming the pen she held down on the desk.

"It's not compensation." I frowned.

"Then what is it? Because that is what it feels like, and you said it was payback."

"Amelia, it was a simple thank you. One I think you should accept, and you will accept it."

"Always so bossy," she muttered.

Our eyes locked for a moment and then I broke away, heading back out of the emergency area, completely bugged that she'd actually think I'd try to pay her for helping.

"Dalton," I heard from behind me and glanced over my shoulder to see Amelia following me.

"Look, just accept the food," I said, spinning around and facing her.

She halted and looked at me. "I don't appreciate being told what I'm going to do or not do. I helped her because I genuinely cared, and for you to think otherwise of me is just…it's just…well, it's not fair."

She went to push past me, but I stopped her, grabbing her arms and holding her in front of me.

"Amelia, I thought nothing other than that. It actually shocked me."

"It shocked you I'd want to help someone?" she questioned. "I'm in the medical field, Dalton. Helping people is what I do."

"It shocked me because I know how you feel about me."

She frowned as she met my eyes. "What is that supposed to mean?"

"Amelia, just stop, okay? I know you can't stand

me. I don't need that to be written for me to understand it. I see the way you look at me, the things you do to irritate me. I just…it was really nice is all, and honestly, in case you couldn't tell, I needed the help. It meant a lot, she um…she doesn't have a woman in her life to help her with these sorts of things. I do my best, but let's be honest, there are just things a girl needs her mother for."

"I agree. That was why I told her that if she needed anything, she could always call me."

"If that is the case, then I insist you keep the lunch."

"Again, Dalton, I didn't do this for any type of compensation. I meant what I said to her."

"I know."

She looked up at me with those beautiful eyes and swallowed hard. We stood there for what felt like minutes, looking at one another, until she broke eye contact. She cleared her throat and looked up at me once again.

"Despite what you might think, Dalton, I don't hate you."

"You don't?"

"No, and I'd never tell a child I'd be there for them if I didn't mean it. So, thank you for the food. I'll see you tomorrow."

She pushed past me and headed into the ladies' room.

I stood there, shocked at her words. Did she actually just say what I thought she said? She didn't hate me? I swallowed hard as I stared at the door to the women's washroom.

AMELIA

Snow was softly falling as I carried my hot chocolate and wandered around the small holiday market. It was a beautiful morning, and I'd taken advantage of my day off to do some Christmas shopping.

I took a sip of my hot chocolate and stopped at a fudge stand, choosing my flavours just as my phone rang. I quickly selected the last two flavours and handed the vendor the cash while I answered my phone. I hoped it wasn't work. I'd already put in the allowable amount of overtime for this month, and if it was, I'd have to turn down the shift. It wasn't something I liked to do, but it would be something I'd have to do, unless Connie would approve the overtime.

"Hello!" I sang into the receiver.

I heard a throat clear and then a cough. "Amelia?"

"This is she," I said, not recognizing the voice.

I heard whispering, followed by a throat clearing, followed by more whispering.

"Um, it's Dalton. I mean Doctor Frost. I mean Dalton."

I frowned. He sounded nervous and unsure of himself, which wasn't like him. I worried I'd missed a meeting or something because I couldn't figure out why else he'd be calling. It was his day off as well, so I knew it couldn't be work related.

"Yes? Is there something I can help you with?" I questioned.

"I'm so sorry to bother you on your day off...but I needed to ask you something."

"It's okay, but I will, um, have to get you the answers tomorrow once I'm in the office," I answered. "I'm not much good without my notes and the client files in front of me, I'm afraid."

"It's not work related," he said, his voice shaking. "I guess you could say it's more of a personal issue."

I frowned. A personal issue. Dalton didn't seem to be the type of person to need help in his personal life. I listened, curious to find out what he could want.

It was then I heard Claire in the background and then a muffled response from Dalton.

"I see. Well, what is it you need?" I questioned,

frowning as I listened to muffled voices again, certain Claire must need something.

"Sorry about the interruption. I have a favour to ask. I'm wondering if you could spare a little time today to come and see Claire. She has a bit of a problem and would like to speak with another woman, as she puts it."

I softly smiled. Claire was a sweet girl, and if she needed someone, there was no way I'd turn her down. I'd hold up my promise.

"Sure, I can. I just need the address," I said, glancing at my watch.

"75 Sycamore," Dalton replied.

"Okay, um, I should be able to be there within the next couple of hours," I answered.

"Great, thank you, Amelia."

"No problem."

I'D TAKEN my time finishing up at the holiday market before heading home to get ready. I showered, pulled my hair back in a bun, and quickly did my makeup before I hopped into my car and made my way over. I pulled up outside the two-story home, put my car in park, and cut the engine. Grabbing my purse, I made my way to the front door, careful not to slip on the snow-covered walkway.

I was about to knock when the door opened abruptly, and there stood Dalton. At first, I thought I was at the wrong house and looked up to make sure it was the right place. I barely recognized him. He wore blue jeans and a T-shirt, and I couldn't help but notice he was barefoot. He looked so different dressed in casual clothing.

"Amelia, thank you so much for coming over," he said, an actual smile on his face.

Where is Dalton Frost and what have you done with him, I thought to myself as I stared at this incredibly sexy man. That was the only thing running through my mind as I stepped into his house and he closed the door behind me.

"I hope you didn't mind me calling you. Claire has been having a terrible morning. Mrs. Jenkins would normally deal with her, but she is on her weekend off and, well, I didn't want to call her, but I didn't know what to do. She insisted she couldn't talk to me about it. She claimed it was a woman's issue."

I smiled, almost laughed. It sounded funny that she wouldn't talk to her father about a woman's issue, considering he was a gynecologist.

"What's so funny?' he questioned.

"I think you know what is funny," I added as I followed behind him, glancing into the living room as we walked through into the kitchen where I found Claire sitting at the kitchen table, her cheeks flushed, her eyes red. Had she been crying?

"Hey, Claire," I said, smiling down at her.

"Amelia, you came!" she said, jumping up and running over to me, wrapping her arms around my waist.

"What's going on?" I questioned, giving her a one-armed hug.

I glanced over at Dalton, who stood there, coffee mug in his hand, watching us. He leaned up against the counter, and for the first time, I noticed how his muscles flexed in his forearms and how strong his hands were. I'd worked with this man daily for a year and had noticed none of this before. When I looked back down at Claire, I noticed she glanced over to Dalton and then back at me.

"Can we go talk in private?" she whispered.

I looked back over to Dalton, who cleared his throat. I was expecting him to force her to talk to me here, but he surprised me.

"You can use the backyard if you like." He nodded, gently smiling at Claire.

"Thanks." I looked down at Claire, who slipped her hand into mine and led me to the backdoor.

Once outside, Claire nodded to four empty chairs in the middle of the backyard. I followed her over, and we both took a seat.

"So, what is going on that you can't talk to your dad about?" I questioned.

Her cheeks flushed, and she shook her head. "It's embarrassing," she mumbled.

"Okay, well, how about you just take a deep breath and tell me?" I smiled.

Claire did as I suggested and, without looking at me, she murmured, "I woke up this morning and there was blood in my bed," she said, almost near tears.

I gently smiled, remembering when I'd gotten my first period. It was almost identical to what had happened to Claire. The only difference was I had my mother to talk about it with.

"Mrs. Jenkins wasn't here, and I couldn't tell my dad." Tears filled her eyes.

"It's okay. No need to cry. I can help you with this, no problem." I smiled, reaching into my purse and pulling out a pad. "You've gone over these things in health class, I take it?"

Claire nodded. "I just had nothing in the house, and I didn't want to ask Dad to take me to the drugstore because I'd rather die. I was going to wait until Monday when Mrs. Jenkins was here, but I wasn't sure I should."

"No problem. How about I take you to the drugstore? We can get you some supplies and you can ask me all the questions you'd like to ask in private. Sound good?"

Claire nodded, smiling at me. "Thank you."

"No problem. Now why don't you head on up to your room, get ready, and I will take you to the drugstore."

"Okay," she said, getting up from the chair and shoving the pad into the pocket of her jeans. "Oh, and, Amelia?"

"Yes?"

"Don't tell my dad, okay?"

I flinched a little, not sure I really wanted to keep something like that from her father. I softly smiled. "Honey, don't you worry. I will talk with your dad, but I'm almost certain he will understand. He deals with this stuff every day at work. There is nothing to be ashamed of."

"I know. I just don't want him to know."

I softly smiled. "It's okay, I will talk with him," I assured her. "Now go on and get ready."

I gave her a moment to head into the house and then got up and made my way inside, where I found Dalton still in the kitchen, still barefoot, drinking his coffee.

"Everything okay?" he questioned the moment I came inside.

"Yes, everything is fine," I answered.

Without asking, he poured me a cup of coffee and placed it down in front of me, which I gladly accepted and took a sip.

"She really had me worried. She's never refused to speak to me before."

I walked over beside him and looked out the back window out to the sprawling yard I'd just sat in.

"She doesn't want you to know, but you need to. She got her period," I said.

Almost immediately, Dalton's cheeks flushed as he tore his eyes from mine. "I see. Well, that definitely called for needing another woman."

I'd never seen him act this way before. "Are you okay?" I questioned.

"Yep, thanks for coming over," he said, swallowing hard.

"Dalton, are you embarrassed? You deal with these things for a living."

Dalton met my eyes. "Not embarrassed. Guess I forgot how old she really was. Most days I look at them and still see them as five years old."

"Gotcha. Well, I told her I'd take her over to the drugstore and get her some supplies."

Dalton looked at me, relief washing over his face. I was about to ask him if he was okay when I heard footsteps coming down the stairs. I glanced at him.

"Say nothing." I whispered.

"My lips are sealed," he whispered back, gently smiling.

"Ready to go?" I questioned, turning to see Claire standing on the other side of the island.

"Yes," she answered.

I made my way around the island and began following her to the front door when Dalton cleared his throat and called my name. We both turned to look at him.

"I was wondering if perhaps you might like to join us for dinner tonight?"

"Oh, well, I—"

"Please, Amelia!" Claire begged.

I smiled at her and then looked over at Dalton. I really didn't know how to take this at all. First, he was more human than I'd ever seen, and second, he was inviting me into his home to have dinner with him and his kids.

"I mean, if you already have plans, I understand. I just thought it might be nice…"

"Say no more." I smiled. "I'll stay."

"Yay!" Claire screamed.

I couldn't help but laugh as I listened to Claire and how excited she was for me to be staying for dinner as I followed her through the house and out to my car.

DALTON HAD ORDERED in from The Golden Lotus, a new Thai restaurant in Eastport. During dinner,

Claire and Tommy shared stories about their week at school and about some of their favourite hobbies. Once the food was gone, the table cleared and dishes were done, Dalton made us a coffee and left me in the living room while he went to tuck both kids into bed.

I now sat in the living room, sipping on the hot coffee, flipping through a magazine while I waited for him.

"Sorry about that. Tommy wouldn't stop talking about that one kid at school that invited him for the weekend to the cottage," Dalton said, coming over and sitting down on the couch beside me.

"Not a problem." I smiled. "He seemed pretty excited about the invite at dinner, too."

"Yeah, that is Tommy. I haven't even given him a yes or no yet." Dalton chuckled.

"Well, I hope it's a yes, otherwise I think he is going to be pretty upset," I said, thinking back to how excited he looked.

Dalton chuckled. I wasn't sure I'd ever even heard the man laugh before. Dalton was good-looking. I'd always thought so, and he had a really pleasant smile too, and there was a glint in his eyes as he looked at me. Today was the first time I'd seen a personality to match the total package.

The room grew quiet as we looked at one another,

and soon his sombre face returned. I swallowed hard as I placed my mug down on the table.

"Well, thank you once again for dinner. Really, you didn't have to," I said, reaching for my purse.

"It was my way of saying thank you for helping me with Claire."

"Like I said before, you don't need to thank me," I said, feeling annoyed as I dug into my purse for my keys. Finally, I felt them and looked over at Dalton, ready to announce my departure.

"Like I said before, I know you don't like me very much," he said. "In fact, I'm almost sure you probably hate me."

I frowned and sat back, looking over at him. He seemed almost vulnerable.

I placed my keys back down on top of my purse, waiting for him to talk, but he just studied me.

"Like I said before, I don't hate you. I don't have room in my heart for hate. I will say I don't like the way you treat people."

I could tell from the look on his face he knew how he was treating people was wrong, which if he knew that, then I wondered why he continued.

"I think I'm going to head home," I said, shifting myself to the edge of the couch to stand when he grabbed my hand. I looked down to where his hand rested on my arm and then over at his face.

"I...I didn't use to be this way," he murmured. "So short and cold with people."

I could tell from the look on his face that whatever he was about to say was serious and that he needed to share whatever it was. I shifted on the couch and turned my hand around so his rested on mine.

"What happened?" I questioned.

"It was November, snowing bad. I was working nights in the emergency. It was a busy night. Claire had called to say good night right as the EMTs brought in two stabbing victims and a car accident. Immediately, I took the accident, saying good night to Claire. I rushed over to the room where they were working to get the patient stable."

As I watched him, I noticed the colour had drained from his face and knew immediately what he was going to say, but I let him continue, not wanting to stop him. He obviously needed someone to talk to, and if I was that someone he was comfortable sharing with, then I'd be the ear.

"I shoved the curtain to the side and began reading over the extent of the injuries. Broken leg, possible broken pelvis, broken ribs, oxygen levels were low, suggesting maybe a punctured or collapsed lung, possible internal bleeding as well. As I made my way to the head of the stretcher and looked down at the woman who lay there, my world stopped. Every ounce of air that had been in the room was gone, the room spinning out of control as I looked down at my wife."

I closed my eyes, blinking away the burning feeling that was certain to become tears. I couldn't imagine how he must have felt at that moment.

"In that moment, the noise of the emergency room fell away and every memory my mind held flashed before me. The first time we met, the first time we kissed, the first time we…our first home, our first baby, our second baby….the trip we'd just taken to Hawaii. Panic filled me and the room continued to spin out of control. That was when I turned and vomited on the floor. I couldn't ever remember a time that I couldn't breathe, couldn't even think. All I could see was her beautiful face laying on that stretcher as I sunk to my knees in shock. The RN who I normally worked with immediately noticed and she came over and that was when they called the code."

"Oh, Dalton…" I whispered, my eyes filling with tears as I gripped his hand a little tighter.

"It literally felt like hours as they worked on her, not minutes, as it truly was."

Dalton fell quiet as we both sat there. The look of heartbreak combined with sadness pulled at my heart. It wasn't a wonder the man was the way he was. He'd suffered not only a devastating loss, but had seen it with his own eyes. It would cause the warmest, caring person to turn inward.

"When I heard that flatline, I knew my entire world was about to change, only it didn't just change, it literally stopped."

My heart hurt for Dalton and for Claire and Tommy.

"Dalton, I'm sorry, I did not know."

"I wouldn't have expected you to," he quietly answered.

Almost immediately, I remembered all those horrible things I'd said to him that afternoon when I'd lost my composure. How horrible he was, how his significant other must hate being around such a grumpy man. Those words were now that bitter pill I had to swallow and made me feel like a fool.

"I think I'm going to get going," I said, swallowing hard, wishing I'd never said those words to him.

Dalton nodded and whispered, "I understand."

"Before I do, I want to apologize for all the things—"

He placed his forefinger on my lips, silencing me. "No need. They needed to be said," he whispered, meeting my eyes.

Embarrassment and anger flooded me. They didn't need to be said. I should have been fired over those words. I'd overstepped. I'd attacked his personal life, and that wasn't professional in the slightest.

I grabbed my purse and keys and made my way to

the front door where I slipped my shoes on. I could barely breathe at the thought of my words from that night.

When I turned to say goodbye, I didn't expect Dalton to be right there. His body was so close to me, I could feel the heat pouring off it. His eyes met mine, and I felt him take my hand in his.

I had no idea what was happening inside me at the moment. I wanted him to kiss me. I wanted to know what his lips would feel like against mine. I wanted him to take me in his arms and pull me against him. I wanted to feel his body against mine, but most of all I wanted to take his pain away, if only for a moment or two.

My heart pounded as I studied his eyes and silence fell between us. The longer I stood there, the warmer I felt, and the realization that I was about to cross a professional line was staring me in the face.

"I'll see you tomorrow at work," I whispered, as something in my brain forced me to stop thinking that way.

"Good night, Amelia."

"Night, Dalton."

AMELIA

"CAROL, if you'd like to come with me, I'll get you set up in one of the treatment rooms," Charlotte said, taking the file folder from the pile I'd just placed on the desk.

The lady smiled at me as she passed the desk and followed Charlotte down the hall.

It was Friday. It had been five days since I'd been at Dalton's house, and he'd barely even spoken to me. I went back to the file I was working on when Dalton came around the corner and dropped a file folder down in front of me without so much as a word, and then went to go back down the hall when he stopped.

"Amelia, call Mrs. Johnson and share with her the results of her tests," he grunted.

I stopped what I was doing and looked up at Dalton. I'd seen Mrs. Johnson's test results this morning, and it wasn't good news. I knew she'd have questions, as would anyone with a cancer diagnosis. I also knew I shouldn't be answering them.

"Wait," I said, loud enough to get the attention of some patients in the waiting area.

"What?" Dalton barked and rolled his eyes.

Charlotte stepped out of the treatment room she'd just put Carol into and looked at the pair of us, wondering what was going on.

"Can I speak with you in private, please?" I questioned, looking up at him.

I could see the annoyance in his eyes as I continued down the hall and entered his office, waiting for him.

I was looking out the window when I heard his door click shut.

"What is it? If you pulled me in here to tell me you don't want to call Mrs. Johnson, that is too bad. I have asked you to do it, and I'm not taking no for an answer," he sternly replied.

Dalton had been in a terrible mood for most of the week. He'd worked late every night, well past his usual time. I'd have thought that after he'd shared things about his wife with me, he'd have been different, but I'd been wrong about that too.

"What is wrong?" I questioned, cutting right to the chase instead of dancing around it.

"Nothing."

"Oh no, Dalton, it's not nothing. You have been horrendous lately. Worse than usual. Poor Charlotte has been afraid to do anything, and in case you didn't notice, no one even looked your way today while you were in the cafeteria. People are avoiding you more than ever."

"Good, I'm glad they are avoiding me. They at least know what is good for them, unlike you."

I crossed my arms and glared at him. This was Dalton at work. This wasn't the man I'd shared dinner with less than a week ago.

"Dalton, just stop. Now, something is wrong, because the man I shared dinner with—"

"Whoa, you shared dinner with me and my family, and that will be the end of that talk. I don't need rumours spreading around the hospital about me fraternizing with one of my staff," he barked.

"There isn't a non-fraternization policy here, Dalton. Besides, just because two people share dinner together does not mean they are in a relationship of any kind aside from a friendship," I said. "So what gives?"

Dalton looked at me and then turned around. I saw his shoulders rise and fall in a deep sigh.

"Today is…"

His voice was barely audible, and I strained to hear what he was going to say next. I waited, only he said nothing.

"Today is what?" I questioned.

He was quiet, his shoulders rising and falling. "Today is the anniversary of my wife's death," he finally answered.

Heat flooded my body as his words hit me. What on earth was he doing here? He should be at home, spending time with the kids, learning how to deal or cope with whatever was running through his head.

"Why are you here? You should be at home with Claire and Tommy," I cried, realizing that those kids were alone.

"I can't," he quietly murmured.

"You can't? Why not?" I questioned. "Your children need you. They need to be with you, not be alone, or with their nanny."

"You don't understand."

I crossed my arms over my chest. He was right; I didn't understand, but I knew those children needed their father probably more today than ever, and it was bloody selfish of him to be here with his patients than to be at home allowing those kids to cope.

"What I understand is that you are being an ass," I bit out.

Dalton whipped around and looked at me. The look in his eyes almost ripped my heart out.

"I can't be there for my kids, because I do not know how to even handle how I feel, never mind how they feel."

I saw the vulnerability in his eyes and immediately wanted to hug him. Once again, I wanted to take away his pain because it was more than obvious to me he was definitely in pain, only I didn't dare. Who knew how he'd react?

"If you will excuse me, I have patients I need to see," he said and turned and stepped out of the office, leaving me there alone.

I'D JUST HUNG up the phone when Dalton dropped another patient file on my desk and left the office . He took off across the hall and stood at the elevator, pressing the button.

I turned to Charlotte. "I'll be back in a few minutes, just going to grab a coffee."

"Sure."

I grabbed my purse and took off out of the clinic and over to the elevator where Dalton stood. I was about to say something when the elevator door opened. We both stepped inside and waited for the door to close.

"What time is your shift over?" I questioned.

"Why?"

"Well, I've been thinking. If it's the same time mine ends, how about I go with you home?"

I stood there, my stomach in knots, waiting for his answer. He was quiet for so long, I figured I'd hear about this later today before I left the office. He probably thought I was trying to come on to him or something and would probably ask me to clean out my desk and not to return.

"Why would you offer to do that?" he asked. "We aren't friends."

I thought for a moment, unsure how to answer him. He needed someone, that much I knew. I knew I could be that someone for him, if he'd let me. He'd opened up once before.

"Dalton, we don't have to be friends for me to help you and your family, but I'd like us to be."

The elevator stopped, and the door opened. Dalton looked at me, then took off without another word. I would not chase him. In fact, I wouldn't say another word about this ever again. It was the only time I was offering. I pressed the button for the eighth floor and took off back to the office.

I JUST FILED the last of the medical files away and grabbed my coat from the hook, then bent down and pulled my purse from the bottom drawer of the desk.

I'd been on edge ever since I'd returned from talking with Dalton in the elevator. He hadn't said a word to me when he returned. We just went about our day as if nothing had happened.

I let out a sigh and went to shut the light off when my hand collided with another hand, causing me to jump.

"Sorry I didn't see you there," I heard a deep voice say and looked up to see Dalton standing there in his coat, his laptop bag flung over his shoulder.

"It's okay," I said, swallowing hard. "I guess I'll see you tomorrow." I gave him a small smile.

He didn't move, so I stepped out from behind the desk and made my way to the clinic door and was about to push it open when I heard him clear his throat behind me.

"Amelia?"

I glanced over my shoulder at him, not saying a word, just waiting for him to speak.

"I just wanted to let you know that I'm sorry about this afternoon."

I nodded. "Of course."

"It's just that your offer took me by surprise, and I didn't really know what to say. If your offer is still on the table, I'd like it if you would join us for dinner tonight."

I could tell from the look on his face that it took a lot for him to apologize and to ask me to join them.

"I don't know how to be with my kids today," he whispered.

I STOOD in Dalton's kitchen ripping up lettuce for the Caesar salad while he stirred the pot that contained the pasta before moving to the one that held the sauce.

"Do you have any croutons?" I questioned.

"Yep, in the pantry," he said. "Second or third shelf."

We'd been here almost an hour, had said goodbye to Mrs. Jenkins, and hadn't seen the kids once. The house was eerily quiet, almost unsettling.

"Would you like a little music?" I questioned, looking at the small radio on the counter.

Dalton looked at me, then at the radio, and swallowed hard, but said nothing.

It was almost like the man was allergic to anyone having a good time.

"If not, that's okay," I said, grabbing the bag of croutons from the pantry. "Just thought it would add a little magic in the air. After all, Christmas is coming. Might make the kids come out of their rooms and join us."

"Go ahead," he said.

I smiled and turned the radio on. Christmas music flooded the kitchen with one of my favourite songs. I made my way back over to where I was working on the salad and finished ripping up the lettuce and was about to dump the croutons in when I heard a voice behind me.

"Amelia?"

I turned to see Claire standing there with her brother. She smiled, but it didn't reach her eyes, and Tommy hid behind her, not smiling either.

"Hey, Claire!" I said, trying to sound upbeat for them. "Hi, Tommy."

"You're listening to the radio? Dad never—"

"Claire!" Dalton yelled in that familiar stern voice he usually used at the office, causing me to jump and dump half the box of croutons into the salad.

I glanced over at Claire to see tears fill her eyes, and then looked over at Dalton and shook my head.

"Guys, go get ready for dinner," Dalton barked, draining the pot of pasta into a strainer.

I looked over at Claire, her eyes filled with tears, and watched as she took Tommy and headed down the hall to the washroom.

"What was that?" I questioned.

"Is the garlic bread ready for the oven?" he asked, ignoring my question completely.

This time I ignored him and grabbed the tray with the garlic bread and shoved it into the oven.

IT WAS UNBEARABLY quiet at dinner. When Claire and Tommy both returned to the dining room, neither of them even looked my way. They sat there, eyes down, and ate. Dalton sat looking out the window, ignoring everyone. It was the most uncomfortable dinner I'd ever sat through, and wondered if this was what homelife for these kids had been like since their mother died.

The moment plates were empty, Dalton gathered them and carried them into the kitchen without a word to anyone. I looked at both the kids, my heart hurting for them.

"You both doing okay?" I asked quietly. "Your dad told me what today is."

Tommy looked up at me with red eyes. He'd been crying at some point. Probably before they came into dinner, and when Claire looked up at me, she had tears in her eyes.

"Did you guys want to talk about your mom?" I questioned, glancing at the doorway to the dining room.

Dalton was more than likely making coffee and

cutting the cake I'd stopped to pick up on my way here. I didn't care if he overheard; he needed to overhear. He needed to be here for his kids. He should be the one asking these questions, not me, some stranger.

Claire looked at me. "I can sometimes still smell her perfume," she said, her voice barely audible. "It was my favourite. I still have a bit in a bottle she used to use. I don't use it, just smell it when I'm missing her."

"I did the same thing with a bottle of my father's cologne." I softly smiled. I wanted her to know there was nothing wrong with what she was doing, because there was no doubt in my mind that if Dalton had caught her, he'd have yelled.

"What about you, Tommy?"

He shrugged. "I don't remember much. I was so little. I sometimes get this song stuck in my head. Claire told me Mom used to sing it to me."

"Can you hum it for me?"

When he began humming it, I instantly recognized it. That was when Dalton walked in. He stood there, watching Tommy sitting there with his eyes closed, humming. He surprised me as he then looked at me and started saying the words.

"Baby mine, don't you cry. Baby mine, dry your eyes."

He placed the two mugs of coffee that were on the tray he carried in front of me and himself, then placed two glasses of milk in front of both the kids, all while continuing to say the words while Tommy hummed.

Claire looked at me with tears in her eyes. When Tommy stopped humming, he too looked up with tears in his eyes. I was almost certain I even saw Dalton's eyes water a little as he finished.

My throat was tight as I sat there witnessing something I'd never thought I would. Dalton bent down and placed a kiss on the top of both kids' heads, gave them a hug, and whispered something into each of their ears before he sat down and took a sip of his coffee, and probably for the first time he actually started talking to his kids about their mother.

AFTER WE'D FINISHED dessert and Dalton shared some stories about his wife with the kids, it was time for them to get ready for bed. While he went up and tucked them in, I quickly cleaned up the kitchen and started the dishwasher, then poured us two fresh cups of coffee and made my way into the living room, where I sat down just as Dalton joined me.

"I poured you a fresh coffee," I said as he sat down beside me.

"Thank you," he said, grabbing the mug and taking a sip.

"No problem." I smiled.

"No, I mean for today. If it wasn't for you, well, I don't think I would have gotten through tonight."

"It wasn't a problem. Glad to help, but honestly, it was by sharing those stories with the kids that got you through it."

"Well, it meant a lot to me you were here," he whispered, his eyes washing over my face. "No one has ever cared enough…"

"That's because you don't let anyone in, Dalton. For people to care, they have to be allowed to get close to you."

"I'm afraid to let anyone in…"

His eyes studied mine, then they fell to my lips. I felt like we were getting closer, and I fought the urge to lean forward and place a kiss on his lips. It would be wrong.

I tore my eyes from his and looked down at the mug in my hands. I was about to say something when I felt his fingers under my chin. I slowly lifted my head and was surprised when he leaned forward. The room fell away as he placed his lips on mine and my fingers gently played with the hair on the back of his head. I could have easily allowed myself to get lost in him if he hadn't pulled away.

The room was silent. I could hear my heart beating and panic flooded me.

"I've got to get going," I said, jumping to my feet.

I had to get out of there. The second his lips touched mine, I wanted more. The emptiness I felt when he'd pulled away was almost unbearable.

"Amelia, wait…" Dalton said, standing as well. "I'm sorry, I shouldn't have…"

"Don't be silly. It's fine," I said, grabbing my purse and slipping my feet into my shoes, not sure if I was going to panic or kiss the man again.

I was about to pull the door open when I felt his hands on my upper arms. I froze, not able to move.

"Amelia…" he breathed.

"Dalton…"

"Yes?" he answered.

"It's been a long and emotional day. I think it's best if we both say good night."

I didn't wait; I opened the door and stepped out onto the porch, feeling Dalton's hands slip from my arms.

"Good night, Dalton. I'll see you on Monday."

I didn't look back; I rushed to my car, climbed in, and backed out of the driveway.

DALTON

I LET OUT a yawn as I was going over the notes from this morning's meeting. I'd barely slept the weekend after Amelia left. I felt like a complete fool. I'd kissed her, I'd let my guard down, something I'd promised myself would never happen. Then I'd tossed and turned all night, worrying that she was going to report me to human resources today, and if not today, I was sure it would only be a matter of time.

I let out a sigh and closed my notebook, glancing at the clock. It was almost one, and I'd still not seen Amelia today. She hadn't called in sick either, which was unlike her. I left my office and made my way down the hall toward the front desk, where I found Charlotte on the phone. I went into the copy room only to find it empty and then returned to the front desk.

"If you are looking for Amelia, they called and asked if she could come to the emergency room. Apparently, they were slammed, and we weren't, so I told her to go. You were in your meeting."

I nodded. Normally, she would have cleared it with me first, but she hadn't, which normally would have made me angry.

Charlotte looked up at me, waiting for my reaction. Only I had nothing to give. After the other night, I knew I was skating on thin ice.

"I'm going to head down for lunch. Want anything?"

Charlotte looked at me weirdly. What was the matter with me? This wasn't the cold exterior I normally had. I'd never offered to get my employees anything.

"No, I'm good, thanks," she said hesitantly, looking up at me with concern.

"Okay, be back soon," I said, heading toward the door.

Making my way into the cafeteria, I grabbed my lunch and was about to sit down at a quiet table off to the left side when I spotted Amelia sitting alone. I wanted to apologize again, so I approached her slowly. She had her headphones in and didn't notice me until I was almost beside her.

"Dalton, hi," she said, removing one of her earbuds. From what I could tell, she was annoyed with me.

"Mind if I join you?" I questioned, fully prepared for

her to tell me to take a hike, only she didn't. Instead, she smiled and nodded to the chair beside her.

"Please, sit down."

A funny feeling came over me as I sat down and opened my soda. "Amelia, I wanted to apologize again about Friday night. I was way out of line."

She placed her hand on mine and softly smiled. "Dalton, relax. It's okay, given everything that went on that night and what you were dealing with. It's understandable. We both know it was nothing more than a simple mistake."

I couldn't have her thinking that. It wasn't a mistake. It was something I'd wanted from the first time I laid eyes on her, and from the gentleness of her kiss back, the way her fingers ran through my hair at the back of my head, I guessed she'd wanted it as well.

"No."

She looked up at me with questions in her eyes.

"I knew what I was doing. It wasn't a mistake. I'm… I'm very attracted to you and have been for a long time," I said, closing my eyes, feeling a bit of relief rise off my chest.

"What?" Amelia questioned, her eyes meeting mine.

I was quiet for a while, not sure I was ready to tell her exactly how I was feeling. I knew I had to, but it was hard to get the words out.

"Amelia, I have feelings for you, and I have for a while."

Shock immediately flooded her face at my admission. Her cheeks went red, and I realized that the cafeteria probably wasn't the best place to admit this to her.

"Dalton, I—"

"I'm sorry, but if I'm not honest about this, then…"

She swallowed hard, and her eyes watered as she waited for me to continue, only I couldn't. The familiar feeling of choking, like all the air was being sucked from this room, hit me as I sat there waiting for the only thing that I figured was coming my way. Rejection.

"Dalton, please, we will talk about this later, in private," she said, throwing her half-eaten muffin down on her tray before standing up and grabbing her things, leaving me there alone.

AMELIA

Amelia, I have feelings for you.

His words ran through my mind as I hooked up an IV for what I hoped would be the last patient of the day. I was exhausted, and my mind was in overdrive.

"Did you hear what I said?" I heard a woman say.

I looked down at the patient laying on the stretcher, certain there was nothing but confusion on my face.

"I'm sorry, what?"

"I said that hurts."

I looked down to see I was holding the needle a little crooked in her arm and immediately straightened it.

"Oh my gosh, I'm so sorry," I said, trying hard to focus and pay more attention to what I was doing than what I was thinking about. "Sorry about that."

"It's okay. I told you I have a little needle phobia, and I detest having IVs."

"Most people do," I said, placing a piece of tape across the back of her hand, securing the IV in place. "Honestly, I don't know if I have ever met someone who likes them, and I'm normally very good at setting the IV."

"Uh-huh," she said, looking away from me.

I turned on the machine and slipped from the room, depositing my gloves into the trash and my gown into the wash bin, then headed for the desk, where I finished up my notes. The moment I finished, Dalton's admission flooded my mind again.

I let out a sigh. Truth was, I'd been feeling the same way he did, and it hadn't helped that I'd always found him attractive, but since seeing a caring side to him, it had gotten worse. I'd done my best to shove my thoughts to the back of my mind, and it had worked, until we'd shared that kiss.

It was the last thing on my mind last night when I'd closed my eyes and the first thing I'd thought of when I'd opened them, and if I thought about it hard enough, I could still feel his lips on mine.

I finished making the last of my notes, and as soon as my replacement came in, I left, ready to head home for the night.

I was almost to the parking garage when I reached

into my pocket, only to find my keys were missing. That was when I realized I'd left my purse upstairs in the office. I'd been called to the ER almost immediately after arriving and had just left everything there. I let out a sigh and made my way back to the hospital.

The lights were off in the office, which sent a sigh of relief through me. Everyone was already gone for the day. I swiped my key card and opened the door and made my way in behind the desk and opened the filing cabinet drawer, pulling my purse out from inside, then grabbed my jacket from the hook on the wall and slid into it. I turned around and went to take a step when I ran into someone and let out a scream.

"Amelia, it's okay. It's only me. Dalton."

I placed my hand on my chest, my heart was racing. "What are you still doing here?" I cried, trying to slow my breathing.

"I was just getting ready to leave. What are you doing here?"

"The same thing!" I exclaimed. "I left my purse and jacket here. I thought everyone was gone for the night."

"Same here." Dalton chuckled. "Look, I'm glad you are here. I'd like to take you out for dinner, so we can talk."

The look in his eyes was so genuine, and when he reached out and took my hand in his, all I could do was follow him.

WE SHARED a lovely and quiet dinner along with a bottle of wine at one of the best restaurants in Eastport. We talked about our day, laughing and joking, and then Dalton drove us back to his place. He slid his hand into mine as we drove back to his place and when we stepped into the house, two smiling faces and Mrs. Jenkins greeted us.

"What are you guys still doing up?" Dalton questioned, looking over to Mrs. Jenkins.

"We wanted to watch our show," Claire explained, getting up and coming over to me, wrapping her arms around me. "I'm so happy to see you."

"I'm happy to see you, too!" I exclaimed.

"Okay, guys, why don't you head on up and get ready for bed, and I'll be up in a minute," Dalton instructed.

"Can't Amelia tuck us in tonight?" Claire asked, and Tommy agreed.

Dalton looked over at me and then at both his kids and nodded. "Well, if it's okay with Amelia, sure."

"It's fine. Come on, kids, let's go."

I took them both upstairs and waited while they changed and brushed their teeth, then tucked each one of them into bed before making my way back down-stairs. Soft music played on the living room speakers, and Dalton sat on the couch, two glasses of wine poured.

"They go down, okay?"

"Yep, Tommy was asleep the moment his head hit the pillow." I giggled.

Dalton smiled and patted the empty seat beside him. I went over and sat down as he handed me my glass of wine.

"Did you enjoy dinner?"

"Very much," I whispered, taking a sip of my wine.

Dalton took my hand in his and ran his thumb over the back of my hand. He was a completely different man than he was at work. This Dalton Frost I could easily see myself falling in love with. I met his eyes and softly smiled.

"Amelia, I know I'm not always the easiest man to get along with."

"Somehow, though, I can understand. You've been through a lot over the past few years."

"I have."

"I want to let you know that I'm sorry for what I said that night. I know I've apologized before, but if I had known about your wife, I'd never have said…"

He placed his forefinger on my lips, silencing me. "It's okay. Don't worry about it. I deserved it."

"Well, maybe in some ways, but you didn't deserve that comment."

"No, I probably did. Honestly, I probably deserved more than what you gave. I guess the reason I'm always worse to you than anyone else at the office is because you reminded me of Kenzie."

"Really?"

Dalton nodded. "Yes. I guess it scared me because when I first started noticing those things that you exhibit that had originally attracted me to her, my first instinct was to push you away."

I nodded, studying his eyes. He was guarded, which made sense. I could understand that too. If my world had been suddenly ripped from me, it would make me the same.

"Amelia, I've given a lot of thought to things over the past few weeks. I feel there could be something between us."

"What do you mean?" I questioned, taking a sip of my wine and averting my eyes for a moment.

"I mean, I think there could be something more between us than just co-workers and friends. I think I'd like us to explore that option. If you are interested, that is."

"Dalton, I'm not sure we should date. I mean, we work together. You are my boss."

Dalton was quiet for a moment. "You never

mentioned work earlier. It didn't seem to bother you to come here and help Claire, or to have dinner with me before, so that is not what is bothering you. So, what is holding you back?"

His words ran through my mind. Being friends didn't seem to be a problem with the work thing, but what would people think at work if we were dating? I hadn't exactly been silent about how I'd felt about Dalton, and even though my feelings were changing, the thought scared me a little.

He brought his hand to my cheek, and the moment his hand touched me, heat flooded my body. His eyes captivated me, and before I could stop myself, I leaned forward and met his lips.

"We can't be caught at work like this," I whispered.

"Not at work, I agree, but what we do in our personal life is no one's business," he whispered, bringing his lips back to mine.

His kiss this time was a little more demanding as he wrapped his arms around me and pulled me toward him. In one quick movement, he'd pulled me over so I was straddling his lap. As our kiss deepened, his hands gripped my ass and pulled me closer toward him. I could already feel him straining against his jeans. Every part of me was on fire, and I let out a soft moan as his hands began exploring my body.

One hand snaked into my hair, and he gently pulled

as he kissed me again, sending waves of pleasure through me. I ran my fingers through the hair at the back of his head as he kissed his way down my neck and back up, nibbling on my ear.

"You like that?" he whispered.

The feel of his breath on my neck and ear sent chills through me, causing my centre to throb.

"Very much so." I moaned.

Cupping my cheek, he brought his lips to mine again, kissing me slow. A bolt of excitement ran through me when I felt his hand slide under my shirt and brush against my stomach in a tender touch. I pulled away, studying his eyes, then gripped the bottom of my shirt and pulled it off over my head.

I craved his lips but loved watching his eyes as they ran over my body, stopping on my breasts. I reached behind me and unclipped my bra, letting it fall away from my body. He immediately grabbed me, pulling me forward, his mouth meeting my breast. I felt his tongue flick my hard nipple as he sucked the one into his mouth while his other hand explored the other one, pinching and rolling my nipple between his fingers, causing me to let out a moan as I ground my hips down on him.

We were probably moving too far too fast, but I didn't care. Every relationship I'd ever had, I'd always waited and almost tried to plan for the right time.

In a swift motion, he lifted me up, and I found myself

under him on the couch, his mouth now exploring my body. I reached down between us, running my hand over the impressive bulge in his pants, causing him to let out a moan. I pulled at his belt and quickly pulled at the button and zipper on his pants just enough I could slip my hand inside.

"Fuck." He hissed as I took him in my hand, stroking his length.

I watched him; he closed his eyes, his face peaceful as I continued running my hand over him. His breath quickened as I ran my thumb over the bead of pre-cum that had gathered on the head of his cock.

He took hold of my hand, his hand shaking, and pulled my hand away from him, stopping me. When he looked down at me, I could see that his eyes were full of want. He placed my hand above my head and then gripped the other one, pulling it to over my head, and held them both there while he undid my pants with his free hand. In a matter of seconds, he'd slipped his hands into my panties and let out a groan as his fingers slipped through my soaked centre.

"You're fucking soaked." He moaned.

I closed my eyes and let out a guttural groan as his fingers ran softly over my clit, gently circling for a few seconds before he stopped and pulled at my pants. I lifted, letting him pull them down off my hips to give him better access.

Pushing my panties to the side, his fingers danced lightly over my throbbing centre, before he slid one finger, then two deep inside of me, his thumb finding and concentrating on my clit.

I bit my bottom lip as I tried to pull my hands free from his grasp. I was going to come. It would only be a matter of seconds if he didn't stop. Only he didn't stop. Instead, he increased his efforts and met my lips, stifling my moans.

I could feel myself tightening around his fingers. He let go of my hands and removed his fingers, leaving me empty and throbbing. He sat down, relaxed back, and patted his lap as he took his cock in his hand and began stroking it slowly.

I watched him as I slid my pants off. I leaned over and grabbed my purse from the table, reaching in and pulling out a condom. His eyes met mine as I held it out for him to take. Without a word, he opened it and rolled it on himself, then took hold of my hand and guided me. I straddled his lap as he slid down a little, then he took hold of my hips and guided me as he lined himself up at my entrance.

I closed my eyes as I felt him enter me, letting out a moan as I took him all the way inside, filling me and stretching me in ways I'd never been before. Then, with his hands on my hips, he gently guided my motion.

Resting my one hand on his knee, I leaned back a bit

as he leaned forward and sucked one of my nipples into his mouth. I reached down between us and with my free hand, running my fingers over my clit.

I could feel my orgasm building faster as he continued to guide my motion a little faster.

"You close?" he grunted.

I nodded, closing my eyes as he sucked my other nipple into his mouth, causing me to slip over the edge and tighten around him. His muscles tensed as he held onto me, stilling me as he poured himself inside of me.

DALTON

Two Weeks Later

"Something is different about you lately."

"What do you mean?" I questioned, glancing at Connie, the head RN of the hospital.

I glanced down at my watch to see I was running late to meet Amelia for lunch. We'd started having lunch together over at The Cooling Rack. Even though many doctors and nurses ate there, we'd found a booth in the back that was away from prying eyes. We'd only started doing this since we'd slept together a couple of weeks ago. Until that time, we'd eaten in the cafeteria separately. We'd promised each other that we'd keep work life separate from our personal life, but we wanted to spend our time together when we were off the clock, so this was the best way.

"I don't know, you seem….less cranky. Almost as if you've…dare I say it…"

"Connie…don't start that," I grumbled, not in the mood to put out rumors.

Connie was Eastport's gossip column. You wanted to know something about anyone, all you needed to do was ask her. She also had a tendency to make up whatever she wanted about people, which often led to some very nasty rumors being spread around. That was last thing I needed or wanted was rumors to be spread around about my new relationship with Amelia, true or not.

"I've noticed you haven't been eating in the cafeteria…" she continued, as if I hadn't said a word.

"What are you, my keeper? I've been taking lunch at odd hours the past couple of weeks." I shrugged. "Patient load has been heavier than normal."

Connie gave me with curious look. It was a completely viable answer, and one that someone couldn't dispute.

"Is that okay with you?" I questioned, my tone taking on more of its usual sound. Connie said nothing. She turned her head and stared straight ahead. "That's what I thought," I murmured just as the elevator doors opened.

The moment she'd stepped out of the elevator, I hit the close button and pressed the button for the main floor.

AMELIA WAS SITTING in our usual spot when I arrived. She glanced up from the article she was reading in the paper and smiled.

"I didn't think you were coming."

"And miss lunch with you? Never," I said, sitting across from her. "Did you order?"

"Yep, I got you the burger. Is that okay?"

"Sounds great," I said, letting out a breath as I slid into the seat across from her.

She studied me with a curious look. "What's going on?"

"What?" I asked. "It's nothing. Don't worry about it."

"Don't tell me not to worry about it. You look angry."

I reached out and took her hand in mine. I didn't want to spend our time together talking about Connie and her questions. I wanted to spend it with Amelia, laughing and talking about our plans for the upcoming weekend.

"It's nothing. Don't worry about it. Now, I was thinking about this weekend, the family holiday party… what time should we pick you up?"

Amelia looked at me with worry in her eyes.

"You are planning on joining the kids and I, aren't you?"

She swallowed hard and gently shook her head no. "I don't think so, Dalton. I'm worried that people will talk if we arrive together."

"The kids will be crushed," I said, my voice low enough, so no one overheard.

She looked at me with concern. "Dalton, I gave it some thought. We promised not to mix work with our personal life. I feel that if we attend together, that is what we will be doing."

"Whoa, wait a minute. I know what we said, but the kids are looking forward to it. Claire was so excited when I told her you were joining us."

"I know, and to be honest, I probably should have given it more thought when you asked, instead of just agreeing to go. We both agreed to keep our situation under wraps at work."

I studied her. I could tell there was something she wasn't telling me. I suddenly wondered if perhaps Connie had questioned her as well yesterday when she'd picked up the extra shift in the emergency.

"We did, but there is nothing saying you didn't need a lift. Besides, what would be wrong with us inviting you to join us for the day? You do work for me, after all."

Amelia let out a sigh, but I could still see something

was bothering her, but I didn't want to press her into telling me. I wanted her to talk to me when she was comfortable.

"I'll come by the house around four," she said, just as our lunch arrived.

I STOOD outside Santa's Workshop with Amelia, waiting for Claire and Tommy to visit Santa. We'd shared a wonderful afternoon together, laughing, doing crafts with the kids, and singing songs. I could tell both the kids loved Amelia. They'd started coming around more once they caught us kissing one night in the kitchen before dinner. That had taken some explaining, but thankfully, I'd handled it well.

I was afraid of their questions. There was no doubt about it. They'd never seen me with another woman; they'd barely seen me with their mother. However, I remained calm and answered them. It seemed easier when I followed my heart for the answers instead of my head.

"I'm going to use the washroom," Amelia whispered.

"No problem. I'm sure we will be here." I winked.

I wanted to lean over and kiss her before she left my side, but I stopped myself, remembering where we were.

I took pictures of both the kids when it was their turn to speak with Santa and waited while they were both given their special present from Santa himself. They both came running over to me with their wrapped gifts, begging me to open them.

"Well, I think we should wait for Amelia, don't you think?" I questioned, glancing down at my watch, wondering where she could be. She'd been gone for over a half hour. "Perhaps we will save them for home."

"I guess," Claire said.

"What about you, Tommy?" I questioned, looking around the room for a sign of her.

"Fine," he whined.

It was then I spotted Amelia. She came into the room, her eyes red, and immediately made her way over to us.

"What is it?" I questioned, concern filling me.

"Can we just go? Like right now," she said, turning and making her way toward the door.

I glanced down at Claire and Tommy and ushered them both to the coat check, where I grabbed all our jackets and the three of us made our way toward the car.

Amelia was silent the entire drive back to my place. Almost the minute we were inside, I sent the kids upstairs to get ready for dinner and turned to find Amelia still standing at the door, her coat still on.

"What are you doing?"

"I'm going to head home. I'm not feeling very well."

I studied her, knowing full well there was something wrong. I'd worked with her far too long and knew when she was sick. This wasn't sick, she was upset. Hell, I was normally the cause of her anger, so I knew the difference.

"Amelia, if this is going to work between us, we have to be honest with one another."

"Dalton, it's nothing, really."

She met my eyes. She was trying to be strong, but I could see the worry filling hers. Something had happened while she'd been in that bathroom. I studied her, almost not wanting to ask what I already knew.

"Did Connie…"

That was the only word she had to hear. She turned away from me to hide her eyes. Anger filled me. It was fine she'd tried getting to me, but I knew Amelia wouldn't be able to fight her. It wasn't in her nature.

"She confronted you?"

"I've got to go." She sniffled, and without another word, she took off out the front door.

AMELIA

Three Weeks Before Christmas

No matter how many times Dalton had asked, I hadn't told him what it was Connie had said the night of the kids' Christmas party. In the last week, we'd gone to work separately, we'd had lunch separately, and I'd done nothing but pull away. It wasn't because I was confused about how I felt about him, because I wasn't. Dalton wasn't who he was at work. He was a kind man who was capable of love and passion. It was because of Connie and the hatred and threats she'd spewed at me. So, for me, pulling away was the answer.

I knew Dalton was confused. I could see it in his eyes

every time he looked at me. I'd become cold and with-drawn and absolutely hated myself for it. It wasn't like me to be this way toward him, especially without telling him why. He'd even tried to get me alone for an explanation, but each time I had a reason why I couldn't talk.

That was, until last night.

Charlotte had left for the day, and I was busy in the copy room putting away supplies when he'd come in and shut the door behind him. He placed his hands on my hips and placed a gentle kiss on the side of my neck.

Instantly, I thought I was going to break at the feel of him behind me. It was then he confessed to missing me and wanted to know if I would come join him and the kids for the night. Another kiss to the side of the neck and I was his. I couldn't turn him down.

I looked up from the kids' Christmas list and saw Dalton come into the living room carrying a bottle of wine and two glasses. He stopped, turning down the lights, gave me that sexy smile, and sat down beside me.

"Care for a drink?"

I placed the list on the table and smiled. "I'd love one."

He opened the wine and began pouring the two glasses as he met my eyes.

"I'm glad you joined us tonight," he said, handing me my glass, then clinking his against mine.

"Same." I softly smiled as I took a sip.

"I've missed you."

I nodded. "Dalton, I've missed you as well, and I'm sorry I've been avoiding you."

I saw the questions in his eyes, but I also knew he knew it had to do with why I'd run.

"She can be awful," he said quietly, studying me. "She confronted me too, a couple of days before the party."

I looked up at him, shocked that he hadn't told me that night. Perhaps had I not run and talked with him, he would have told me. Although he too could have brought the fact that she confronted him to me as well, to warn me if nothing more.

"What did she say to you?" he questioned.

I took another sip of my wine and looked up at him. "She claimed she knew why you request my help in the ER when you aid down there."

Dalton frowned. "I request your help because you are a fucking exceptional nurse. No other reason."

I felt my cheeks heat at his admission. "I know. She was referring to a conversation we'd had before anything happened between us, but I know Connie. She is great at twisting situations and words around. The things she's made up..."

"You don't need to explain. I've heard," Dalton said,

taking my hand in his. "You also need to stand up to her."

"I don't know. She's my boss." I shrugged, worried how this could turn out. "She is the head RN."

"Who could be viewed as harassing you. Especially if she is making things up about your personal life, which in turn is affecting your work life."

I knew Dalton was right, but I also worried what would happen if she reported us to human resources. However, since we hadn't made our situation public, we could just deny it and it would go away. They may watch us for a while, but not forever.

"Just hold your ground, okay? She is your boss at the hospital, but also remember I am as well. Just remember that."

I nodded and welcomed his lips to mine.

THE NEXT MORNING, I walked through Eastport Mall trying to find a Christmas gift for Claire and Tommy. I'd picked a couple of ideas off their lists with Dalton's help, and since it was my day off, I figured today was a good day to find something.

I stood inside the toy store singing along to

"Grandma Got Run Over by a Reindeer" when I heard someone call my name. I turned around to see Connie. Irritation filled me as she approached me with a smile. I swallowed hard as I smiled back.

"Hey, Connie," I said, doing my best to focus on finding exactly what action figure it was Tommy had asked for.

"So, what are you doing here?" she questioned.

I gave her a questioning look, wondering why she was so interested in why I was here, and she let out a little laugh. "What do you mean?" I asked.

"Well, what I mean is this is a toy store, and you don't have kids."

I took in a deep breath as I picked up a box I was certain was the correct toy and began looking it over. "Shopping for a friend," I bit out.

"You realize I'm not stupid. There is word floating around the hospital that has me a little concerned."

"Oh? What would that be?" I said, picking up another box and giving it a once-over, trying not to react to what she was saying.

"That you and Dalton are seeing one another?"

"Is that so?" I questioned, doing my best to keep my composure.

"Yes."

"Well, people have their lines crossed because we are nothing more than friends, Connie," I said, putting the box back on the shelf, continuing to look at the other ones.

"You realize I see how you two look at one another?"

I picked up the next box. "How would that be?"

"Don't pretend you don't know. Plus, I've never seen Dalton recommend anyone, yet he has recommended you time and time again."

"Perhaps it's because he thinks I'm good at my job. Did that thought cross your mind?"

Connie studied me, saying nothing, but wore this small smirk.

"What?" I questioned.

"That's it isn't it. I'm correct. You're seeing him."

"No."

"Yes, you are. You don't lie well. Plus, if you knew he thought you were good at your job, it wouldn't have shocked you the day I told you about him recommending you. You yourself know what he is like to work for. Which leads me to believe that is why he was recommending you to begin with. Because the two of you are together."

I shook my head. I could feel my cheeks heating, and I knew there was no way I could play into this anymore. She'd be able to tell from my expression that what she was saying was true.

"That's it, isn't it? You two are together." A funny look washed over her face as she stood up a little straighter. It was enough to frighten me. "Amelia, you realize that it's against hospital policy to date a superior, don't you?"

"For the hundredth time, we aren't dating. We are friends," I gritted, my irritation growing bigger by the second.

Connie studied me, and I almost thought she believed me until she gave me an evil smile and shook her head.

"You know, Amelia, I've always liked you, and I'd love to believe you, but one girl mentioned to me a couple of days ago that she saw the two of you at The Cooling Rack together, eating lunch."

"So what?" I said, shoving the list into my back pocket. "We were two colleagues having lunch. What's wrong with that?"

"Nothing, if it were true. However, I've never known someone who hates someone to have lunch with said person, or to help them with his kids, or to hold hands."

I went to walk away, tired of listening to this craziness. She was trying to get me to crack, and I couldn't allow her to know how close I was to doing so.

"I'll be talking to the proper channels later this week at work," she called out.

"Do whatever you feel you need to do, Connie," I said as I turned and made my way toward the exit, worry filling me.

I rushed to my car and then sped out of the parking

lot back to Dalton's, ready to tell him everything, but when I got inside, he was on the phone and it looked serious.

I poured myself a hot coffee and sat down, fretting about the news I had to tell him. I listened as he spoke; it sounded like it was about a patient. Finally, he said he'd be there soon and then hung up the phone.

DALTON

It was nice of her to leave one light on when I'd returned from the hospital. I'd felt awful about having to leave her with the kids when I'd gotten the call. One of my patients was being admitted into the hospital and had insisted on speaking with me. When I'd told her about the call, she'd insisted she agreed with me that I should go.

I'd offered to call Mrs. Jenkins to come stay with the kids, but Amelia absolutely refused and said she'd stay and get their dinner. I'd messaged her an hour ago just as I was wrapping up and she'd told me they had all gone to bed with no problems, to take as long as I needed. I'd expected her to be up when I arrived, but the house was dark and quiet—all but the one light.

I slipped my shoes off and shut the light off, heading

upstairs to my bedroom. I could see light spilling into the hallway from under the bedroom door and quietly opened the door, expecting to find Amelia awake, but she was on her back, dressed in one of my T-shirts, sound asleep, with a book open, resting across her chest.

I softly smiled and went around to her side of the bed, gently taking the book from her chest, careful not to wake her. I'd just bookmarked her spot and shut the light off when she let out a soft moan and opened her eyes, looking up at me with hazy eyes.

"Dalton? What…what time is it?"

"It's late," I whispered. "Go back to sleep. I'll just be a minute." I cupped her cheek and placed a kiss on her forehead.

When I returned, she'd slipped under the covers and was lying on her side. I crawled in under the covers and wrapped my arms around her, pulling her back against me.

"How did it go?" she asked quietly.

"Okay," I whispered, pressing a kiss to her cheek.

I wasn't sure I wanted to discuss what had happened at the hospital tonight. It had been so long since I'd had a close interaction with a patient who was dying; I wasn't sure I knew how to deal with it anymore.

She rolled over, facing me, studying my eyes in the dimly lit room, then without a word pressed a kiss to my lips.

"I know it was hard for you to go, but I'm glad you went."

"Me too."

I pulled her into me, holding her tight. I needed to feel her close to me right now. I needed to know she was here.

"Tommy and Claire were talking to me about getting a tree tonight."

I couldn't help but chuckle. "Is that so?"

"They wondered if I would join you guys on that venture."

I looked down at her moonlit face, waiting to hear her answer. We'd barely been seeing one another a month, but to me it felt as if we had been together for much longer, and I already knew I was falling for her. Hell, if I were honest with myself the day she walked into my office for her interview, I'd thought about what it would be like to have a relationship with her. That had scared me so bad I could do nothing but be an ass to her, but she'd finally broken down my barriers.

"What did you tell them?"

"Nothing. I wasn't sure how you'd feel about me tagging along for that family time."

I frowned. "You weren't sure?"

She looked up at me, those large brown eyes staring back at me, and shook her head.

"I'd love to have you with us." I winked. "If you want to be, that is."

"I'd love to join you."

I pushed myself up onto my forearm and looked into her eyes. Placing my hand on her cheek, I lowered myself and placed a kiss on her lips, my tongue washing through her mouth. She wrapped her arms around me, and as I deepened the kiss, she let out a tiny moan.

"HERE'S a hot chocolate for you, and one for you, Tommy, and one for you," I said, handing Amelia her cup.

"Extra marshmallows?" she countered.

I smiled and winked. "You know it. Now, let's venture off and find a tree, shall we?"

"Yes!" Tommy shouted, slipping his gloved hand into Amelia's as Claire shoved hers into Tommy's.

I smiled at Amelia as the four of us walked through the gates of the second largest tree lot in Eastport. Christmas had always been a hard time ever since Kenzie died. The kids and I had done our best, but the three of us had struggled through the holidays. I knew my attitude hadn't helped things, but this year with Amelia in my life, I felt lighter than I had in a long time.

As we walked around, she started singing Christmas carols, which got the kids going, and soon the four of us were all singing "Jingle Bells" as we walked around the lot together. Finally, Claire pointed at a tree, claiming it was the perfect one, which, upon closer inspection, we all agreed.

"Is this the tree?" the attendant at the tree lot asked.

I looked down at both kids, who both stared up at me with goofy smiles. I couldn't help but chuckle and nod.

"Sure is. Can you wrap it for us? I'll go get the vehicle and pull it up to the gate over there," I said, pointing at the loading area.

"Sure can," he said, grabbing the tree and taking it over to the wrapping station.

I was just about to leave when Claire grabbed my hand.

"Dad, don't you think we should take a picture?"

Pictures were something we used to do when Kenzie was alive. The kids hadn't asked since she'd passed. However, I normally stopped at a grocery store lot and picked a tree from whatever was leftover two days before Christmas, and it was out by boxing day. I realized now I'd missed out on capturing memories that used to be important for the past few years.

I looked at Amelia and handed her my phone. "Would you?"

"Oh, sure." She smiled, pulling her glove off as she set her hot chocolate down on the ground.

"No, Dad. Amelia needs to be in the picture, too," Claire cried.

Dalton looked at me and smiled, then pulled his phone from my hand, stopping a couple who were walking by and asking them if they would mind taking the picture. They took his phone and waited for us to get into position.

I wrapped my arm around Amelia, while Tommy and Claire moved in front of us. The four of us smiled as the couple took our picture, then Claire whispered something to Tommy, which made him laugh.

"What's so funny?" Amelia questioned.

Tommy looked up at the two of us and grinned. "Claire says you two should kiss in the next picture," he said, covering his mouth as he giggled.

I couldn't help but smile and asked the couple if they'd mind taking a couple more pictures, which both of them smiled and shook their heads.

I grabbed hold of Amelia and brought my lips to hers as Tommy looked up at us with wide eyes. It was then the couple snapped the picture.

"Thanks," I said and wished them both a Merry

Christmas, only to turn back to see Amelia standing there with a worried look on her face.

I frowned as I made my way back over to them.

"What's wrong?" I whispered so only she could hear.

She looked up at me, her skin a little pale, and shook her head. "Nothing, I think we should just get the car," she said, giving me a weak smile.

I'D ASKED Amelia many times after we'd gotten home what was bothering her, only she refused to tell me, quickly changing the subject or focusing on the kids. She was going to head home after they'd gone to bed, but I convinced her otherwise, and she'd spent the night with me.

I'd just poured a cup of batter into the waffle maker when Amelia came into the kitchen.

"Morning," I said, as she helped herself to a cup of coffee.

"Morning." She softly smiled, only it barely reached her eyes.

She went to walk by me, but I stopped her, leaning in for a kiss.

"You ready to talk yet?" I whispered, not wanting the kids to think something was wrong.

She looked up at me with worried eyes and placed her hand on my chest. "I should have told you, but the day I was shopping, I ran into Connie. She was all over me, threatened…"

"What, that she was going to report us?" I questioned, looking at her.

She nodded.

"Did you do as I suggested and stand up to her?"

She nodded. "I did. I denied everything, but she was there last night. She saw us take the photo. She saw us kiss," she whispered, fighting back tears.

As I thought about what to say, the phone rang. I grabbed the receiver and answered it. As I listened, my heart raced, and I hung up the phone without saying a word. I stood there for a moment, trying to gather my thoughts, when I finally felt Amelia's hand on my arm and turned to look at her.

"Dalton, what is it?"

"That was human resources. They've asked that I attend a disciplinary meeting today at three."

Amelia looked at me, tears in her eyes, and was about to say something when her cell phone rang. She looked at me, grabbed her phone, and listened intently, then hung up.

"Who was that?" I questioned.

"Same as you," she whispered, giving me a worried look.

"Just remain calm and follow my lead, okay?" I whispered into her ear as she climbed out of the car. I placed my hand on her lower back.

She looked up at me, concern in her eyes. "Dalton, do you really think it's a good idea that we show up together?"

"Just remain calm and follow my lead. We have done nothing wrong."

"I'm not sure they are going to see it that way. I'm your subordinate. They could constrew this as me trying to keep my job or something." She shrugged.

"Amelia, please. They can say what they want. We know what the truth is." I leaned forward and placed a kiss on her forehead.

"Do you enjoy having your head on a chopping block?" she questioned.

"My head isn't on a chopping block. Come on, let's go," I said, guiding her toward the door.

Once inside, we made our way to the administrative floor and toward the Human Resources office. I wasn't backing down, and I wasn't putting up with any shit at this first meeting.

I allowed Amelia to walk into the room first, and then I followed to see Connie sitting in a chair across from Rose, the head of human resources.

Irritation flooded me as Rose nodded toward the two empty chairs.

"What is this about?" I barked, opening my suit jacket and sitting down beside Amelia.

"Well, Dalton, Amelia, a formal complaint has been brought to my attention and what it contains is rather disturbing," Rose said, opening a folder on her desk.

"Care to enlighten me?" I questioned.

"It's been brought to my attention that you are currently involved in a relationship with Amelia, your nurse on staff."

I kept a straight face and waited for her to continue.

"That you have been caught engaging in sexual relations in many parts of the hospital?"

I saw Connie turn and look at the pair of us from the corner of my eye. I cleared my throat and stood up, causing Rose to stop speaking.

"I think this meeting is over for now. I'll be getting in touch with my advocate, and I'd recommend Amelia do the same thing."

Rose looked over toward Amelia, who at first didn't move, but then stood up and nodded.

"I'll be getting in touch with mine as well."

I didn't hesitate. I opened the door to the room and walked out. Once I heard the door close, I turned and saw Amelia coming up behind me.

"I'm glad you followed my lead. Those accusations are…"

"Ridiculous," she finished.

"Yes. Let's head on home and call our—"

She held her hand, which stopped me from continuing. She looked to the floor, then to the wall behind me, anywhere but directly at me.

"Amelia, it's going to be—"

"No, Dalton, it won't be okay. This is a disaster. To be honest, I just want to be alone so, I think for tonight, and for the next little while, I'm just going to stay at my place instead."

I didn't know what to say to her. I didn't want her to be alone, to have to deal with these things on her own, but I knew it was probably for the best, so I let her go.

AMELIA

IT HAD BEEN five days since the meeting with Rose. When I'd gone into work the next day, she met me outside of the elevators and told me I would no longer be working in Dalton's office. Instead, I was being moved to the emergency department until further notice. I wasn't allowed to go in and get any of my things from the office until after hours, and I was to have no contact with Dalton, either.

As I made my way past the office, I saw Connie wave at me from behind the desk. Irritation flooded me, followed by anger.

I made my way into the emergency department, thankful that today was the last day of my work week, and was immediately greeted by Sawyer.

"Hey, Amelia. Constance is here to see you. You can use my office."

I frowned, not having a clue who Constance was. Sawyer must have seen the look on my face because he stopped and gave me a small smile.

"Constance is your employee advocate."

"Thanks."

My stomach turned as I made my way toward Sawyer's office. I did not know what to expect, what sort of things had been said in that formal complaint because when I'd gotten my copy yesterday, I was too upset to read it. Instead, I'd drank down a bottle of wine and passed out after work.

I stopped outside of his door, my mind racing with all the things that I imagined Connie would have or could have said in that complaint.

I took a deep breath and then pushed the door open, stepping into the room to see a woman sitting behind Sawyer's desk making some notes. She looked up, lowered her glasses to the tip of her nose, and cleared her throat.

"Amelia White?"

"Yes," I said, swallowing hard, certain I probably looked as if I were going to be sick.

"I'm Constance Granger. I'm here to aid you through this hearing. Why don't you have a seat?" she said, standing up and pouring me a glass of water from the pitcher on the desk.

I slipped into the chair and placed my purse at my feet, thankful to sit down as it helped the room to stop spinning.

"So, why don't you start by telling me about your relationship with Dalton?"

What did she want to know? Panic filled me now that I realized I probably should have read the complaint. Since I did not know what it even said, I did not know how to answer her question.

"What about my relationship?" I questioned.

"Oh, I guess I should be a little clearer. About your working relationship. How long have you been working with him?"

I nodded. "I've been working for him for a year."

"And how would you describe him as a boss?"

"I enjoy working for him."

She wrote my answer, then looked up at me. "Some of the staff around the hospital say he can be difficult to get along with. Would you say that is true?"

I shrugged. "Maybe at first, but once you get to know him and what he expects, it gets easier."

"Amelia, you have worked for many doctors in this hospital. Wouldn't you say that every doctor expects the same standard of work?"

"Of course."

"Do you not provide the same work ethic to them all?"

"Yes."

"Then what is it you mean by once you learn what he expects."

Alarm filled me. I'd clearly chosen the wrong words.

"In the report, it was mentioned that you often complained about Dalton to others. Then suddenly you stopped. It was shortly after he requested you specifically to come to the emergency department one day. After that, you helped with him and his daughter in the cafeteria. You were also seen holding hands and kissing in public places, not to mention being caught in the act. So exactly what does this man expect?"

I frowned. That was the day his daughter had the meltdown over her hair. That was the day I'd helped fix it for her in the change room.

I smiled, trying to hide my nerves. "Yes, the cafeteria. His daughter had somewhat of a hair catastrophe and was having a meltdown. I helped fix her hair for her."

"I see, and you were spotted with her shortly after that in the pharmacy on West Road," she said, looking back at the complaint.

I frowned. Had Connie been following me? "Well, yes, she was having a female emergency."

Constance looked up at me and stopped writing.

"I was simply helping her get some female hygiene

products. Since her mother died, she felt better speaking with another woman. I'd told her it was fine to call me."

"Dalton is an OB/GYN, do you not think he could take care of that for his own daughter?" she questioned, looking me straight in the eye.

"Well, yes, but—"

"But what? What it looks like to me is that perhaps Dalton called you because he wanted to get closer to you, and the only way he could do that was to get you out of the office and perhaps into his own private space. Or maybe you were looking for a promotion that Connie wouldn't give you?"

"That is ridiculous."

"Is it? People tell me Dalton is hard to please, so it only makes sense that promotions wouldn't be handed out quickly. Also, word around the hospital is that he works long hours, leaving his children at home with nannies, so he doesn't need to deal with them. It was also reported that you were Christmas shopping in a toy store, yet you have no children of your own. After being confronted and denying the allegations, someone saw you out with the entire family looking for a Christmas tree, where it was reported the two of you kissed for a photo, which apparently, when you noticed, there was a look of discomfort on your face."

The room spun out of control. The look of discomfort

had been because I'd seen Connie watching us. There had been no other reason.

"Also—"

I cut her off. I didn't like what she was suggesting, nor that she was siding with the complaint. She was supposed to be here to hear my side of the story and look at the entire thing objectively, not have a preformed opinion.

"I'm sorry, but I need to use the washroom for a moment." Getting up and grabbing my purse, I left the room.

Once I was in the washroom, I locked the main door and went into one stall. I pulled my phone from my purse, panic filling me at her suggestion. I did not know what to do, and since I hadn't seen or talked to Dalton all week, we hadn't come up with a plan.

I was about to dial his office when I realized Connie would be the one answering the phones. She was probably already aware of the fact that Constance was here to see me as well. So, I dialed his personal cell phone, hoping and praying he wasn't in his own meeting or in with a client. Only it didn't ring. Instead, it went directly to his voicemail.

I covered my mouth, trying to stifle my cries as I listened to his message. Once I heard the beep, I sniffled and tried hard to regain composure, only I blubbered into the phone, no doubt not making any sense, then I hung up, wiped my eyes, and went to the sink. I splashed some cold water on my face, took a few deep breaths, and then headed back to the meeting.

I sat back down in my chair and waited for Constance to look up from her notes. When she did, I cleared my throat. I wasn't sure how she was going to react to my next statement, but it needed to be said.

"I don't like how you are twisting what I say around to make Dalton look bad. He has in no way influenced me or preyed upon me, if that is what you are trying to get me to admit. He also has never passed me up for a promotion, since I've never applied or expressed interest in any," I said, trying to stand my ground.

Constance removed her glasses, then sat back in her chair. I could see she was thinking before she said anything, and when she did, I felt all the air leave the room.

"Amelia, it would be in your best interest for you to get on board with the narrative, especially if you'd like to keep your job."

What was she talking about? Did she really just give me this ultimatum, to turn against Dalton and go with the story or lose my job? I crossed my arms in front of me, trying to work through everything.

"Tell you what. Here is my card, you think about it. Call me no later than Monday and let me know what path you are going to take."

She bundled up the folder she had in front of her and shoved it into her case and then left the room. I felt nauseous and like I could faint. There was no way I could work today.

I reached over and grabbed a pen and pad of paper from Sawyers' desk and quickly scribbled a note, then gathered my things and slipped out the back door.

DALTON

I LISTENED to her muffled message and sobbing cries once I'd gotten into my car, trying to make out what she was saying. It was so garbled, I had to replay it.

As I listened carefully to the message, my heart raced. She mentioned something about being forced to follow along or be fired. When I got to the next message, it was her again, only the second message there was no way I could understand. It sounded as if she'd been outside when she'd called and left the message.

I gripped the steering wheel of the car, debating what to do. I'd been forewarned by my advocate not to have contact with her, but she was hurting and needed me. I hated the position Connie had put us in.

Almost as if on cue, Connie appeared, walking in front of my car on the way to hers. She held up her hand

and waved as if we were best friends, then signalled for me to roll my window down.

I hit the button, the cold winter air hitting my cheeks.

"Have a great night, Dalton. I am glad everything went well today with all the patients, and I look forward to getting more hands-on tomorrow!" she yelled as she waved.

Irritation flooded me. She was a horrible nurse, horrible with the patients, paperwork and reports hadn't been filed all week, I couldn't find anything I needed, and she was lazy as hell. The moment the office closed, she was out of there. How the hell she'd ever become the head RN baffled me. I now remembered why I'd denied her promotion when we worked together at the last hospital I was at.

My phone rang just as I started the engine. I grabbed it immediately, seeing it was Amelia. Only when I answered, the line went dead.

That was it. I didn't care that I'd been warned; I was going to her. This was absolutely ridiculous and beyond anything I could ever imagine could have happened because of this.

I knocked on the door of her apartment, waiting in the hall. I heard nothing as I listened at the door. Perhaps she wasn't home, I thought to myself. I was just about to turn and leave when I heard the door unlock. I stopped, turning in time to see her red, swollen eyes.

I pushed the door open and stepped inside, shutting it behind me before I grabbed her and wrapped her in my arms. Almost immediately, she cried heavy sobs as I held her in my arms.

When she finally stopped and I let her go, she looked up at me.

"You shouldn't be here."

"I know, but when I got your message, I had to come. This is all my fault."

"What? No, it's not," she cried, getting upset again. "I just want this all to go away. It was so horrible today." She sniffled.

I'd never seen her this upset, not even when I'd had my worst days, so I could only imagine how bad it must have been.

"It will soon, and it is my fault. I was the one who pursued you. This is all on me."

"What are you saying?"

I'd battled internally all day with my thoughts on how to deal with the situation. This was Amelia's livelihood, and I knew if they gave her any type of ultimatum, which, from what I'd made out in her message, they had, that they meant what they said. She'd be without a job before Christmas if she didn't side with them. Even though this was my livelihood as well, I was in a far better position to give it all up.

"What I'm saying is that I've given things a lot of thought and—"

"I'm not siding with them, Dalton, I'm not. They are accusing you of things that never happened. I refuse to allow them to do that to you."

I placed my hands on her shoulders and met her eyes. "You don't need to side with them because there is nothing to side with. I'm just going to come clean."

"About what? What they are accusing you of? That isn't fair, and I won't let you do that," she said, crossing her arms in front of her, that stubborn, fiery side of her that I loved so much coming out.

"Look, I know how much you love this job. It's your passion. What you need to do is put a little trust in me and not worry about how things turn out for me. I will not be angry at the outcome. It will be what it is. It will change nothing between us."

"I'm not siding with them. I'm not accusing you of something so heinous. You did nothing. All they did was twist my words to fit the story they want to hear. It's wrong. I don't understand how you can tell me to do what they want."

"Whoa, I just said you don't need to side with them. You need to put your trust in me and what I'm about to do."

She got quiet as she looked at me. I could tell she wanted to say something, so I waited.

"What are you going to do?" she finally questioned, her voice shaking.

I couldn't help but softly smile at her. If it meant that everything would go away, I'd do this over again if ever it came up again.

"I need you to put your trust in me. I'm going to protect you in any way I have to," I said, swallowing hard.

"What? What are you talking about?"

"I'm going to do whatever it takes to protect you because when you love someone, that is what you do."

It was the first time I'd said it, and even though we hadn't been dating all that long—less than six weeks I'd fallen head over heels for her—truth was, I'd fallen for her a long time ago, way before we'd ever even become friends. I'd only realized it today, as I looked around my office, at the mess before me, waiting and wanting to hear that playful giggle she always gave when she was working so hard at annoying me with the say please and thank you speech.

Tears filled her eyes as I looked at her and she brought her hands to her eyes to clear them away.

"I'm in love with you, and that is what I am going to tell them," I said, bringing my lips to hers.

When I broke our kiss, not another word was said. I slipped from her apartment and took off down the hall, leaving her until the hearing.

AMELIA

I STOOD in front of the disciplinary committee, my hands together as I waited while Connie gave her update to them. How the hell they even allowed that was beyond me. The woman was going to go to hell if karma truly was a bitch, I thought to myself.

Since I hadn't liked Constance or her ultimatum, I faced the board on my own, and to be honest, ignoring all that had been said once I'd finally read the complaint. I planned to file my complaint against her with Dalton's help once this was all over.

I took a deep breath as I watched Connie speak with the members of the committee. Each time she said something, she glanced at me over her shoulder, giving me some form of a smile. I could only imagine what she was telling them.

When she finished making up more lies, she made her way to the chair she'd been sitting in and took a seat, waiting while they made some notes and then turned their attention to me.

"Amelia, would you care to say anything before we begin?" one of the board members questioned.

I nodded. "I came to work for Dalton Frost a year ago. While to begin with, he was difficult to work with, we soon fell into a routine that worked. Over the course of the year, I got to know him and started helping with his family when his daughter had a hair emergency for a school dance. I found out that Dalton was a widow, and being a girl who'd lost a parent at a young age, I took to his daughter Claire quickly and told her if she needed anything she could always ask me.

"Soon after that, she'd called with a bit of an emergency that only a girl would be comfortable sharing with her mother. While I knew she didn't have a mother, I figured I'd help her out. Over time, spending time with Dalton and his family, things developed slowly into more. Neither of us planned for that to happen, but I fell in love with him, and while I'm not proud of the fact that it was being broadcast to my fellow employees the way it has," I said, glancing over to Connie, "I'm not sorry that it happened. You all yourself know you can't help who you fall in love with."

Connie rolled her eyes at me as I let out the breath I was holding. The board members then turned toward Dalton.

"Dalton, anything you'd like to add?"

Dalton stood up and smiled at me. Then cleared his throat. "All Amelia said is true. There was never any intent behind her helping me with my children. The claims of the situation are false. We have never, nor would we ever, have any sexual relations during working hours. That was something the pair of us laid out immediately when we started dating. However, the truth is I fell in love with her, and I will accept whatever comes my way from all of this because she is more than worth it."

He reached over and took my hand in his, softly smiling at me, not caring what the board members thought.

It was then I heard Connie mumble, "Oh boy."

When I turned to look her way, she was rolling her eyes as she crossed her arms in front of her chest. The board members even glanced at her as they spoke amongst themselves before looking to us.

"If you'd like to take a bit of a break while we discuss our decision, you may. We will continue in ten minutes."

Dalton placed his hand on the small of my back and guided me to the door. Once outside in the hall, he pulled me in for a hug and whispered in my ear that he was proud of me. We both watched as Connie moved down the hall and took a seat far away from us.

Almost twenty minutes later, Rose stepped out of the room and nodded toward us. We both went back in and took our seats. As Connie approached the door, Rose shut it to shield whatever it was she was saying to her and then came in without her. I couldn't help but look to Dalton with curiosity as to why she wasn't allowed to return, but the look I got from him told me to calm down a bit until we heard the end.

Rose sat down and then looked at us both. She softly smiled and held out a copy of the employee handbook.

"First, I'd like to start by saying that the committee and I have decided the there was no wrongdoing here at all. You both have been given a copy of this handbook, and I know you have both read it."

"We have," Dalton and I said in unison.

"So while there is nothing wrong with dating co-workers here at Eastport, we have a clause that states that there will be no relations allowed between boss and employee. Now, we have gone over everything, and since Amelia, yes, works in your clinic, you are not her direct boss. The head RN is, which is Connie."

I glanced over to Dalton. The clouds finally seemed to lift.

"Now, we don't see any issue with what has transpired between the pair of you. What we have an issue with is this complaint and the fact that it seems Connie has been harassing Amelia. Everything in this complaint leads me to believe that she maybe has even been following you around, looking for things."

I couldn't believe my ears. Dalton was right, he'd said it first, that the board may see this as just that. I looked over at him, but he kept his eyes forward.

"So, we plan to investigate that after the holidays. So, your new boss, Amelia, will be assigned to you next week until we do this investigation. Now, we need you both to fill out this paperwork, just so we have it on record that you are involved, but we see no reason you both cannot continue to work together in any capacity."

Dalton stood up, taking my hand in his. I too stood, and we both thanked the entire committee before leaving the room.

We were partway down the hall when Connie came walking toward us, sneering at us both as she passed. I couldn't help but turn around and watch as Rose waited for her at the door, which was closed once Connie stepped into the room.

I turned to Dalton, relief flooding me as our eyes met. It was over; we weren't in the wrong, and it looked as if my Christmas wish had come true. Karma had shown its face.

"What do you say we head over to the store, grab some wine and some dinner, and head home to the kids?" Dalton questioned.

"I'd love that," I whispered as his lips met mine.

AMELIA

CHRISTMAS NIGHT - 1 year Later

THE KIDS WERE ALREADY in bed.

I sat in the living room, admiring the ring on my hand. After the hearing last year, things moved rather fast for us. I ended up moving in with Dalton and the kids at the beginning of summer and never looked back.

"Think you can tear your eyes away enough to have some wine?" Dalton questioned, holding the glass out in front of me.

I let out a tiny giggle, taking the glass from him.

"Sorry, it's just so beautiful," I said, looking back down at my hand.

"I know. Looks even better on you." He winked.

He placed his arm on the back of the couch, and I shifted so I could lean into him. The moment I rested against him, he placed his arm around me and kissed the top of my head.

"You happy?" he questioned.

"Am I happy? You aren't seriously asking me that, are you?" I asked, taking a sip of my wine.

"I am. I just want to make sure."

"I am," I assured him. "I can't wait to plan our wedding."

"Same here, and I think the first person we should add to the guest list is Connie."

I couldn't help but laugh at his suggestion.

"I'll get right on that."

Connie had been fired from Eastport at the beginning of the year. Apparently, when she lodged another complaint against Dalton at the beginning of this year, they had her followed and found that she had been following both of us. Turns out she was seeking Dalton's approval since she'd never gotten over the fact I'd passed her over for promotions time and time again. When I confronted her on the second complaint she finally broke down and told human resources that. It didn't matter that she held a high position at Eastport, she hated Dalton with a passion and wanted to win his approval.

"You know what I think?" he whispered in my ear as music quietly played.

"What?"

"I think I'd like to see you in nothing but that ring," he said, pressing a kiss to the side of my neck.

"Is that so?" I questioned, swallowing hard as a wave of excitement rolled through my body.

"Right there, in front of the fireplace," he whispered.

My mind shot back to the first time we'd been together, right here on this couch. How I'd known he was for me and I was for him. We'd fit so well together.

He stood up, placed his glass on the table in front of us, and then turned, taking my glass from my hand. He then took hold of my hand, grabbing the blanket that lay on the back of the couch. Walking around the table, he spread the blanket out on the floor then wiggled his forefinger at me, in a come-to-me motion.

I shyly smiled as I always did and got up to go to him. He pulled me in his arms and kissed me deeply. This was how I wanted us to be forever—in love, with no one in our way.

At first, I thought the name Frost was so fitting, but I'd been wrong. He had a wonderful, caring heart, and he was warm and passionate, and I had never been so happy to be the owner of his frost-less heart.

GET A FREE BOOK

Sign up for my newsletter and I'll send you a free book.

https://geni.us/NLSignupBackMatter

Follow S.L. Sterling

Did you know that bookbub has a feature where you can follow me and it will send you an alert when I release a book or put a title on sale? Sign up here and make sure you stay in the loop.

Bookbub:
https://geni.us/SLSterlingBookbub

Website
https://www.authorslsterling.com

Facebook
https://geni.us/SLSterlingFB

Twitter
https://geni.us/SLSterlingTwitter

Instagram
https://geni.us/SLSterlingInstagram

Tiktok
https://geni.us/slsterlingtiktok

Reader Group

ABOUT THE AUTHOR

USA Today Bestselling Author S.L. Sterling was born and raised in southern Ontario.

An avid reader all her life, S.L. Sterling dreamt of becoming an author. She decided to give writing a try after one of her favorite authors launched a course on how to write your novel. This course gave her the push she needed to put pen to paper and her debut novel "It Was Always You" was born.

When S.L. Sterling isn't writing or plotting her next novel she can be found curled up with a cup of coffee, blanket and the newest romance novel from one of her favorite authors.

In her spare time, she enjoys camping, hiking, sunny destinations, spending quality time with family and friends and of course reading.

To be notified of new releases or sales, join S.L. Sterling's private Mailing List. https://geni.us/NLSignupBackMatter

Get even more of the inside scoop when you join S.L. Sterling's private Facebook group, Sterling's Silver Sapphires: https://geni.us/SapphiresReaderGroup